HONEYSUCKLE AND BONE

HONEYSUCKLE AND BONE

TRISHA TOBIAS

SWEET JULY BOOKS
A zando IMPRINT

The characters and events in this book are fictitious. Any similarity to real persons, living or dead, is coincidental and not intended by the author.

Copyright © 2025 Working Partners Limited

Licensed by Working Partners Limited through its Dovetail Fiction division.

Zando supports the right to free expression and the value of copyright. The purpose of copyright is to encourage writers and artists to produce the creative works that enrich our culture. Thank you for buying an authorized edition of this book and for complying with copyright laws by not reproducing, scanning, uploading, or distributing this book or any part of it without permission. If you would like permission to use material from the book (other than for brief quotations embodied in reviews), please contact connect@zandoprojects.com.

Sweet July Books is an imprint of Zando.
zandoprojects.com

First Edition: January 2025

Text design by Neuwirth & Associates, Inc.
Cover design by Tal Goretsky

The publisher does not have control over and is not responsible for author or other third-party websites (or their content).

Library of Congress Control Number: 2024943293

978-1-63893-102-7 (Hardcover)
978-1-63893-103-4 (ebook)

10 9 8 7 6 5 4 3 2 1
Manufactured in the United States of America

*In loving memory of my father
and in heartfelt honor of my mother*

HONEYSUCKLE AND BONE

CARINA: You've always been the better one.

CARINA: So I'm going.

CARINA: Thank you.

Not Seen

ONE

I'm looking for a sign. Literally.

Outside Sangster International, travelers lug dented suitcases, yell directions into cell phones, wipe sweat from their brows as Jamaica's humidity swallows us. I glance up and down the yellow-lined curb, take in the older cars and tour buses crowding for pickup. Just under the symphony of car horns, music plays. And I know that bass, those drums. Bob Marley and the Wailers' "Three Little Birds." Every other Saturday morning at home, while the house was still dark, Mom and I would scrub the place from top to bottom, this song in the background.

Now, as I stand in a whole different country, it's the one familiar thing I cling to.

The airport scene is laughing staff, bright summer dresses, and every conversation happening at once. I could get lost in all this movement, all this life waiting for me to join.

Here, I'm one girl out of a million.

Normal.

I just have to act like it.

The Hall family's house manager, Thomas, said to find him when I landed. His emails were short and dry, so I figured I'd get picked up by some stern-looking older man.

But the person waiting for me is no old man.

Tall and slender, the girl might be around my age. Dark skin covered in colorful bracelets and gold necklaces. Hair shaved down, real clean. Deep-red lipstick on pouty lips. Her jewelry jingles as she waves a black-and-white JOY CARTER sign over her head. A patrolling policeman lowers his sunglasses and glares at the show she's putting on.

I jog toward the poster board, my stuffed messenger bag hanging off my shoulder and my heavy-ass suitcase dragging behind me. The young woman smirks as I approach. "Oh, pretty girl, then?" I just have clear brown skin and large eyes. Together, they're an "undeserved compliment" cheat code. I've actually looked like a bridge troll the last few weeks. The girl reaches out and toys with the lengths of my braids, pulls them over my shoulder. "Much fun."

"You hitting on me, Thomas?"

She cackles. "No, no. Thomas get called away. Name's Ora. I work for the Halls, clean up during the day." She studies her poster and arches an eyebrow. "You don't look like a Joy."

Blunt. Very blunt.

"You know, everyone but my parents would agree with you. I go by Carina. Middle name."

Ora grins. "Carina-rina? Yeah, I can work with that. Love a nickname."

The gleaming blue-and-white emblem on the car freezes me. The articles and videos seem true. The Halls must have *some* money. "So you clean *and* chauffeur?"

"No. But when Thomas say him need someone to pick up the new girl, I jump and change out me uniform. I have to escape the house." Ora takes me in, makes a little face that says what I already knew: my travel outfit is trash. An old white Tuff Gong tee and some off-white sweats. A ghost next to all her color. "And had to see who come. We need fresh blood. Most of staff already shaking hands with Lord Jesus himself."

Oh, I like her.

We struggle to load my two bulky bags in the back of the car, then hop in—after she nudges me to the passenger seat on the left. I'm getting used to this when Ora extends a brown oil-stained paper bag toward me. "Long drive, so I got you beef patty. But don't get no crumbs on the floor. Mrs. Hall will lecture me for the mess, believe that."

That warning is the first thing Ora's said that didn't sound like a joke, and after what I've researched about the Halls, I believe her. But I'm so hungry, I'm willing to risk that lecture. Before I boarded my flight at JFK, my stomach was doing flips, so I didn't try to eat. Now? One peek of that flaky yellow crust, and my mouth's watering.

"Oh, but it's Juici beef," she says. "And you're from New York. You probably like Tastee then? Or Golden Krust?" I don't know the difference, didn't know there was a beef patty brand war. It's a small thing, but the tinge of embarrassment is there. If I don't learn this shit quickly, I'm going to get my Jamaican American card revoked.

There's a knock on Ora's window. That police officer with the sunglasses. My pulse skyrockets. I press my back against the seat, hug myself. His raised voice carries through the glass. "You cannot idle here, ladies. Busy, busy. Time to go."

"Of course, sir," Ora replies with a smile. There's a gap between her front teeth. Ora offers me the paper bag again, and I take it. She puts the car in drive, mutters "Kiss my ass" before pulling away.

Ora cranks the radio volume to blasting. I lower the window, let the breeze cool my face. Dancehall booms through the speakers, and the world rushes by.

I'm surrounded by vivid flowers in bloom, sunset orange and blush pink painting the petals. The flowers give way to unassuming little stores behind chain-link fences, plastic chairs scattered by front doors. The wide blue sky is streaked with power lines. Ora weaves through the tightly packed streets, avoids hustling deliverymen on bikes and pedestrians too impatient to cross at the light. In the distance, I see mountains crowned in lush grass—and a horizon I could chase forever and never reach. I imagine myself walking along city sidewalks, sipping a bottle of champagne soda, the hours dripping away like melting ice.

For the first time in a while, I imagine what it's like to feel okay.

Ora dials down the music. My fantasy dissipates like smoke.

"So, Rina, let me explain something," she begins. "The Halls' house? It big, yes, but also very small, if you understand. So if we're working together, we need to know each other. And good."

I take a careful bite of the still-hot patty, shift in my seat. The Scotch bonnet pepper torches my tongue—hotter than I'm used to. I fight back a cough. "What do you want to know?"

Ora shakes her head. Her dangling teardrop earrings hit her cheekbones. "I hate small talk. Bore me to death. How 'bout . . . Two Truths and a Lie?"

A knot forms right at the base of my throat. I gulp. It doesn't move.

"I'm not that interesting," I reply.

"Nah, don't do that." She peers at me out of the corner of her eye. "Come. Play."

It'll get awkward if I keep protesting. I'm trying to make friends, not push them away. And I used to love this game at parties. Rarely lost.

I nod.

Ora shows off that tooth gap again. "I'll do you a kindness. Me first." She hums for a moment. "Okay: I'm late to everything. Been confirmed or baptized at least five times—looked at a lot of churches. And . . . been to a nude beach."

Interesting. Well, she had to be at the airport a little early to be waiting on me, so maybe not that one. She doesn't seem shy about her body with her cropped tank top and cutoff shorts, but . . . I scan the bundle of necklaces draped around her neck. Almost all of them are that greenish yellow-gold color—probably fake. But one is a cross.

Tarnished, so, real gold. It means something to her, and she's had it for ages. Which just leaves . . .

"The nude beach. Lie."

Ora kisses her teeth, but she grins right after. "Them big eyes see everything?" She laughs, like she's impressed. "Yeah, no beach. *Yet*. God made this body too tight for me to keep to myself." She isn't wrong, either. "You go?"

Careful.

"I have a tattoo *somewhere*. I'm Jamaican but I've never visited the country before. And my brother taught me to drive."

Ora takes quick peeks at me like she's unsure which I am: a little sister, a girl with hidden ink, or someone with a passport full of empty pages. Today, I'm a mystery. I decide what's revealed. Who I get to be.

"I think . . . Lie's that this your first time." She juts her chin at me, pointing at my Tuff Gong tee. "That shirt ratty as hell. You got it long time ago, been wearing it morning, noon, and night."

Not a bad guess. "I'm an only child."

She swears as we cruise down miles of smooth road. We've cleared the city limits already. Nothing but open highway now. "So how you never come here?"

"Parents just never got the chance. Busy, you know?" But not that busy. Mom and Dad could have brought me to Jamaica during Christmas breaks, could have squeezed in a little trip during summers off. I asked dozens of times to see Mom's hometown. And Dad's nearly cracked more than once. He's American, but he'd move us to Jamaica for half the year if Mom would let him. He loves the country that much.

But Mom is Mom. She lays down the law and expects you to follow it without question, or else you're disobedient. And her explanation is always the same: between the gangs, the drugs, the cost to travel, and the long-told tales of family gone missing, I have no business being there.

When I turned eighteen, it must have killed her. I could do what I needed without her knowing. And she had to stand by and watch.

I come back to the game when Ora asks, "So where the tattoo?"

My heart rate drops. "Nope. You go."

"And you said you were boring. Fake quiet. I see you." Ora adjusts her grip on the wheel. "Okay. Little harder now: I won third place in a primary school spelling bee, I'm talking to two men right now, and I give nicknames to everyone. Go on, best guess."

Her words make me pause. I don't want to get hung up on them because a normal person wouldn't. I lick patty crumbs off my lips, try to think, try to remember that this is just a game. But my brain shuts off. The wind whips through the window, fills my ears with white noise. My mind is white noise.

One second.

Then another.

I've been quiet too long. I spit out an answer, any answer. "You didn't place third in a spelling bee."

"Girl, what? I look like I can't spell? Big vocabulary, you know."

"Didn't say you can't spell. Just that you didn't come third. Maybe first place?"

Ora makes a grating buzzer sound. "You flatter me, but no. You see the lie? The men. Not seeing anyone."

I clear my throat. "Bad breakup?"

"Just don't need two." We drive by a pulled-over SUV, its windows open. I catch a piece of the passengers' screaming match as we whiz past. "Men are dogs."

Agreed.

"One more?" Ora prompts. "If I get it right, gimme a bite of your patty."

It's like we've been friends for years. Ora's frank. Candid.

Good to know.

"I've worn all white for the last month or two. I think the Halls seem very cool but very mysterious. And . . . I love the reggae singer Irie Blaze."

"Well, Mr. Hall in politics. Head of his party. Got him under lock and key. Family all over the news, but nobody *really* know them." My googling suggested the same. Longtime politician with a powerhouse wife. Three children, though one's older than me by six or seven years. The press loves talking about them, but the articles weren't super useful to me. Mostly speculating about the upcoming election or what brands Mrs. Hall is dressing the children in.

Speaking of: Ora inspects my shitty outfit again. "All white." Won't lie, I miss some of my old clothes. The colors. The shimmer. But they needed to go. These clothes are some of what little was left. "And you said you never been here before? Too easy. Has to be Irie Blaze. So underground, even I hardly know him." She holds out her hand, waits for me to drop her reward into her palm.

"Honestly? They're all true."

She lightly slaps me on the knee. "Cheating? You feisty, Rina." But her smile betrays any annoyance. She's an open book. If I had to guess, she probably liked that I took a risk by being honest.

Maybe that makes up for the lies I've already told.

I hold the paper bag out to Ora. She takes a bite without ever pulling her eyes off the road, enjoys the patty, even lukewarm. Despite the breeze, not a crumb on the console. And the pepper doesn't trip her up.

"Well, if you like Irie Blaze," she says, "then I have to take you out next time the Halls them set us free." She ramps the volume back up, practically shouts over the thumping bass. "Gonna make you listen to some live music, straight from the island."

For the first time in a long time, I'm okay. Good, even. And if I stick to my plan, I'll stay that way.

Because I didn't come this close to freedom to fall apart.

It's nearly sunset when I see it. Out my window, an estate's high stone walls loom. The dark wrought iron gate slowly creaks open on its own. Ora pulls through and cruises along the extended paved driveway, tall palm trees and manicured lawn on either side of us.

My new home.

Maybe, with time, I can settle in here.

Maybe, with effort, I can start over.

And maybe, if I play this right, nobody has to know that I'm not Joy.

TWO

"Welcome to Blackbead House."

Blackbead towers over us, a massive two-story mansion of bone-white stucco and coal-black shutters. A grand stone staircase leads to the front veranda, framed by columns. There's a double garage attached at the side. The mansion's lit from within, and there's nothing but stillness behind the sheer curtains. Like the home's blank eyes are staring back at me.

Nausea pulls at my stomach. I'm staying *here*?

Ora parks in the mansion's long shadow at the bottom of the stairs, and I hop out of the car. Take everything in. All around the house, there are red-orange mangoes, spiny green soursop, and fresh limes on leafy branches. I grab my shoulder bag from the back seat. Ora yanks on my suitcase handle, but it doesn't budge.

"Rush, you got no sense," hails a tense voice from the front door. Two young people—a guy and a girl—hurry down the steps. The girl waves at Ora to quit pulling at my luggage. "Let Scoob get it before you hurt yourself."

Ora kisses her teeth, tugs harder. "I can do it, Juney."

"Not an inch of muscle on your whole body, but you can do it? Unbelievable." Juney takes note of my presence. Crosses her arms, looks me over. The slight sneer says she isn't impressed by what she sees. She has a soft face, box braids, and she's a little taller than I am. "Joy, yes?" she asks.

My eyebrow twitches. Ora's right: the name doesn't suit me. Never thought it fit Joy either, though. "Actually," I start. And I stop. The words came easier when I spoke to Ora. But Ora didn't seem as scrutinizing as Juney, that's for sure. "I mean, I prefer Carina, if that's cool. Middle name. Joy feels a little childish, maybe."

"I see . . . Well, nice to meet you." There's a sharpness to her words that makes me think that's not the case. She's not sure about me, I guess. Can't blame her, can I? "I'm Simone," she says, pointing to her name tag. "I clean with Ora during the day."

Juney's her pet name, then. They all probably have one. So nobody should find it weird that I want to go by a different name too.

The guy, "Scoob," nudges Ora out of the way and dislodges my suitcase with one pull. He grins at me, proud. "Call me Josh. You can find me in the kitchen anytime before six o'clock." He lifts the hot-pink luggage with one hand. Almost everything I care about is in there, and it's nothing for him to toss around. Says a lot about my life. "I'm strong, sharp, cook good—might shock you," he continues. Each word is breezy, unserious.

"If you don't hush and carry the bag before the Halls come home," Ora scolds.

"What? Mad I don't flirt with you?" he asks.

Ora pulls the keys out of her pocket and drops them in Simone's hand.

"Now Juney can park the fancy car. Why? 'Cause you a dumbass."

Josh just smirks. "Can't be kind, no? Will let the Blackbead duppy deal with you then." Ora smacks his shoulder before he hauls my suitcase up the steps, and Simone climbs into the BMW for a trip to the garage. Ora fusses with her earrings. Josh gets under her skin, and she can't hide it. She's an open book.

I miss when I could be like that.

"Sorry," she says. "Simone and Josh are nice, but them love to vex me."

"They'll keep me on my toes."

"Don't encourage them." Ora heads up the stairs, and I follow. "The family will be back soon for your welcome dinner." Thank god I have time to change out of these clothes. "For now, I'll take you 'round. Show you the real Blackbead."

We reach the patio, decorated with classic black and cream furniture. Ora stands to one side of the ornate double doors, each decorated with an engraving of a massive tree, its overarching branches drooping with some kind of fruit. Etched onto a tiny plaque above the doorframe, the phrase *Servitium et Honorem* shines. Ora gestures me in. "Come."

I step over the threshold. A fever flashes across my skin.

Blackbead suits its name.

I imagined color flaunted across every bedspread, rug, and tablecloth, like how Mom decorated our town house. That's the stereotype, right? That we Jamaicans aren't afraid to dress our homes in crimson and gold, to do it up with all-out patterns and designs that demand attention. But Blackbead's all work and no play—black and white, wood and stone, silver and crystal. The grand foyer has clean lines, a circular staircase, and a sleek chandelier that gleams. The one thing that feels familiar? The antiseptic scent of Dettol burning my nose. The staff probably used it to clean the floors.

"Shit," Ora says, "forgot to ask. What's your number?" I rattle off the digits. "You got WhatsApp?"

"Why?"

"So I can add you to the group chat later." Ora curls her lip, throws this "duh" look. "Just four of us—Simone, Josh, me, and Aaron. You make five. We call it the Young Birds." She smiles with pride. "Now, let's start the tour."

"That won't be necessary, Miss Williams."

Ora and I spin around. There's an older woman there, light skin contrasting with her black silk blouse and knee-length pencil skirt. She folds her hands in front of her, posture tall and long, like a ballerina's. I've seen her photos online. There'd always be some asshole who questioned how she got her skin that color or why she refused to relax her hair. But otherwise, the comments were loaded with praise. All of it seemingly well deserved.

Turns out Ruth Hall is way more beautiful in person.

"You're home early, Mrs. Hall," Ora says, dipping into a curtsy despite wearing literal pum-pum shorts. I hike my messenger bag higher on my shoulder before joining Ora in a bow. I stare at my sneakers, focus on the scuffs near the toe.

"I had business to attend to at home and hoped to greet our newest guest," Mrs. Hall replies, clear and steady. "Thank you for picking up Miss Carter on Thomas's behalf. I will take it from here." She holds her gaze on Ora for a second longer. "And please wear more appropriate clothes in the future, Miss Williams."

"Yes, ma'am. Sorry, ma'am." Ora quickly side-eyes me before scurrying through an almost invisible door that I didn't notice before because it had been flush with the wall. Secret passageways? The surprises keep coming.

Now it's just Mrs. Hall and me. What do I do without Ora to hold on to? I'm not ready. I haven't gotten any serious info on the Halls from Ora yet. Haven't had a chance to refresh my hair. Haven't even changed out of these raggedy travel clothes like I wanted.

On stiletto heels, Mrs. Hall slowly pivots toward me. I smile, widen my eyes so I seem excited and ready to work. But it's as if she's already running calculations on me, whether I fit the picture she had in mind when she hired Joy. "I've already spoken with Mr. Green—Joshua—and had him deliver your luggage to your quarters. You'll unpack before dinner. For now..." She clears her throat. "Follow me, please, Miss Carter."

It's like someone used Blackbead to smash past and present together—state-of-the-art speakers in the corner of a room covered in mahogany paneling, a shiny 4K television atop an ornate embroidered rug. We pass the formal living room, decked out with glass doors open to a manicured backyard, an in-ground pool, and a view of the turquoise-blue ocean beyond the property's cliffs. Never thought I'd get the chance to live by the water, catch the waves as they come and go.

If Joy had come, she might have slowed down for once to notice everything here.

The kitchen's bustling with folks quickly and quietly preparing for dinner. There are stainless steel appliances, and one of those big fridges with a touch screen, but they're still using cast-iron dutch pots on the stovetop. A white candle sits in the windowsill, its flame burning. At the sound of Mrs. Hall's clicking heels, everyone pauses, faces her, and bends at the waist.

"As you were," Mrs. Hall says lightly. The staff returns to their work as we drift away from the busyness. A well-oiled machine that's back on course.

I try to take in the sights of the house, but it's impossible to catch it all. So I switch to the obvious things. Like how every wall has some massive mirror or prestigious award acknowledging the Halls' contributions to the country. I even spy a stately portrait: two kids, a young man, an older couple—Mrs. Hall and her husband—each poised and proper.

A little royal family. The opposite of my own life.

My mom's an aide on a school bus. Dad's an accountant. Half my clothes are hand-me-downs from Joy. How can I fit into this? How can I *stay* in this?

If I keep it together, play it cool and polite, I'll be in the clear. Then this fresh start is mine to have, and Joy's gift to me doesn't go to waste.

Simple. Easy.

Mrs. Hall escorts us into a sitting room, a darkened space illuminated by the remaining sunrays and some warm lamplight. She lowers herself into a plush armchair, and I sit on the velvet sofa across from her. It's firm, like it's never been used. Probably hasn't been. Rich people seem to love useless, decorative furniture. I rest my bag on the floor. It topples in an awkward, loud clatter as my stuff shifts inside. My breath catches, holds. Clumsy. I feel clumsy compared to Mrs. Hall.

A young woman hurries in, balancing a silver tea tray. It's Juney—Simone. She skillfully pours two teacups—doesn't ask how I like my tea—and passes one to Mrs. Hall and the other to me. I keep the cup and saucer on my lap so nobody hears how badly I'm shaking.

I can do this. I can have a conversation. I can have a totally normal conversation without spooking this woman.

"Thank you, Simone," says Mrs. Hall. Simone curtsies, deadass gives me the stink eye, and exits as quickly as she entered. Damn. She is really not feeling me.

Mrs. Hall exhales, like she can finally relax. "Now that we're alone, we can truly talk. One-on-one. Tell me: Do you prefer Miss Carter or Joy?"

I swallow. "My middle name is fine, ma'am. I usually go by... Carina."

"Really." It's not a question. "Thomas didn't mention a name preference on your paperwork."

"Probably just an oversight, ma'am." Whether I'm suggesting it's an oversight of mine or Thomas's, I don't say. But Mrs. Hall doesn't say anything more either.

Pretty sure she hates me. Or doesn't believe me. I should have let her call me whatever she wants. But it'll be easier if I'm responding to my real name and not *just* the pretend one. I have to make this easier for me to pull off. I press my thumb against the rim of the saucer. Stay grounded.

Finally, Mrs. Hall offers a small grin. "Well, we don't generally use nicknames, but you will be like family, and we want you to feel comfortable. So Carina it is." That's more grace than I expected. And that kicks my anxiety into overdrive. Understanding is foreign to me. I grip the teacup handle and force myself to take a sip. Not enough sugar. No milk. I hide my wince. "We're happy to have you in our beautiful home for the next few weeks. My husband and I will be busy with election responsibilities, but we don't want our children feeling neglected while we wait for our more permanent caretaker to arrive in late August. That's where you come in."

"Of course, Mrs. Hall."

"Monday through Saturday, you will care for our two youngest children, Luis and Jada." I set down my cup, try to subtly wipe my clammy palm on my sweatpants. My grungy, nondesigner sweatpants. Christ. "Between the hours of seven a.m. and eight p.m., we ask for your full attention—this means maintaining routines, overseeing productive play sessions, some light housekeeping." Better that I'm here than Joy, then. The word *routine* would make her break into hives. "We will provide for all your needs, and as our au pair, you may freely enjoy most areas on the property. Sundays will usually be your own, but exact days off will depend on the scheduling of special events that may require your participation. Oh, and you will receive your salary every Friday."

I don't care about the schedule. I don't even care about the money. I've got my foot in the door, and that's enough.

"There's more," Mrs. Hall continues, "but you'll learn all about Blackbead standards in due time. Enough of that. Please, tell me a bit more about yourself. I admit, I'm quite curious." She puts down her teacup, peers at me with an eager, open face. "Your Cultural CareScapes profile said you were familiar with our . . . lifestyle. Is that right?"

Careful.

I hesitate, slow my words before I misspeak. "Yes, ma'am. My parents are blessed to be . . . comfortable." Joy's preferred response when I'd joke about her insane collection of luxury wristwatches she never wore. "And I was lucky to be raised in such favorable conditions. So I definitely understand." I glance around the sitting room, and I hope my expression comes across as awe and respect rather than uncontrolled queasiness. "But I admit you and your husband have built something truly spectacular. Never seen anything like Blackbead. I'll have to send my mother your decor tips."

Mrs. Hall smiles demurely. "You flatter me, dear. Now, could you remind me of your experience with children?"

This is where my past can actually shine for once. Joy never had much experience. She applied for this position because she thought being a fill-in au pair for a couple months sounded fun. And her parents seemingly had no intention of taking her to Jamaica on their own; they never found it as enticing of a vacation spot as Aspen or Rome. Make that make sense.

But Joy knew the only person who wanted to visit Jamaica more than her was me.

"Well," I say, "I've worked with children for years, babysitting privately. I also spent a year and a half monitoring kids at the local gym nursery."

It's not a sparkling résumé, but it's something. And it's the truth: easier to remember.

Mrs. Hall hums. "Our eldest son, Dante, is also dedicated to his mission. Right now, he's deeply involved in his father's reelection campaign, acting as our community outreach representative." She gestures to a framed photo on the table beside her, a spotless picture of a straight-faced young man—the son in question, I guess. She rests her hand on top of the frame, as if patting the crown of Dante's head. "He's already preparing to follow in his father's footsteps by connecting with the people of our parish so we can better serve them. It's important work."

"I can only imagine."

"We want all of our children to use their time and abilities wisely. So it's interesting," she goes on, "that your parents would allow you to perform such... challenging labor. After all, you seem just as bright as my Dante."

Damn. Does she think I'm lying about having money? Because I've had jobs before?

Time for the power of bullshit.

"That's kind of you to say," I reply. "I just... adore children. It's not about the money, obviously, or how difficult the work might be. It's about shaping and supporting young minds. That's just so fulfilling and... and gratifying. And I really give my all to that. It's so important to me."

Bullshit so strong I can smell it.

Mrs. Hall places her teacup on the side table. "And we look forward to seeing that passion in action, Carina."

Dodged that speed bump. Let's avoid another, okay?

"I know these discussions can feel tedious," she says, "but it's important that I personally speak with everyone who works closely with us. Especially our caretakers."

"Of course, Mrs. Hall. You'd want to protect your children most of all."

"It's hard to know the intentions of others when one is... of a certain status. I couldn't tell you how many nannies we've had to report and let go because Dante discovered their misbehavior, their stealing, their lying." Mrs. Hall chuckles to herself. "What am I saying? You know how these things go."

Sure I do.

Wish I knew what happened to the last nanny, though. Did she get cut for the stealing or for the lying? Doesn't matter. I keep my hands on my lap, where Mrs. Hall can see them.

Mrs. Hall rises from her seat, a queen vacating her throne. "Follow me, please. I'll show you more of Blackbead House and bring you to your quarters. Oh, and leave your cup; Simone will handle it."

She leads me back through the long corridors of the mansion. In one glimpse, a gorgeous glass coffee table that's probably worth more than everything I own, closed doors to offices belonging to people more important than me. In another, a shady corner filled with paint cans, a balled-up tarp, and stacks of old newspapers featuring grayscale photos of Mr. Hall orating.

Blackbead is beautiful and midtransformation. Glamorous yet faded. Joy would hate it. Not enough bling, even with the chandelier. Not enough noise.

Mrs. Hall calls my name. "As discussed, you have free rein of most of Blackbead—the jerk pit in the backyard, for example, or the gym and theater in the basement." I'm sorry, a *movie theater*? "However, some areas are reserved for family use only. That includes the offices on this floor, the reading room, as well as my husband's and my bedroom. I also apologize for the mess. Renovations have been slow going." Explains the paint and tarp. "Blackbead will be lovely again once everything is brand new, but this has taken some time. Unfortunately, we were unable to complete the basement au pair suite before your arrival. We've sectioned off our best guest suite upstairs for you in the meantime."

Upstairs? So I don't have to hole up in the basement? I'd gush but I don't think Joy would gush about something like this. Upgrades in life were always expected. "You're too kind, Mrs. Hall, thank you."

"We give the best we can and we expect the best in return," she replies.

There's movement to our left as we pass the kitchen again. A tall guy with cornrows pulled back in a bun comes through the back door, maneuvers around the working staff, and pours himself a glass of water. He nearly overflows the cup when he sees Mrs. Hall with me in tow.

"Aaron, glad we caught you before end of day," Mrs. Hall says. "Come, please."

Ora mentioned an Aaron, didn't she? Another Young Bird.

He jogs to us, looks over Mrs. Hall's shoulder.

At me.

Mahogany skin. Sharp brown eyes. Full lips.

Mrs. Hall steps to the side. "Carina, meet Aaron Miller. He and our longtime gardener, Gregory Daley, share the guesthouse in the back and work across the property." She pats his shoulder; there's warmth in it. "Together, they keep Blackbead looking stunning with flowers and shrubs. It's art."

He doesn't seem like someone in the business of making beautiful things.

He seems like trouble. For me.

Aaron bows his head low out of respect and maybe some shyness. "Just doing my job, ma'am." His voice is rich, mellow. It stirs something familiar in my belly. I pretend I don't feel it.

Aaron holds out his hand, and his calloused palm grasps mine. "Nice meeting you, Carina." The warmth makes me linger.

Careful.

"You too."

Aaron grabs his water and heads back outside. He takes a long sip; liquid drips down his chin, his neck, and darkens the collar of his gray shirt.

"Now, upstairs, please." It's the first time that I've wanted to rebel against Mrs. Hall. I don't.

The portraits on the second level form a history of the Halls. The kids get bigger, the clothes get finer, the poses get stiffer. Mrs. Hall leads me to the far-east side of the floor and opens the door at the end of the corridor.

My new home.

The room is completely old-school compared to most of the house. Dark wood floors, wood dresser, wood bookshelf. Tall wood bed I can hide my lockbox underneath. Everything's clean but dated, a reminder of what the house was like before. The Halls decorated the walls with different paintings and art prints—depictions of Jamaica brushed in greens and golds, sky blues and Scotch-bonnet reds. For a second, I miss the mini Polaroids I pasted on the walls by my bed back in New York. Candids of Joy, snapshots from our favorite diner, that shot of the Statue of Liberty from the one time we bothered to visit.

The lump in my throat swells.

There's a scent on the air, strong and sweet. The smell of flowers and citrus. I can't place it. Maybe it's coming from the wood furniture. It all seems handmade and sturdy as hell. The aroma sends heat through me, though, a strange warmth that sits in my chest.

"Carina, a few more practical matters before you settle in," Mrs. Hall begins. "While you are not required to wear a uniform like the rest of the staff, we do expect you to present yourself respectfully. That means—"

There.

Under Mrs. Hall's speech.

A whisper so faint.

But Mrs. Hall doesn't react to it. She drones on, quickly doling out bedtimes and sickness protocols.

The murmur is there, though.

Persistent.

Phrases I can't make out.

Stress has me slipping. I cannot slip.

Be normal.

I dig my jagged nails into my palms. I focus as Mrs. Hall speaks, like her words are the center of my world. "The run-up to this election will be busy. For the next eight weeks, we will require excellence from every member of our staff. Excellence and discretion."

Slowly—too slowly—the whisper falls back. The scent fades. My shoulders finally relax.

Mrs. Hall picks up a name tag pin from the vanity and holds it out to me. JOY in all caps. Mrs. Hall stands before me. "I'm sure this goes without saying, but we will require the utmost professionalism until all votes are in. Is that understood . . . Miss Carter?"

No drama. No foolishness. Or else.

I've had enough drama and foolishness for a lifetime. I don't need any more.

I take the name tag. "Crystal clear, ma'am."

She smiles. "Perfect. We'll see you at seven for dinner. Do not be late."

YOUNG BIRDS

Carina was added.

ORA: rina join us in the chat!! reminder that this an asshole free zone!!

SIMONE: Welcome

SIMONE: Sorry about the Mrs. Hall surprise

ORA: it was a ambush!! but we manage!!

JOSH: carina run from the place while u still can lol

ORA: scoob if you hate BB so much you can leave!! stop trying to scare off rina!!

SIMONE: Ignore him

CARINA: 😩 Thanks for the add!

ORA: chicken where you at?? what kind of host are you??

ORA: rina part of the live-in crew with you!! come chat with the girl!!

AARON: we already met.

AARON: hi carina. glad you're here.

AARON: and rush, some of us is busy. can't all take long breaks like you.

ORA: LOL god alone can judge me and even he rested!! stay mad!!

Everything depends on this welcome dinner.

Mrs. Hall seemed okay with me by the time she left my room, but there's still the rest of the family. And if they hate me—don't trust me, realize there's something wrong about me—I'm done for. I don't know what life after Blackbead will look like, if I'll be ready to go home once this job is done. I wasn't excited about community college, but the thought of not being able to go because I screwed up too badly here makes me sick. Imagine: no more restarts. Just confiscated belongings and a confusing phone call to my parents.

But if the Halls like me, I'm safe. I can stay.

After meeting the Young Birds, after touring some of this mansion... I *want* to stay. Everything with Joy fell into place so I could be here.

Standing around the corner from the formal dining room, I set down my oversized gift bag and try to hide the bra strap that peeks out from my too-big white dress. I wore this outfit for my cousin's baptism last year. Now, it's loose up top; I lost weight these last few weeks, and it shows. But most of my event clothes are minidresses and short shorts. This is, unfortunately, the prettiest thing I own.

Deep breath.

Don't be like me tonight. Be like Joy. If I'm like Joy, then this will be easy. Everyone loves her. Socializing and charming people? Second nature. These are respectable folks. I can be respectable too.

The silver-and-black pendulum clock on the wall says it's seven. No more hiding. I shake out my hands, pick up the bag, and enter the dining room.

Six pairs of eyes hone on me. They size me up, dress me down, take in my too-large outfit, my worn ballerina flats, my gold earrings and silver necklace.

I recognize the expression that crosses every adult's face. I've seen it dozens of times.

Judgment.

An older man to my left blinks hard before he breaks from his freeze. He's tall, suited up, real refined vibes.

Meanwhile, my bra's showing.

"Miss Joy Carter, welcome to Blackbead House. I'm Thomas Allman, the house manager." I reach out for a handshake, but instead, he swivels close, like he's pulling me into a polite hug. He leans toward my ear. "Remember this, Miss Carter: being on time is being late. Do not make the Halls wait on you again. Yes?" I give a wobbly nod.

Oh, I'm cooked.

Thomas pulls away, glares at me for a split second, then gestures a sweeping arm toward the statuesque group standing across the dining room. "Please meet the Hall family."

They each have a role.

Jada, the Baby: five years old, doe eyes like mine, lush twists with purple beads, thumb-sucker. I wave. She wiggles her four unused fingers back. Shy.

Luis, the Middle Child: nine years old, mischievous smirk with missing teeth and knobby knees. He wears Trouble's face.

Dante, the Eldest: twenty-four according to online articles, tawny brown skin, low fade, lanky with rounded shoulders. He lifts his chin, stares down his nose like I've violated his peace with my presence. I fight the urge to shrink.

"And this is the Honorable Ian Hall and his wife, Ruth."

The Halls match the grandeur of the room, the immensity of the entire estate. Straight backs, practiced presence, fine-spun clothes.

His dark skin contrasts with her light tone. A king and queen, ruling with an iron fist from a modern-day palace. And with style too—Mrs. Hall changed into a striking white pantsuit, and Mr. Hall's in a fitted sapphire-blue suit with white pinstripes. The clear gems on Mrs. Hall's blood-red nails catch the overhead light. Mr. Hall's Rolex calls me broke with each silent tick of the second hand.

They're nothing like my parents. Dad's super kind but hopelessly goofy. Family meals were never fancy, but he'd always do some cheesy song and dance while making everyone's plates—"because y'all deserve dinner and a show." Which, admittedly, was very cute. But I could never see Mr. Hall doing stuff like that; he seems more smooth and put together. Composed.

And Mrs. Hall is about as strict as Mom, but without all the volatility. Like, Mrs. Hall is stern because she has to protect her family. She has something to show for all the rules she has. But Mom? It's like she tries to control everything so she feels better about how hard her life is. And what does she have to show for that?

A tired-looking town house, a stack of bills on the kitchen table, and one runaway daughter.

I pull my presents from the gift bag, kneel to the children's level and offer the gifts like I'm Santa. A kid-size Superman cape for Luis, and a talking stuffed Ellie the Elephant for Jada. Hopefully, they enjoy the presents—and hopefully, so do their parents. I had a tight budget, a small suitcase, and two grainy candids of the children to study for clues about what they like. Their parents have these kids' images on lock.

"Imagine if this were a Batman cape," moans Luis.

"Ellie has big ears like Dante," coos Jada.

"Focus, please," Dante interrupts, rubbing a palm over his face.

"Our guest is here," Mr. Hall adds. "What do we say?"

"Thank you, Miss Joy."

Mr. Hall returns his gaze to me, and his eyebrows raise. Like he's surprised to see me here. Then a switch flips, and Mr. Hall opens his arms wide. "Welcome to our happy home, Joy. You've come at the perfect time." He motions to the dining table, filled with precisely placed silverware and dinner plates rimmed in red and gold.

Mr. Hall must be in his forties or fifties. He grins graciously with perfectly straight teeth, and I breathe. Just a little.

I give him my well-practiced babysitter face, beam at him like the sun shines out of my ass. "Mr. Hall, it's an honor to be here. Happy to help any way I can." I turn to Jada and Luis. "And you two can call me Carina, okay? That's my special nickname, and you're totally allowed to use it."

"But that's not your *real* name," Luis murmurs. "Mama said no pet names."

"It's pretty, though," Jada whispers to him.

"Just like yours," I say. Jada's eyes widen, like she's surprised I heard her. Then she smiles. Cute kid.

"Well, *Carina*, your service during this time is more than appreciated," Mr. Hall continues. He sounds genuine. It's hard to imagine I'm doing this man—this family—any real favor. That they could actually need me when they already have so much.

But I really hope they do.

Luis runs to his mother's side. "Mama, can we show Carina the playroom after dinner?" Jada says "please" over and over before Mrs. Hall quiets them each with a gentle touch on their heads. A gesture so normal but surprisingly tender.

Mrs. Hall twists her rose-gold bracelet, showing off more brilliant diamonds than I can count. She eyes me like she's seeing me for the first time, reevaluating. "The children seem to like you already, Carina." When she talks, it's almost musical.

"Like I said, just good with kids," I say. "Watched them all the time."

Nobody needs to know I haven't had the strength to care for anyone's kids in weeks. Which sucked because I loved to do it.

But I can make up for lost time with Jada and Luis. I'm not the au pair they were supposed to have, but I can be the au pair they deserve. They're probably like most children: they care about fun. Attention. Love.

I can provide all that.

"We look forward to witnessing your skills *tomorrow*," Mrs. Hall says. She stares pointedly at the kids. They get the hint and deflate: they'll have to wait and pester me in the morning.

Everyone finally takes their seats. Thomas hovers nearby as the head chef and two servers float around the dining room, a ballet of beautiful bone china and wine pours. Thomas pulls out my chair at the end of the long table, opposite Mr. Hall. "Before we enjoy this delicious meal," Mr. Hall says. "A toast." He raises a crystal glass, prompts the rest of the room to grab theirs. All those glasses reflecting light onto the walls, a glittering night in a glittering home. All these people who live without shame, without fear, without regret.

I want what they have. I want to be one of them.

"To Carina," Mr. Hall calls out. "Welcome to the family."

In that moment, I make a promise to myself.

The Halls are going to love me.

I've done it.

I crawl into the king-size canopy bed, sheets already turned down, and burrow myself beneath the covers. Egyptian cotton.

Tomorrow is my first real day. The Young Birds took me under their wing. The Halls seemed impressed. Even the kids were mostly nice.

I let my head sink into the pillow, finally release my grip on my new image as a responsible rich girl who can definitely be trusted with someone's children. Everything is going well. Everything is working.

There's a twinge of guilt about that, deep in my gut.

Do I deserve this opportunity, this cordial family, this cushy job? No.

If I deserved it, I wouldn't have had to do so much questionable shit to get it. Lying to people, adopting Joy's name, racking up a laundry list of decisions I'm not proud of.

But it all had to be done.

Now, I have to prove that I can do right by this position and by this household. I'll make myself deserving. Everything else is a distraction.

I click off the nightstand lamp. The room transforms into a void, the dark wood walls absorbing any moonlight. In the night, there's the sound of my breath, the hum of the central air, the creak of the floor. A fly zooms by my head, its teeny wings buzzing in my ear.

Of course I can't sleep.

The scent of honey fills my nose. The furniture still? Or maybe those flowers in the garden?

A shock of heat rushes over me. A familiar feeling. Shame, probably. The warmth lingers. Settles on my skin. Sweat beads across my brow.

It'll take a few nights to get used to the island's heat and stickiness. But no reason to suffer in the meantime. I climb out of bed and shuffle to a window, unlock it, and pull up to open.

It doesn't budge.

I pull harder.

Nothing.

Sweat drips into my eyes, stinging. A fever seeps through my pajamas, through my skin, sinking deep into my muscles. Is it getting hotter? I suck in a deep breath. The air's dense with some cloying scent.

Am I sick?

I run to my door, twist the knob, and step into the hallway, a single foot over the threshold.

Shivers from the chilly air bring goose bumps to my arms. My breath is still loud. The AC still hums. The floor still creaks under my weight. Not a single scream or yelp of concern. It's not the house that's on fire.

It's only my room. It's only me.

I close the door. Just like that, I'm enveloped by the swelter again. Locked in a furnace.

Is this what guilt does? Turns a person inside out, makes them suffer things that others don't? My tongue sticks to the roof of my mouth. Can't breathe.

My fingers shake. It's my nerves. I'm cracking.

What if Joy found me here, one night into taking her name, her history, her job—and already a wreck? She'd stand in the corner, mad as hell. And what would she say?

It's like I almost see her. Arms crossed. Lips moving. No sound. But I don't need to hear her to know how she feels.

The world darkens around the edges.

No.

I'm not ready to break. Not yet.

I lurch to the en suite bathroom. My hands slip as I grip the shower's knob; I run the water ice cold.

And I throw myself into the stream.

A freezing spray pelts me, soaks through my clothes. My teeth chatter. I grit them together. A scream bubbles in my throat, and I don't let it out. I stand there, whole body shaking.

Calm down.

I'm begging myself.

Breathe.

I climb out of the shower and spill to the tiled floor. Water leaks into the grout. And when I stop panting, I feel it. The air is brisk. Light. No more honey.

It's over. I'm not a lost cause yet.

I stagger back to my bedroom, a line of damp footprints in my wake. Duck and peek beneath the bed. The coal-black lockbox sits, same as ever. The lid's cold. Its contents protected.

That was close. Fear had me by the neck. A panic attack, maybe? Can I sleep this off?

I hold my breath. So does the room.

My guilt is real. My lies and worry are real, as real as everything hidden in the box.

But hidden means safe. And all I need to do?

Be careful.

THREE

The kids haven't stopped shouting since dawn.

Are my ears ringing? Sure. But it's a small price to pay for a normal morning. Especially after last night.

It was a blessing in disguise that I hardly slept. Made the sound of the a.m. bell less jarring. I cleaned myself up, dressed, waited for Thomas outside his office so I could get the day's schedule. The man stepped out, locked his door, and handed me a printout of the agenda without even a "good morning." Instead, he just said, "Review this carefully. Follow it."

Yes, sir.

After I grabbed Luis and Jada from their bedrooms and got them ready, they finally showed me their overstuffed play area and introduced me to their little potted cacti in the sunroom. I even convinced Luis to spend a grand total of four minutes playing "Hot Cross Buns" on his recorder.

Then the kitchen treated the three of us to a full breakfast, traditional ackee and saltfish mixed with onions, tomatoes, and thyme. Chef Wesley made it right: creamy, buttery, with that kick from the Scotch bonnet. It's easy to forget you're eating fruit and cod. Mom never liked ackee—preferred breadfruit with her salted fish—so we rarely ate it at home. I hate to say it, but I'm starting to think she just didn't know the right tricks.

In the backyard, the ocean breeze cuts the rising heat of the day, leaving us toasty but not melting. And the kids are behaving.

"Don't run close to the pool, please!"

Mostly.

Luis is a top whirling across the backyard, yelling about the game he's made up, one with rules that evolve every minute. To him, I'm background noise.

But not to Jada. We sit under the umbrella-shaded patio table. She's fixed on my face. Every once in a while, she pulls out her thumb to pepper me with questions.

How old are you?

Eighteen.

Do you live here forever now?

No, just for a couple months.

Why not longer?

Because your real nanny will be here when summer ends. I'm just here to help until then.

What if I miss you after you leave?

That's okay. Missing someone means you care about them.

Do you miss your friends?

That last question might have gutted me if anyone else asked it. But I don't mind it coming from her. I even tell the truth.

Yes.

Years of sleepovers and adding her shitty exes to our "Fuck You" book. Sneaking into warehouse raves and cruising in Joy's car on warm summer nights. We did everything together, shared everything. She even shared this job.

But I'm here alone.

There's that thickness in my throat. *Careful.* I need a minute.

"Why don't you play with your brother?" I suggest.

She doesn't bother removing her thumb to answer. "He won't let me."

"Tell him I demand he play princess with you." She scurries off, yelling Luis's name with a smugness that almost makes me laugh.

I sit up straight in my chair, check that Luis's inhaler is still next to me. The most enormous mango tree I've ever seen sways nearby, heavy with fruit, just like the trees carved into the front doors. The pool ripples. I sip the smooth soursop juice Wesley kindly made me after I asked for more at breakfast. A little sour from the extra lime, a little sweet from the brown sugar. Ice-cold liquid hits my stomach and nearly masks the unease pooling there.

Nearly.

Last night's dinner was perfect. Mrs. Hall had Wesley give me his sweet potato pudding recipe since I loved it so much. Mr. Hall shared a hilarious childhood story about how he accidentally picked weed from the garden instead of mint, brewing this crazy tea for his mother's church friends. Luis told some terrible jokes he'd learned before school let out for the summer, but he couldn't remember the punch lines. Jada and I laughed anyway. Everything went well.

Then stress turned my bedroom into a broiler.

It was as if the good night went up in smoke. And in my mind, as I tried to sleep, I dreamed of concerts without music, a funeral, the red ribbons my mother used to tie into my braids when I was small. I woke with thoughts as tangled as they were a couple hours before.

The sunlight glints off my JOY name tag.

Blackbead is beautiful. And I don't belong here.

But here I am, under a patio umbrella, watching two rich kids play in the backyard of a fancy mansion. And nobody here even knows my real birthday.

Of course I feel like the sky is falling.

But if I keep behaving like the perfect au pair, maybe I can hold up the sky for a little while longer.

Two figures turn the bend into the backyard, carrying shovels and bags of fertilizer. One's a much older man, stubble across his square jaw, frowning hard.

And the other's Aaron. Squinting against the sun, clean-shaven. I remember the water from his glass slipping down his chin.

Why am I remembering that?

I pretend to fully focus on my drink. But from the corner of my eye, I notice the pair drop their things and start working on some flower beds. Aaron tugs his sweaty shirt away from his body. It clings to his torso again. He sucks his teeth, checks to see if anyone's spying, then pulls the shirt off completely.

My mouth goes dry. He must not have seen me. Right?

The kids run to Aaron. "Do you have time to play?" Luis asks. "It's knight and princess."

Aaron stands with his hands on his hips. I wait for him to politely decline and get to his tasks.

His work pants hang low. Something inside me wakes. Bares its teeth.

"Depends," he says. "How fast can you save the princess from . . . a dragon!" He throws Jada over his shoulder, sprints across the yard while Luis chases. Jada's giggles pierce the air as Aaron dodges the jabs from Luis's imaginary sword.

He looks like he spends his free time boxing or hiking, not playing storm the castle with silver spoon kids. But they seem to love Aaron. And he seems to love them too.

Aaron gently places Jada on the grass and collapses. "You got me." Jada escapes and Luis deals his killing blows. *Stab, stab, stab.* Aaron gasps in fake pain. And with the threat neutralized, they're off to play something more fun.

He hauls himself off the ground, grabs his T-shirt, and tries to wipe the stuck dirt and grass from his body. He joins me under the patio umbrella. I'm cool. I'm chill.

"Thought you were gonna save me," he says.

I lean back in my chair, act like I don't care about him or his pretty brown eyes at all. "My responsibility is to care for the kids. Barely noticed you."

"Think you notice plenty."

Warmth rushes to my face. Maybe he did see me before.

Back home, when Joy and I would catch guys staring, we'd call them out: "Get caught, get shot!" We wouldn't shoot anyone, obviously, and almost everyone likes attention. But it made the guys think twice about leering at strangers. And here I am, doing the same thing. History shows my brain stops working when boys are involved.

Note to self: get caught, get shot.

"Sorry," Aaron adds. "Too soon to be messing with you like that."

"Bet you do that with everyone."

"Not true." He holds my gaze. Whatever he's trying to say, I refuse to translate.

In the background, the older guy scowls, shades his eyes, and peers around like he's searching for something.

Or someone.

"That your boss?" I ask. My voice cracks because I'm pathetic. "I think he wants to get back to work."

Aaron peers over his shoulder, waves at the man who must be Gregory. "Thought I *was* working." He winks at me. Then off he goes, digging beneath the Jamaican sun, sweat running down his broad back. Gregory's squinted glare stays on me for a second too long.

I didn't imagine it yesterday. Aaron's seeing me. And I'm seeing him.

Yes.

No.

Shit.

"Yo, Carina! You still hungry?"

There's Josh, scurrying through the glass doors like a thief with loot, arms full of plates. Ora and Simone slowly trail behind.

"Breakfast wrapped. What's this?" I ask.

Josh simply says, "Brunch."

"Leftovers he stole from the kitchen," Simone clarifies. She stares uncomfortably as Josh places the dishes on the patio table. "Tried to stop him. Wesley will have Scoob washing up all day when him find out."

"And him better hope that's all he suffer," Ora adds.

I shoo Josh away. "I'm not getting caught with all this. What if Thomas docks my pay or something?" Nobody specified what the consequences were for breaking "Blackbead standards," but I'm not trying to find out on day one.

"If we don't eat this," Josh says, "it'll go straight into the trash. Staff not even allowed to take none of it home. But Rush and Juney just complain they're hungry. It's a waste."

"The Halls can waste what they want," I reply. "They bought the food. That's their business."

"That's true," Ora murmurs.

But still, Simone and Ora ogle the platters. It's like I can hear their stomachs growling. And there it is: guilt. Because I had my fill at breakfast. I'm allowed to eat as much as I want. That's one of the gifts of this nanny gig, the benefit of being the foreigner who's "like family" to the Halls. I'm part of the house staff, but I see the difference between me and the housekeepers, or me and the cooks.

Like how those guys all start work so early. I'm not sure if they have time to eat much before their shifts. And sure, I bet Ora and Simone brought lunches to eat during their assigned break, but that won't be for a while. It'd be a shame for them to starve while the Halls throw out all this food.

The perfect nanny probably wouldn't do this. But the new me? She would.

I glance at the back door. Nobody there.

Please, don't make me regret this.

I subtly nudge a plate toward Simone. "Can't work well if you're hungry," I say. Simone pauses. Stares at me hard.

Then, she says, "Thomas nosy and mean. Eat fast."

I let the others take most of the food, wait until it seems everyone's satisfied before I grab a piece of spiced bun nobody wanted. I nibble, eat around the raisins but savor the molasses and cinnamon. While the kids play tag, Josh waves Aaron over. Aaron bites into some pear-shaped apple I didn't recognize at breakfast. His teeth break the burgundy skin, exposing pure white flesh.

Aaron notices me noticing. "You see how the skin blood-red?" he asks. "That how you know it sweet."

Ora does a little shimmy as she eats, like she can't stop herself from dancing, even when she's at risk of getting in trouble. Go back in time, and Ora and I could have been two halves of the same person. She makes a better Joy than I do.

The plates finally clear. Aaron heads back to the flower beds. I check the back door.

Someone's watching.

Dante.

What's that saying? No good deed goes unpunished?

"The son's here," I warn. The son who isn't afraid to report the help, according to his mother. The pressure in my head builds. Move. Fix. Behave. I start gathering dishes. "Help me clean."

Everyone twists to see him looming through the glass.

"He like to lurk, that one," Simone says as she grabs forks and spoons. Her eyes linger at the back door. "Him see a lot but don't usually say much. But you never know, do you . . ."

Josh snickers, then tosses a grape into his mouth. Simone hits his shoulder with the utensils, practically begging him to act right, at least while one of our bosses is surveilling us. Instead, Josh lazily strolls around while we tidy the mess he so kindly gifted us.

"Wait," Josh starts, "Rina don't know who's who yet. Let's teach?"

Ora slides into a chair next to me, pretends like she's all about piling up these dishes. "We start with Thomas. Fenky-fenky, you think. Stuck-up, don't do a thing wrong. But you know he used to be a peeping ... Thomas?"

"He what?" There's a tiny window high on my shower wall. I thought it was for show. Did he see me last night, drenched in sweat and icy water?

"Rush, behave." Simone turns to me. "It's just what we've heard."

"So, a rumor?"

"Lies can start in truth," Ora states. She jerks the grapes away from Josh and puts them on the opposite end of the table. "So maybe he isn't spying on the girls *now*. But in his youth?" She shakes her head like she can't bear the weight of her disappointment.

"And Gregory?" Josh points him out, working in the yard with Aaron and grumbling all the while. "He get all the pum-pum 'cause the women know he won't leave them with child."

Gregory? Grouchy old Gregory? He's really pulling women that easily? He hardly even talks.

"How do you know that?"

Josh shrugs. "Don't know it. But believe it."

Simone offers me a kitchen towel, and we wipe down the table. Dante's still there. He's got his arms crossed, vague expression—he's too far away to overhear anything. But he's clearly inspecting us. Maybe calculating the damages of all the food we ate. Maybe mentally drafting the speech he'll give when he fires me for theft and sends Cultural CareScapes after me for employment fraud. "And what else should I know about Dante?" I ask.

Something wild sparks in everyone at the mere mention of him. "He keeps to himself," Simone starts. Diplomatic answer.

"Think he's too good for us," Ora adds. "He's always kept a distance, like we have disease."

"Him keep a candle lit in the kitchen window all day long," Aaron says. "He makes the staff check that it still burn."

"It's true!"

Then everybody goes off, almost too quick for me to follow who's saying what.

"Heard him have a secret family. That's why he's hardly here."

"Nah, Dante's busy talking to demons. His energy's wrong. Cleanse him, Lord."

"The family do Obeah since before Dante born. Probably dress themselves in chicken blood and make deals with demons. How else you explain the wealth? Strange."

"Not strange. Mr. Hall pay off all kind of people to keep squeaky clean. No one else in Parliament this rich."

"You mad. The money come from Dante running drugs to the States now his father can't. That's the only 'community' he concern with."

Jokes overlapping, laughter all around. I force a chuckle.

It's funny to them, the rumors. And I get it. What's a little hearsay amongst the help? What's some silly gossip to a man who could fit four of your house inside his mansion? And Ora's right. There's some truth in almost any lie.

But that grain of truth doesn't make the lie hurt less.

I search for Dante at the back door.

But he's gone.

YOUNG BIRDS

JOSH: dante is a sneak fr. halls dem cut my pay becuz me take sum food they dun need

CARINA: You're joking.

SIMONE: But we all had some

JOSH: said me bad role model bc me been here longest. dem xpect more from me

JOSH: maaaaaaaad

JOSH: let the duppy deal wit em then

AARON: damn. sorry man.

ORA: didn't mean to get you in trouble!!

SIMONE: Nothing we can do now

SIMONE: First day OK Carina?

CARINA: 😪

JOSH: cant handle it? lemme hav ur job then

CARINA: Over my dead body.

ORA: back up, scoob!! rina cant die yet!!

AARON: we have to take turns annoying her, ya hear?

CARINA: Feeling so welcome. 💀

SIMONE: And we just get started.

FOUR

By day four, I slot into two parallel routines at Blackbead.

The Halls: Rouse the kids at 8:00 a.m. Get the day's schedule from Thomas. Keep away from the locked offices. Share meals with the children and find increasingly creative ways to explain that their parents are too busy to join ... again. Ensure Dante's kitchen candle is still burning; don't actually talk to Dante. Enjoy a glimpse of the cliffside through the above-sink window. Play and teach and make it through the day while being harmony made human. Hurry the kids to bed before the curfew bell rings.

The staff: Wake with the morning bell and check the weather. If a storm's coming, cover the mirrors with white cloth. Pretend you understand why. Tidy up after Luis for hours at a time because most of the house mess is his. Silently mock the contractors trying to fix up the au pair suite in the basement. Leave any messages you don't want the Halls to find in the staff passageways. Before dinner, steal a single Icy Mint from the candy dish in the living room. Draw all the curtains at sunset because the Halls value their privacy.

Right now, I'm somewhere between bedtime and the curfew bell.

Jada's already been asleep for half an hour. Now, Luis crawls into bed while I pick up playthings and action figures to throw in his personal toy box. Turns out I was right. The kid's very into superheroes. In fact, Luis's room is plastered with *Avengers* posters. There's a Superman logo stuck to his wall. Green glow-in-the-dark stars twinkle from the ceiling. I'm shocked Mrs. Hall allowed them. Doesn't fit her aesthetic, and if there's one thing I've figured out by now, it's that Mrs. Hall takes a lot of pride in this house. No wonder the unfinished parts irritate her so much.

"Can I have Spider-Man?" Luis asks.

Didn't see him as the type of child to sleep with a toy. He's never asked for one before, and Spider-Man's missing an arm. It's cute, though. I hand over Spidey, and he murmurs a small thanks. I don't know about the rest of the family, but I've at least won some of Luis's trust. That's progress.

He goes, "Can I tell you a story?"

"You know, you've already told me a few." Like, seven. In the last hour. His thoughts spew out of his mouth, a faucet that runs until it floods the bathroom.

"Well, who else am I supposed to tell? Papa and Mama won't let friends come over." His mouth twists to one side. "They said they don't like strangers in their business."

That... does sound like something the Halls would say. Can't blame them either. They're public figures, yes, but they deserve privacy as much as anyone else.

I check the time on my phone. Rule is that he has to be in bed by eight. And he is. Technically. "Okay, one more story while I tidy."

Luis sits cross-legged on his bed, Spider-Man in his lap. "Have you ever heard of the Rolling Calf?"

"Nope."

"How 'bout the Roarin' Calf?"

"Is that different?"

"Same thing. One of the nannies told me 'bout it once," Luis says. "It's a bull, but not like a normal bull. It's a duppy, and s'got red fiery eyes and chains all over."

My whole body stills. My skin tingles. Sharp horns, loud hooves . . .

Stop. It's a ghost story. Jamaicans love using duppy tales to make kids act right. Even Josh has teased about the Legend of Blackbead House aka some stupid ghost shit.

When Mom was in a good mood, she told duppy stories. Talks of obeahmen and cotton trees, of rituals and possessions. Stuff she claimed happened to her as a little girl growing up in the bush. Like getting followed home from church one night by a giant ghost wolf. Or watching Grandma tie a measuring tape around her waist to keep Grandpa's spirit from feeling her up from the afterlife. Her spirit sagas were amusing, sometimes scary. But even Mom ended the stories with a hint of mortification. And if I asked too many times for her to take me to Jamaica and show me where everything happened, she locked up those tales tight again.

"There's an evil spirit inside the bull," Luis whispers. He waves around the action figure like it's a phantom haunting the bedroom and not a toy missing a limb.

I gather dirty clothes from the day, throw them in a basket to carry out when I leave. The nooks and crannies in Luis's room seem especially dark tonight. My hands twitch a little. "And how'd that spirit become evil, you think?"

Luis hums to himself, thinking. "The nanny said the Calf is always a bad person. They hurt others when they were alive. Now they're dead and still hurt people."

The nanny must have been desperate to control Luis if she was feeding him this mess. If she was fired by Dante, I can understand why. "That sounds really terrifying. Good thing Rolling Calves aren't real, right?"

"I saw one!" It's insistent. It's also bullshit. But he's a kid. What can I expect?

I place the laundry by the bedroom door. "Okay. Where?"

"In the backyard." Luis stirs on the bed. "I snuck out one night," he says. "Was trying to catch peeny-wally." Fireflies. "Was looking, and I whistled. And then I heard this sound behind me. Like chains rattling."

"And the Calf was there?" I ask.

A long pause. The ceiling fan whirs, sends a chill through the air.

"You said you saw it."

"I almost did," Luis admits.

I grab the laundry basket and smile a little. "And you almost got me. Good one." I use my free hand to rub his head, then I shut off the fan light. "Night, Luis."

Luis groans loudly enough for me to hear even after I close the door.

A tremor runs down my spine. Of all the stories for Luis to tell, why did it have to be one about a bull?

When I was fourteen, Dad won some tickets at work and insisted on taking me and my new friend Joy to see this rodeo at Madison Square Garden. I'd told him she used to take horseback riding lessons, and he just ran with the yeehaw.

Life with Joy was still fresh, and up to that point, all of it had been spent in her corner of the universe. That corner had lots of extravagant dinners with her tycoon mom and private screenings of yet-to-be-released movies. That's what Joy was used to.

And here I was, dragging her to a rodeo I didn't want to go to. That's what I had to give.

I worried she'd hate it. We'd go home afterward, and she'd block my number with a quickness for being a broke-ass loser, nothing to offer but dopey cowboys and barrel racing. She'd get over whatever weird charity interest she'd taken in me and go back to hanging out with people more on her level. How else could our friendship end?

But Joy took to the show like it had been her idea to come. She cheered and screamed and chuckled from her stomach, full and real. She fit in even when she didn't. Even in a Gucci cowboy hat.

I tried to do what she did. Hollered and taunted all the horses and bulls from my seat. Laughed even though this wasn't fun to me.

Laughed even though I was uneasy about the animals, the crowd, the possibility that Joy might be humoring me.

Halfway through the show, one bull tossed his rider. A gasp rippled through the spectators. The bull rampaged around the ring, dodging the cowboys trying to contain him.

The bull charged right at us. It's like he found us in the crowd and singled us—me—out. Eyes lit with rage, hooves stomping and kicking dirt into the air. Like a demon on the hunt. Ready to crash through the barrier, impale us with his horns.

That was the end. I knew it. I shrieked until I tasted blood.

At the last moment, the bull swerved.

I couldn't stop shaking. Dad held me tight, asked me if I was okay, then told me that I was. Joy didn't say a word, seemed more amused than frightened. She watched the staff restrain and haul the fucker away.

We all bailed once I could stand. And I knew: this mess was absolutely payback from the universe for trying to bring Joy into my world, for trying to give her anything of mine when I knew I didn't have shit.

And for being a pain in the ass.

I know better now. I try not to tempt trouble. Most of the time. But trouble finds me anyway.

Exhaustion bleeds into my bones. My quarters are on the east end of the floor, far from all of the Halls' rooms. Good thing the laundry chute is on the way. I shuffle down the darkened corridor, past Mr. and Mrs. Hall's bedroom. Warm light spills under the door.

So do voices.

"This is a problem." That's Mrs. Hall. She sounds tense, frustrated. It's so strange to hear, it makes me slow down. "You see it too, don't you?"

Mr. Hall shushes her. It's not comforting. "Breathe, Ruth," he says, speaking with a rumble. "I see it, I do. But be calm. This is a controlled situation. There is nothing for us to fear."

"Ian, this could uproot every—"

"Everything is perfect," he says firmly. "Yes?"

There's a drawn-out silence. Thin shadows shift, fluid as ink. Then: "Yes, love. Of course."

There's that skin prickle again, a tension in my jaw.

What if they know?

The bull rampaged around the ring...

Their doorknob jiggles. My heart's in my throat.

The curfew bell will ring soon. If the Halls think I'm eavesdropping, violating their privacy rules, they'll send me back to New York without a second thought. I'll have done all this work for nothing. Worn this mask of perfection for no reason.

I'm not tempting trouble tonight.

So I move.

I toss the dirty laundry and any memory of what I've heard down the chute together.

FIVE

YOUNG BIRDS

ORA: rina, you done work yet??
ORA: promised you live music. rum bar TONIGHT!! can pick you up if chicken not home!!
JOSH: only nite we all have off 4 long time. need a break fr.
JOSH: come so me n rush not bored w/ juney n chicken lol
SIMONE: The dependable ones is boring? Figures
SIMONE: Been saving up to dance though
AARON: shouldn't miss bar night with the young birds. it's rare.
AARON: and the music good. trust me.

Should I be going out five days into my new job? Probably not. Yeah, for my hard work so far, I was gifted a curfew-free night, but I still have to come back to Blackbead once the party's over. Still have work tomorrow morning. And it feels like the mansion is studying me, even though the nights have been comfortably quiet.

But I've also been on edge since I arrived. I've done my best to be the nanny that the family needs. Attentive, enthusiastic, always positive.

But the Halls have rules upon orders upon decrees—no white flowers in the house, respect the mango tree, never touch the family portraits. I spend each day tiptoeing around Blackbead, trying to complete my tasks without disturbing the family or letting my upright image slip. I'm lucky to be here, and being here is hard as hell. Exhausting, even.

The truth? I miss parties. The music, the people, the freedom. Blackbead is isolating, removed from the rest of the island. Joy would have been disappointed if she'd stayed here; there's been zero time to really experience Jamaica. So, a night to let loose a little bit? To finally get out and lock myself into the Young Birds for good?

CARINA: I'm in.

This is me.

Loud drums. Strong drinks. Close bodies.

The bar's a true hole-in-the-wall—grimy lemon-yellow walls, old concrete floor, a bunch of discarded sun hats and abandoned flip-flops tied to the ceiling as decor. All the way in the back, behind the counter, there's shelves of Appleton and Wray & Nephew. There are four or five wooden barstools, a couple small tables on each side of the open entrance, two more outside. Every other spare inch is for the band—and the makeshift dance floor.

It's like the whole world's crammed inside this little bar, a few dozen people ready to get lost in dancehall, rum, and sweat.

I'm pure energy.

The band ends their song, and I pout, already missing the lead singer's crooning tone. Scattered applause, some whoops and hollers. Now that the room's calmer, the bare light bulbs overhead quit swinging like wrecking balls. Ora takes my hand and pulls me through the crowd, to the bar in the back.

"Them boys by the door been watching you all night," she shouts over the noise.

Oh, I noticed. They're wearing sleeveless white shirts that show off their arms, tattoos on display. One caught my gaze, rocked a self-assured smile. Probably cocky because he's sure he could get a girl like me.

But I'm not just a girl.

He should be more careful.

"Not here for them," I reply flatly. And I mean it. Ora squeezes my hand in solidarity. It's a fuckboy-free night.

The rest of the group trickles our way as Ora slaps the counter for another round of shots. I steal a barstool and rest my sore feet. I'm out of practice. Simone finishes her beer. Josh wipes the sweat off his face. And Aaron nurses some water. Don't think he's had a drink all night.

This is the first time I've really seen Aaron out of his work clothes. I like the way his shirt fits across his chest, the scar by his eyebrow, the toothpick clamped between his teeth. I pretend like I'm more concerned about the dirt staining my white denim shorts than how good he looks.

"Know what I figure?" Ora asks. She peers at me sideways. "Time to give the girl a pet name, yeah?"

Ora did say she makes nicknames for everyone. And she uses them just as much as their government ones. Simone is Juney because she's born in June, like me, and Josh is Scoob since he has the same energy as Scooby-Doo. Ora's is Rush because she doesn't slow down for anything. And Aaron's is Chicken. I can't imagine how he fell into that one. He seems more like a King or a Don.

And now it's my turn. This will be fun.

Ora holds up a finger. "One idea, each of us. Go."

From Simone: Princess. Which isn't fair, because I don't even act stuck-up or snooty or anything.

Ora's choice: Singa. She must have realized I sometimes sing to myself when I'm nervous.

And Josh—smart-ass—offers Bugeye. Ouch. So much for my eyes being a compliment cheat code.

"What happened to Rina?" I ask everyone. "Or even CiCi?" Those used to be my go-tos back home.

Ora does her witch cackle. "Oh, she no like them." She pinches my cheek like I'm Jada. "How 'bout Screw Face, then, since you wanna frown so?"

"Bambi."

Aaron's suggestion cuts through.

I like it.

"I vote for Bambi," Simone says.

Josh studies me closely, thinks it over. "Did say Bugeye for the big eyes them. Bambi works too. My vote."

"We don't vote," Ora says. "I decide." She looks up at Aaron, sighs. "It fit, though . . ." She raises her shot glass high. "To Bambi!"

"Big up!"

I throw back the rum, feel it burn my throat on the way down. The taste makes the hair on the back of my neck stand on end. Makes me feel alive. The others follow. Aaron salutes me with his water glass.

And just like that, a whole new family.

My second in under a week.

We're sitting at one of the tables—Josh knee-deep in a wild story about working for the Halls—when the night goes sideways.

"Mad shit go down in the kitchen," he says while we're still chuckling. "Don't know how it all follow me."

"Because you make it happen," Simone replies. "You bring chaos 'pon yourself and then act surprised."

"Nah, I get into a normal amount of trouble, for real. The Halls them intense for no reason. No, for the wrong reason." He takes a swig of his beer and slams the bottle down a little too hard.

"You upset still?" Ora asks. "About the pay? Already bought you drink to apologize. Let it go."

"Is not about the money, Rush. It's the rule. It stupid, selfish, wasteful—"

"Didn't know you care so much about these things," Aaron murmurs. "Justice, fairness, on and on."

"You don't know because you guys hear me but don't listen. Hard ears, all a you."

"That a true," Ora replies. "Why we want listen to you?"

There's music to how they speak—the melodic lilt of patois spoken easily between close friends. Up to now, most people have used Standard English to talk to me, to help me understand. And I appreciate it. And it feels strange. Embarrassing.

My ears were raised on mostly American accents. Mom's patois is a language that's slowly escaped her over the years, one she has to reach a little further for with each season. But it's still her birthright, still suits her. Growing up, I'd try on Jamaican words that fit like all my hand-me-downs—well-worn by others, but a joke on me. Like I'm playing pretend. Mom taught me a curse once, and the second I repeated it, she laughed herself to tears. She apologized, of course.

But now I know to keep my mouth shut.

"Well," Josh says, "hear me now: the Halls them immoral. Morning, noon, night. Call themselves Jamaican, but I would rather die than be compared to them. I'll tell you a joke, but never tell you a lie. I see what goes on. I pay attention."

My mental profile of Josh so far doesn't include the trait perceptive. Silly, laid-back, even bighearted, okay. But maybe I'm missing something, because I'm not seeing what he's seeing.

The Halls have been what I expected: very rich, somewhat demanding, but altogether polite. Yes, they're wealthy, but they aren't evil. They're privileged. Being out of touch isn't a crime. And I know crime. If Scoob were truly paying attention, maybe he'd see *that*.

Simone shushes Josh, peeps around the bar like she's praying nobody can hear us. "Okay, so what would you have we do?" she questions. "You say they evil, yet still you work for them. Why? Because you need them. Just like Jamaica need them. We worse off without. You think Badrick and them bleeding hearts can do better?"

"But don't it bother you to see Hall run the parish so?" Josh asks. "Dante young, working in the community. Could use his power and change everything, you hear? But what him do? Same as his father: nothing. That doesn't burn you up, Juney?"

"I skin my teeth and do my work. Be smart, not loud."

"Nah, loud up the thing."

"Then be fair about what good they do," Aaron urges. "They give scholarships, buy school uniforms—"

"—Okay with sending the children to school hungry, though."

"Even me," Aaron continues, "living on their property for free."

"But nothing's free. We pay with work. It's slavery all over again, and everyone know it. Whole parish bow to their face and suck teeth in private."

"And where all the people who agree with you, yeah?" Ora asks.

Josh curses. "Most people are not like me. They afraid to speak out in case the Halls them bite back. Then them outta job, money, food."

"You drink too much," Aaron says. "Mr. Hall would not ruin someone like that."

"How so? Man took the money I earned from me. Why not you? Or anyone else?" Josh wheels around to me, practically pleading. "These people don't care 'bout none a us. They wear the fakey Rasta hat. Shake white man hand and say, 'Yah, mon.' It's all bullshit!"

A young man strolls over from the bar, eyes peeled on Josh. "We cool here?" The guy's cute with his full lips and slightly crooked nose. He places a hand on Josh's shoulder. "Think 'bout take a walk? Calm yourself."

"You don't tell me what to do," Josh spits back. But a few seconds later, he pushes back from the table and stalks out the back door.

Aaron stands, offers the guy a "Thanks," and chases after Josh.

Ora watches Aaron leave. "Chicken will talk to him, and he'll be fine. Liquor make Scoob testy."

"The rum gets us all soon enough," says the young man. He looks at me. "I hope he didn't scare you. You seem quiet while he was going off."

"No, I'm good." I'm self-conscious about my words, my accent, how I fit into this occasion. "Can handle myself okay."

"Foreign girl?" he says with a smirk. "Yeah, bet you handle yourself fine."

He's flirting. He's interested. And it feels good. It always did. What's not to like about the little fantasy world two people build for the few minutes they talk? A wave of sadness washes over me. I miss things being this uncomplicated.

Ora leans onto the table. "Anyway, thanks, brother. The girls need to talk now." He gets the message, and after one final glance at me, he saunters away.

"Problem?" I ask her.

"No, he seem okay. But you said no men tonight." She got me there. Ora winks at me like a proud older sister. "Yet see you. Pulling them so." I feel a dull pang in my gut. Like I know I should feel shame for even talking to that guy. But for the first time in a while, the shame doesn't come right away.

Proof I'm not ready to be left to my own devices.

I peek at Simone. She sits on my left and glides her thumb across her drained water glass. Her brow's furrowed like she's thinking about something she can't stand. And I guess she feels me staring because she looks up, looks me right in the eye.

There's this hard stare like I've done something wrong. Like she knows me. My mouth becomes dry as dust.

Then she blinks, and it's gone.

Simone leans over, her voice nectar-sweet. "Everything good, Bambi?" I nod, try to swallow. Ora throws an arm around my shoulder, drags me out of the uncomfortable moment. But not entirely.

Am I paranoid? Or perceptive?

Do I see everything that goes on?

Drink count: unknown.

I sway in my chair at the table and nudge a stranger's empty cup with my elbow. Almost everyone's disappeared for bathroom breaks or fresh air. The band's long gone, so the standing speakers reverberate with reggae classics instead. Overhead, a light bulb flickers. Some older men chat loudly outside as their domino game heats up. The booze slows everything to a crawl.

This was a good night. Not perfect, but fun. The kind Joy and I used to live for any weekend we could. She'd love this place.

But she's not here.

How fucking sad.

Aaron pulls up a seat beside me, distracts me from my pity party. "So, how your first night as an official Young Bird?" he asks.

We're alone. We've never been alone before. Maybe that should worry me.

"Been okay," I tell him. "Helping me settle in."

"You must miss home," he says softly.

An ember of something I don't want to name kindles in my belly. I've enjoyed the few days I've been here, but Aaron's been the only one to wonder if I'm adjusting well. The only one to ask—minus Jada.

"I do miss home," I say. *Careful.* That warning is quiet, but it's there. "I mean, it's great. But ... the energy's different at Blackbead." Josh mouthed off about the Halls enough already, so no need to pile on. But he was right about one thing: the family and the mansion are ... exacting. Never mind that dense heat I feel all around the property, that honeyed scent on the air. Still not sure what that's about. "I don't know. The vibes are just kind of ..."

"Strange?" Aaron offers. Damn, is that rude to admit? But that's how I feel. The Halls have opened their beautiful home to me, they treat me well even though I'm still learning all their rules, the kids like me almost too much. But something's not clicking. "Wealthy people live different," Aaron explains. "And living with them? Make you feel off. Trust me."

He's not wrong. With Joy, I saw firsthand how rich people live. And the Halls have their own unique concerns with the whole politics thing. So maybe I just need time. And by the end of the summer, who knows? All the weirdness could vanish. I scan the bar's deserted concrete floor.

"Do you ... wanna dance?" Aaron asks.

"With you?"

"Why not?"

"Not sure you *can* dance," I tease. "All you've done is people watch."

"Hey, I've spent half the night just noticing you."

Oh.

See, talking to Aaron isn't like joking with Josh or flirting with some guy in a bar. It's like Aaron really tries to see me. I don't have to guess if he's genuine. He makes me feel sure that he is. It's simple with him.

"So, you're just going to admit that?" I ask.

"Admiring how island life suit you, that's all. Now come." He stands, holds his hand out. Even in the hazy light, his smile devastates me. "Can teach you how to move like a Jamaican."

Careful.

I shouldn't go with him. But I've been good tonight. Who does one dance hurt?

We go to the floor.

Aaron slides behind me, grasps my hips with calloused, warm hands. The bass crashes against my chest. He guides my body, rolling me against him. There's his breath on my ear, my neck. I close my eyes, imagine it's just the two of us here.

Something within winds its way around my rib cage, recalls how powerful it used to be.

I used to never say no to myself. Now I remember why.

I'm not weak in the knees. No butterflies, no floating on air. But it's hunger, and it's got teeth. It's fun to want but even better to have.

The thing with teeth glides through my drunkenness and my thirst and it rises to life.

So alive.

Without warning, my skin prickles. Like something's wrong. I open my eyes.

There's Ora, sitting at our table. Watching us.

Her glower is so intense, I feel like I've been caught cheating on a math test. And for what? I freeze. Aaron leans down, whispers in my ear. "All good, Bambi?"

I shiver. I'm not cold. "Feel a little sick. Gonna sit." His hands drop off my waist, and he lets me go. I don't want to go.

I grab a seat next to Ora. "You were gone forever. You okay?"

"Long line for toilet." I can't read her expression. She leans toward me. "Can I be honest with you?"

"Of course."

"You know how I told you most men are dogs?" She spies Aaron and Simone talking across the bar. "Not him."

Oh.

"You . . . like Aaron." And she just witnessed the two of us, bodies pressed against each other like we'd die if air came between us. Is that why she brought it up? "I had no idea." Ora's concealed her feelings well. Or maybe it's been totally obvious and I didn't want to face the facts that were right in front of my face. Both powerful possibilities.

"I try to hide it," she admits. "Been friends since he was a skinny little chicken." Guess that's where the nickname came from, since he isn't scrawny now. "Seen each other through everything: death of my brother, shit with his parents. To him, we're family."

There it is. "But not to you."

Ora sighs. It's so lovesick, so girlish. So unlike her. "Dating pool here small; everybody know everybody. And everybody know he never play games. Body built for sin. But he won't even look at me." She shrugs a little. "Maybe if I'm patient, he'll see me." And I know how good it feels to be seen by him.

But this is Ora. Bold, bright, loud. "Why not tell him now?"

"No, no. Bad time." I wait for more explanation. It never comes. Ora rubs my knee, half smiles. "But I told you 'cause you seem like a safe. Words go in your ears, but nothing come out your mouth. Lock up tight."

Guilt tries to drown me. I almost let it. God, I've missed having a friend to gossip with, dance with, be real with. Ora's perfect. And here I am, days into our friendship, crossing the line. Hurting her.

Joy would do a lot, but she wouldn't do this.

The flickering light bulb sparks, burns out. Ora curses in the darkness. Worry settles into my mind.

I have to leave Aaron alone. Or I'll be alone.

Again.

My stomach twists.

Ora points her phone's flashlight in my face. "You look like a ghost. What's wrong?"

"Gonna throw up."

Ora twists the top off a shaker on the table and grabs a pinch. "Open wide." I listen, and she sprinkles salt on my tongue. "That's the remedy, Bambi. This'll soothe you."

But her help's just salt in the wound.

SIX

I need to go home.

Crickets chirp, their song surrounding me as I sit on the curb outside the bar. It's humid as hell. Mosquitoes eat me up, and their bites swell across my legs and arms. Under the green-tinged lights, they look disgusting.

I want to slide into my room, wash my face, and put the night behind me so I can forget every awkward, screwy thing from the last hour.

"Hey," someone says. Low voice, a bit hoarse. Josh, maybe, finally done raging about work. "What you need?"

Water. A ride home. Clothes that fit. A time machine. Some common fucking sense.

"Honestly?" I ask. "Chicken nuggets and fries. From Burger King."

He laughs, and the sound would knock me on my ass if I weren't already sitting. That's not Josh. It's Aaron. No, not now. Anyone but him. "You Jamaican, come live in Jamaica, then ask for Burger King?" And despite myself, I laugh too. Hysterically. It feels good to get a break from my own drama.

"I'm not making any sense," I sputter as I wipe away tears.

He stands over me, his profile dipped in shadow. "Come. Ora ask me to take you home."

"Ora did?"

"Them three sober up and help Leon close shop. But I'm good to drive. And you... look a little rough. The Halls them have rules about staff drinking. Hope they don't catch you."

I try to track Aaron's face in the dark. Ora seemed serious about him. She's a firework, but talking about Aaron made her so soft—like candlelight. I don't want to get in the way of them, don't want to put a single concern in Ora's mind. So how would it look if she saw us leaving together?

A headache blooms in my temples. But if Ora told Aaron to help me... maybe it's fine. Maybe she'd rather I get home safe, even if that means getting a ride from the guy she's into. The idea that people could be nice to me simply to be nice is clearly hard for me to imagine.

Okay. The sooner we leave, the sooner we're done.

I investigate the near-vacant lot. "Which car's yours?"

He points to a spot near the bar's entrance, and I follow his finger.

That's not a car.

That's a motorcycle. A reflective little two-wheeler in blue and black.

My lungs hitch. "Nope. Not going anywhere near that." I've never ridden a motorcycle before. Sure, I've always wanted to, but this feels like the wrong time to try.

"You have another way?" he asks. "We already headed the same place."

He's not wrong... I stand, surrender. "Okay. Let's go."

Aaron leads me to his bike and helps me onto the rear seat. He fits his helmet onto my head. His fingers brush the underside of my chin as he clicks the clasp into place.

"What about you?" I ask.

"Hard-headed. Don't worry 'bout me."

Aaron hops into the front, pulls my arms around his waist. "Hold tight. Like life or death."

I've lost my mind. I really latch on. "Life or death."

We roll away from the rum bar.

And then comes the terror.

My heart's in my throat. The few streetlights we pass zip by in a blur. My braids fly behind me as we speed through the sultry Caribbean night. I can't breathe as the wind hits my cheeks, pulls tears from my eyes. I can't think while the bike rumbles down these long, half-lit roads. I hold on to Aaron tighter, wonder when we'll topple in some catastrophic crash.

"You're okay," Aaron tells me, raising his voice over the roaring engine. "You're safe."

And then the panic lets up. Just a little. And underneath that is this feeling like maybe he's right. That the adrenaline rushing through me isn't an omen saying that I'm at death's door.

It's proof that there's still blood running through my veins.

I whoop into the night air and hear myself echo.

I lean into the warmth of Aaron's body, the softness of his shirt. I catch his scent—a bit of mint, a bit of rum, a lot of him.

Temptation still calls to me, and I hate that I want to answer.

Minutes later, we pull into Blackbead's driveway, right up to the staff's side entrance. A few feet away, the veranda lights illuminate the front of the house.

"This your stop, Bambi."

I know. But once I let go of him, I let go of this moment. Letting go is impossible.

But I should. So I do.

I free Aaron from my grip and hop off the rear seat. Unclasp the helmet myself. "Thanks for the ride, Chicken." I hand the helmet to him, and he grabs it. We hold it between us.

His eyes meet mine. Then they travel down—to my lips. And back up. A stare that consumes me, roots me in place.

Walk away.

"Night," I say.

"Be careful."

And I run into the house, closing the door behind me.

I pray the dark hid my flushed face.

I pray the dark remembers this moment that will never happen again.

Apparently, the cost of that motorcycle ride was one of my earrings. Guess nothing comes free.

I tiptoe into my bedroom, quietly close the door behind me so nobody in the Halls' wing hears me—shit, so Blackbead itself doesn't hear me scuttling around like a shameful, drunk crab. And right when the door clicks shut, I get that feeling again, like I did on my first day here. That warmth in my chest, down my backbone. A spike of nausea.

Maybe the alcohol. But probably the guilt. For spending time with Aaron. For liking him in the first place. Maybe I'm lucky that my one punishment for that is an upset stomach and a lost earring.

My limbs feel too heavy to move. But I still shuffle to the bathroom, desperate to splash cool water on my face and scrub away some of the bar grime. I flick on the light.

On the mirror.

Deep red marks.

The face of a bull, horns sharply drawn.

And a word—*Run*—scrawled across the glass.

Run.

Run.

Run.

Someone's been here.

"What the fuck?" I hear my own voice, louder than I mean it to be. Is this blood? Can't stand blood. I retch. Did someone on the staff do this? Shit, maybe the Young Birds lured me out for the night on purpose. I mumble—"no no no no no"—and my breath comes too quick.

Even freaked out and disgusted, I don't hesitate. All of this needs to go. I scramble to wipe everything off the mirror. Bottles tumble from the counter and crash against the floor. The bull's snout smears under my fingertips.

Lipstick. In Ora's usual shade.

Could it be her? But that doesn't make sense. She was with me all night, and she wouldn't do something like this anyway. And I didn't know about her and Aaron until an hour or two ago.

I search the shadowy alcoves of the bedroom, hunt for the outline of an intruder in the sweeping window curtains. My muscles tense, like I'm ready to sprint.

A thought staggers into my brain, and I can't unthink it. What if somebody here knows the truth?

It's almost impossible. I've been careful. I've put on the performance of a lifetime since I landed in Jamaica. Covered my tracks by deactivating my social media, wiping all my profile pics, even switching to fake names so nobody can search for me. Hardly anyone knew about Joy's work assignment, and nobody could know I took over her job. My own parents have no clue.

But . . .

I think of the lockbox. Unassuming black steel holding half my secrets. I imagine a key shoved into the lock, the lid thrown back, everything within uncovered.

What if?

What if someone here knows the truth about me?

Outside my room—footsteps.

But nobody sleeps on my side of the house.

Careful.

There's a sharp knock.

"Hello?" I hear myself again, scared this time.

I close the bathroom door and whirl around to face whoever comes. It's Dante.

He stands in the threshold, irritated. He's in a navy polo and dress pants, his face warped into a scowl. Like having to check on "the help" is the biggest disruption from his golden life. "Problem?" he asks.

This is the first time we've ever spoken, and I'm fighting the urge to puke. Aaron warned me to not get caught. But here I am, drunk, covered in someone's red lipstick, with an earring missing. Days into building trust with these people, and I'm blowing it up. I clear my throat, try not to look at Dante directly.

"Well?"

I don't know what's going on, but I know I don't need Dante involved. I glance at the bed, where I hope the box still rests underneath. Just need Dante to leave so I can think, so I can check.

"I am so sorry, sir," I start. "I didn't mean to . . . to bother you." Get it together. I swipe my tongue over my cracked bottom lip. "No problems here. Just a little . . . I got startled by a . . . lizard . . . sir."

Dante's eyes hold on my face. My cheeks warm. That judgment again. My mind imagines Dante evaluating me with equal parts revulsion and disdain. Now, a vision of Dante taking detailed, handwritten notes about me and every infraction I've broken just tonight. Then, Dante telling his parents that the new au pair is ghetto and untrustworthy and needs to be terminated immediately.

Then everything else coming out. The fake papers, the stolen IDs.

Do not call the agency. Please.

He takes one step into my room. Pauses. My spine's stiff.

Run.

Run.

Run.

Finally, Dante says: "This is your one pass. To bed, please, Miss Carter."

"Yes. So sorry, sir. Good night." He idles for a moment longer before leaving. I listen as his footsteps fade away.

Then silence.

Blackbead is silent.

I bolt for the bed.

The box is still there, lock intact.

My body goes slack; my knees wobble.

That honey-sweet scent hits my nose.

I vomit in the toilet.

SEVEN

All I've done before the morning bell is hunt for pain meds and Windex my bathroom mirror.

Dawn creeps across the sky as I hike outside of Blackbead and stand by the pedestrian gate. Open road stretches to my left and right, and it's as if I'm alone in the world. I turn my phone over and over, dig the pads of my thumbs into any nooks and crannies on the red and silver case, any sensation to distract me from this ice-pick migraine.

I woke and almost didn't remember last night. Had a few tranquil seconds before it all flooded back.

The music, the dancing, the motorcycle ride with Aaron through the cool Caribbean night. The night I became Bambi.

Then: Ora. The bull drawn in lipstick. Dante chastising me. I was so close to tearing down everything I've tried to build, and it would have been my own fault.

I switch on my phone screen, scan all the unanswered private messages from yesterday and this morning.

AARON: sleep tight, bambi.

JOSH: sry 4 last nite. rum hit different

SIMONE: Tell me if need help with kids today

ORA: bambi let me know you're ok!! will hunt you down if you ignore me!!

I quickly let everyone know I'm alive. They all checked on me. Even Josh, in his own way. And this morning, there was no pink slip under my door, so I'm not unemployed yet. Everything seems fine.

Which makes yesterday more confusing.

Someone came into my room and drew that bull. To send a message, I guess. To scare me. But why? Could the kids have teamed up to mess with me? Did the staff haze me? I even consider asking the group chat if anyone knows something. But I've had a target on my back before. The more that people know they're upsetting you, the harder they push. If the asshole hears that I'm rattled, they might escalate. And the asshole could be nearly anyone in Blackbead.

I'll keep this to myself. And until I figure out who did this, I'll be on high alert. If someone knows I'm not Joy, what I do next will depend entirely on who found out and what I think they'll do with the info. Watch and be watched. That's the game now.

There are two more unread messages. From Mom.

MOM: Dad wants to know what you thought of Scotts Bluff.

Right. Forgot that picture hit their phones yesterday. I set a photo to send at 11:03 a.m., proof that I'm exploring open Nebraskan prairies. Scheduled messages come in clutch.

I'm not sure what my parents would do if they learned where I actually am, aka Not Nebraska. But I can guess how they'd feel. Mom would be livid realizing I'd disobeyed her, and Dad would be hurt that I'd lied to him. They'd both be confused how I wound up in Jamaica after all of Mom's demanding that I stay away. But to understand, they'd have to know more. And I can't tell them more without disappointing them. Despite the tension between us over the years, I do love my parents. Hurting them isn't something that I'd ever purposely do unless I had no other choice.

So instead, they know what they need to.

They know I was depressed toward the end of the school year. They know I spent all day cooped up in my bedroom, thinking. And they know what I said a few weeks ago—that I was ready to get back out there, shake this low mood. A cross-country road trip with a friend would be good for me. Limited Wi-Fi and cell phone reception. Plenty of free time to sort myself out. Trails and natural wonders and fresh air. I'd come home a whole new person.

I showed them the free camping gear I grabbed off someone local to prep for the trip. I gave them my itinerary, which national parks my friend and I planned to visit, which campgrounds and motels we'd stay at.

But I was never going on a road trip. I had other plans.

Jamaica.

Joy's job in Jamaica, I mean. I got the call, the opportunity fell in my lap, and I went for it. How often does a clean slate just come to you?

So instead of taking a rideshare to a friend's house so we could pack into her van, I paid for a trip to the airport. Because there was no friend.

Hadn't been one in a while.

Mom and Dad were doing their best with me, but I don't think they know what it's like to be lost. To drift. They wouldn't understand why I had no choice but to go on this trip. Why I needed to lock into someplace else and start anew. They don't realize the shit I'd put myself in back home.

Mom's second text?

MOM: Need to know you're alive. Is everything OK?

Guilt pulls at my chest, tightens it. Is everything okay? Well, that's up for debate.

"Carina, good morning!"

I leap out of my skin. Turns out it's just Wesley at the staff door, his loud and thunderous voice carrying through the morning air. Probably waiting to hear my requests for the breakfast spread. But I don't know how to act normal yet. Not with my nerves this raw. So I croak out a reply—"Morning! I'll be in soon."—and then scroll through my phone like I'm searching for something important. I look busy.

And then I *am* busy. Careening down the rabbit hole. Flipping through my photo gallery packed with screenshots of tweets, DMs, and texts, vivid memories of how I'm remembered back home.

@LANARJONES
If you're mutuals with me and Carina, you're getting blocked.

@BREANNNNNNA07
messy bitches stay messy. 👀 the truth always comes out.

@GLITTERBITCHNY
don't bother blocking me. got tons of accounts. and if I see you, it's on sight. swear to god. i will FUCK YOUR SHIT UP.

UNKNOWN NUMBER
Carina. I don't get it. Why?

On and on. Picture after picture. Everything I wish I could erase. But I can't.

It's everything I know that I deserve.

Maybe I should have been strong enough to stomach a month of people attacking me, but I couldn't. The barrage was relentless. I hardly slept, and when I did, I'd wake up to so many messages like these, each ripping me to pieces. Most from strangers, some from girls I grew up with, people I called my friends before everything. I made a mistake—a huge one—and I've been paying for it.

Dad used to worry that all of my partying and drinking with Joy was my biggest problem. That the alcohol might kill me if I wasn't more careful. But those texts? The tweets? Nearly took me out.

After last night, should I leave Blackbead? Apparently, someone here thinks so. But there's no going home. I'm not ready yet.

I need this to work. I will make this work.

I turn on my phone camera, angle the lens so it shows only my face and none of my surroundings. Press Record.

"Mom, consider this proof of life. I'm *fine*. And Scotts Bluff was very cool. Now don't worry about me. Everything's perfect." I force a smile. "I'll update you soon."

The video slowly loads into our thread.

I make sure my next scheduled road trip update is ready to send in two days. A picture I found of steam rising from white rock terraces and pools of hot water. The Mammoth Hot Springs, apparently.

Hope my parents love seeing me in Yellowstone.

EIGHT

Centerpieces blooming with yellow roses and purple hydrangea. Ice clinking in glasses full of sweet rum cream and tart sorrel. Plates of mango cheesecake and curry goat, smoky jerk shrimp and creamy coconut drops. Silk and chiffon, exquisite dinnerware, an ice sculpture cut in the shape of Jamaica's hummingbird.

And me, on a Friday night, in a shimmering white-and-gold shift dress, chosen by Mr. Hall just for the evening. ("A former employee left this dress behind, but please wear it tonight. It looks like it was made for you, my dear.") It feels strange to be in something other than all-white boring shit. I'm shining for this event at one of the parish's most opulent banquet halls—the Hibiscus.

Tonight is the kickoff for Mr. Hall's campaign fundraising push. It all starts right here, surrounded by at least a hundred devout supporters with long histories and deep pockets.

It's only been two days, but I miss that dirty-ass rum bar already.

I wrangle the kids to a back corner and check my phone, stuffed into the gold-beaded clutch Mrs. Hall gifted to me. No calls, no texts. The Hibiscus is a total dead zone, so nobody will be reaching me tonight.

"We can't disturb the guests," I explain to Luis and Jada, "so let's play quietly, okay?"

"But what do we do?" Luis asks.

Yeah, about that. I grab some napkins off a nearby serving table and hand them over with the small pack of crayons I was just barely able to stuff into my bag along with Luis's inhaler. "How about you try drawing each other?"

They break away, clearly ticked. And I don't blame them. I should have tried to bring a game, or at least an actual coloring book. Joy would have thought of something fun to keep them busy. But my head's not in it tonight. Hasn't been in it for a couple days now.

Everyone at Blackbead has been acting so regular lately, and it's stressing me out.

The Young Birds joke with me in the chat daily. Wesley gives me an extra-large dessert every evening. Clive, one of the live-in housekeepers, started leaving towel animals on my bed every night. Even Dante has been gracious enough to avoid me and pretend that bizarre moment in my room never happened.

But somewhere, someone is observing me. Someone wants me gone. How do I focus on coloring books when I know that?

So I sidle into the corner and look. I can keep watch too.

Bodies glide through the space. I catch snippets of conversation: questions about a recent vacation to Monaco, someone's latest business venture in Kingston.

"Where's Whitney?" asks a bubbly young woman a couple steps away. She must be talking to her friend by her side. "Thought she'd be here tonight. We never miss the Halls' get-togethers."

I avoid eye contact, fixate on her shoes instead. Black with red-bottom heels.

"Swayed to the other side," her friend whispers. Her crystal-drenched pumps come to a point so sharp, they could double as a weapon. "She fell for Badrick's 'A Better Jamaica' con. Donated the moment she heard him speak."

Gossip amongst the elite is both bougie *and* boring. But I listen. Because I remember what Josh said at the bar, how he felt the Halls were out of touch. Like they weren't doing enough and people deserved better than them. Does better exist? Are the Halls all that bad?

Miss Louboutin huffs. "Whitney too? I don't understand. A boy shows up with almost no credentials, says he's going to make a difference. All this empty talk of progress and change. And now he's skyrocketed to party leader?" There's this nervous pause. "What if everyone votes for his side? Then we'll have some nobody for prime minister."

Lady Jimmy Choo hums in thought. "I'm not worried. Ian's waited for his turn. Invested in the community, in tradition. Jamaica needs stability, and everyone with a brain knows that means we need Ian. We'll win majority and have him as PM soon enough."

"We'll make sure of that," Miss Louboutin titters.

A new pair of shoes strolls into view. Responsible black slip-ons with serious grip. Shoes for a server.

I look up and see Simone's face.

Not flying solo after all. I break into a smile. "Juney, what are you doing here?"

"Bills need be paid. Simple." Simone doesn't smile. I think I'm slipping again . . . I blink, try to reset my image of her like I did at the bar. But this time, her face doesn't change. Behind her, the kids attempt to draw on each other's arms. "Get them back to the table. Have them sit proper."

"They're so bored, they're practically bouncing off the walls," I tell her. "They need to tire themselves out."

"I'm helping you, Joy," she says. My body freezes. Not Bambi. Not even Carina. *Joy.* "The Halls will have words if you don't take my advice. But up to you." She walks off, her serving platter perfectly balanced.

Simone's taken the longest to warm up to me. It's like her spirit doesn't accept me yet. But besides glaring while serving tea to Mrs. Hall and me, she's never been straight-up hostile before.

Run! Run!

That's impossible. We were at the bar together. It couldn't be her . . . could it?

No. Simone must be having a rough night. Hell, so am I. Even if she dislikes me, she wouldn't go after me like that. I'm letting paranoia spin out weird shit that doesn't even make sense.

I push the thought away and nudge the kids. "Let's go." Luis moans and drags his feet. I hold Jada's little hand.

Mr. Hall and Dante stand by the table, showing out in their tailored suits and dress shoes. They're deep in conversation, but I can't hear them over the buzz of the crowd. Mr. Hall leans in, murmurs something in Dante's ear through clenched teeth. Serious expressions all around. Dante shakes his head, clenches his fists. When Mr. Hall pulls away, the two stare at each other, hard. Then Mr. Hall spots someone in the crowd over Dante's shoulder. A giant politician's grin bursts across his face. He lifts his chin and walks off, already prepped to shake hands with a supporter. Dante watches him go.

Okay, that was incredibly weird. I've never seen them interact like that. So I file that moment away. In case.

At the table, Luis starts picking at the centerpiece flowers before I even get a chance to sit. Yellow and lavender petals mix with green leaves on the gold tablecloth. I start gathering the petals, softly beg him to stop. But he's antsy. And so am I. Be calm. Stay calm.

"Hey."

Dante's voice cuts through.

He pulls a wad of plastic bills from his pocket, waves it in the kids' faces. "Treasure hunt: first to find a twenty-five-cent coin in the next three minutes gets all this to buy snacks."

Their eyes light up, and off they go.

Except I learned the other day that Jamaica doesn't use twenty-five-cent coins anymore. Dante's sent the kids on a wild-goose chase. Why? To give me a minute to get my shit together?

Well . . . I need it.

Dante takes his seat, leans back in his chair, and folds his arms. He's laser-focused on the stage, where his parents and the emcee quietly talk. I sit next to him, keep my knees and ankles close together like Mom taught me. "Thank you, sir," I say. "For the help, I mean."

He nods, barely glances at me. His mind's clearly on other things.

Relatable.

A couple minutes later, the kids come back with sour faces—and no twenty-five-cent coin. "Nobody has one," Jada whines.

"We asked everybody," Luis adds. "I think you tricked us."

Dante gives them each a fifty-dollar bill, probably just enough to buy some coco bread. Jada seems the most thrilled with her loot.

Screeching mic feedback draws everyone's attention to the stage.

"Ladies and gentlemen," the emcee starts. "Please sit for a few words from the Honorable Ian Hall."

No one listens. The room rises with applause as Mr. Hall shakes hands with the emcee and gives Mrs. Hall a kiss on the cheek. She stands back, regards him with love. He holds the mic with an easy, practiced grip.

"To my respected and generous guests, thank you for joining me and my family tonight. We are so blessed to have you by our sides as we embark on what I know will be a phenomenal campaign." Mr. Hall offers a wide grin. "This is just the beginning, for all of us."

I jump when the crowd erupts with cheers and claps. The air is electric; he's barely even said anything and people are already leaping to their feet. These people love Mr. Hall like he's Jesus, back from heaven.

And I get it. Mr. Hall doesn't stutter. No lazy posture, no cracks when he speaks. That's a man with a spine. And he's well-matched by his wife, dignity incarnate, pristinely styled. I've never seen two people so sophisticated. But it's like I'm seeing something not quite real, like one of Mr. Hall's portraits at Blackbead has come to life on stage.

"I understand that there is much to worry about," Mr. Hall says, his words weighty with empathy. "We are a nation built on family, community, and caring for one another. Yet with each passing day, and in the face of foreign influence, we forget ourselves. Our beautiful country struggles with its identity."

"You mean Jamaican? Caribbean? West Indian? There's three."

Dante is face forward, expressionless. But that *was* him talking. To . . . me?

"But we are a proud people," Mr. Hall continues. "A strong people. And with the right leadership, we will find ourselves again. We will rise up, at home and abroad. We will not only tell the world who we are, we will show them." He places a hand over his heart. "That is my promise to Jamaica, the land I love."

I'm learning to love it too. Jamaica's in my blood, but actually being here is special. Because for years, I believed there must be more to this country than the stereotypical stuff I'd taken, trying to fill my own culture gaps. Like, I'd tell people Sebastian the crab was my favorite Disney character when it's Ariel. I did the "cool girl" thing and sewed a marijuana leaf patch to my backpack until school admin made me remove it. Even wore Rasta hats for Halloween because everyone thought that was funny. It wasn't.

It's humiliating to feel like you're role-playing your identity because you don't know better. But slowly, I'm seeing more.

Dante sucks his teeth. "People clapping because my father knows the national anthem," he says under his breath. "Unbelievable." Can anyone else hear this? But all eyes are firmly—lovingly—on Mr. Hall.

Then Dante looks right at me. He looks so uncomfortable. But... also like he's trying?

After our last run-in, I need to get back in Dante's good graces. But making fun of his father? That's risky.

"This is a critical moment in our nation's history," Mr. Hall declares, "and our next steps will decide our future."

Let's hope the risk pays off.

"Did ChatGPT write his speech?" I whisper.

"Doubtful. He probably studied some parody remarks and thought they were good enough to copy," Dante replies.

"That's fine. He can still win everyone's vote by giving away Air Jordans."

"No, he'll serenade them with 'One Love,'" Dante whispers back. "Jamaicans love that. Not pandering at all."

Dante smirks a little. I barely know him. Definitely didn't think he was even capable of joking. But I guess his father is the one thing he'll poke fun at. A sore spot.

Noted.

The emcee gestures toward the Halls' table. "Come up for family photos and a bit of Q&A, please," he says. Luis wastes no time running to the stage. I prod a sleepy Jada to join him. Dante rises and straightens his jacket.

Once Dante stands before everyone, he transforms. Suddenly, he's working his angles. A politician in the making, a sounding board for his community. In front of all these cameras, he's Dante Hall, son of the Honorable Ian Hall.

Son of the man vying to become Jamaica's next prime minister.

Dante and I aren't in the same age group or tax bracket, but we *are* the same. We bury what's painful. We play the game. We hide our truths.

But that's everyone, right? I wonder how Ora lost her brother, where Aaron's parents are. Why Josh hates working at Blackbead but won't quit, and why Simone has to hustle so hard all the time. I wonder how the Halls became the legends they are. Hell, I wonder if my mom misses living in Craighead, her hometown, even after all these years in the States. When I've asked her, she's refused to answer. Like admitting yes or no aloud would damage her beyond repair. And perhaps it would.

There's so much about us that goes unseen. No wonder we're all so lonely.

Something slinks into my rib cage. It feels like heartache.

My phone rings from deep inside my clutch. Shit. There hasn't been a signal all night, but now, a call wants to sneak through while Mr. Hall is taking questions. He forges ahead while I dig into the bag and jam the side button to silence it.

Nothing.

I hit the button again, hard. Mr. Hall pauses for a second. A few people glower. Mrs. Hall's eyes cut to me.

The phone keeps going.

I snap shut my purse and beeline for the doors. My knees quake as I stagger through the dark, the clutch mashed against my chest to muffle the sound. Murmurs flood my ears. They have to be talking about me. Citrus and honey fill my nostrils. A woman jeers as I squeeze past her, digging my heel into her toes. I see her shoes. Lady Jimmy Choo.

"Watch yourself," she spits.

Simone stands by the exit, hands primly folded behind her. She pulls her concentration away from the stage. She stares at me.

That piercing, cold gaze. Like at the bar. Like earlier tonight.

"Thank you for your thoughtful questions," Mr. Hall says, his words reverberating through the speakers. "And now, a toast."

Simone lifts her chin, sees my huddled run out of the banquet.

Careful.

I try to slow the double doors as they close behind me. No more noise. No more staring. I pace the cream-colored tile.

Of course my phone malfunctions. I hold the power button to shut it down completely. "Come on, come on, come on . . ."

It. Won't. Turn. Off.

Another call comes through, lighting up the screen.

No name. No number. Just white.

The cell grows hot in my palm. I don't know if it's somebody here or back in New York, but someone is fucking with me. Running some autodialer. My phone vibrates with a voicemail. And then another, and another.

I'm hit with a wave of nausea. A weight on my chest as if my ribs could cave with my next breath. My hands tremble as I fight to play even one message.

Just one.

The reception hall erupts with cheers that shake the walls. They almost sound like screams.

I hold my breath. Bring the scorching phone to my ear.

A feminine voice.

A faint voice.

". . . Leave."

Leave.

Leave.

Leave.

An echo in my head. Time slows to a stop. My body breaks into a cold sweat.

Run. Leave.

In the banquet room, the emcee's command stops me. "Back to the celebration!"

I need to return to my post. But I can't bring this phone back to the party.

I hunt around. By the doors of a different reception hall, there's a tall green plant in a tan-and-black pot. I run and stash the blistering cell in the soil. It's ringing, but at least nobody inside should be able to hear it.

Inside. I have to go back inside.

I steal into the ballroom, step carefully. My heart rate won't slow.

The Halls crowd their table. Luis goofs around; Jada giggles at the funny faces he makes. Dante pulls out a chair for his mother while Mr. Hall takes a photo with a well-dressed gentleman.

The banquet is alive. Alive with excitement for Hall's campaign, Hall's family, Hall himself. There's so much hope.

And I'm scared.

The night can't end fast enough.

We hang back so Mr. and Mrs. Hall can personally say goodbye to everyone as they exit. The kids sleep atop the tablecloth in a puddle of drool. I lift from my seat, start to hustle toward the door so I can check on my rogue phone.

That catches Mrs. Hall's eye.

With ease, she excuses herself from her conversation and heads straight for me. "Carina, my dear, I just remembered something."

"Yes, ma'am?"

Mrs. Hall rests a hand on my upper arm. Her hold tightens, ever so slightly, and I suck in a jerky breath. "Miss Carter, may I remind you to silence your phone during these events?"

Miss Carter? Oh, she's mad.

"Of course, I'm so sorry, Mrs. Hall. That will never happen again."

"No, it won't." She gives a tight-lipped smile. "Starting Monday, you'll be under Thomas's careful supervision. Temporarily, of course. To ensure you're understanding Blackbead standards. Are we in agreement?"

Thomas up my ass for who knows how long? Kill me.

"Very agreed, ma'am."

"Marvelous. Now, if you'll excuse me." She heads back to her husband, back to charming the last stragglers.

Finally, I run out to pick up my phone. It's not ringing anymore, a blessing. I peer into the plant's container.

Nothing but dirt.

My breath shallows out.

"This belong to you?" I whip my head across the hall.

Simone. With my cell in hand.

She crosses the floor, studies the phone case. "It's yours, right?" She flashes it at me—a red background and a metallic silver phoenix rising from its ashes.

"Yeah, thanks." After earlier, I don't know whether to call her Juney or Simone, so I call her nothing.

Simone surrenders the cell and looks me in the eye. A knowing look. "Wouldn't want it stolen now."

It's warm in my hand. And the screen's no longer stark white. Instead, I'm faced with what I missed while inside.

Three hundred and forty-nine calls.

And if Simone's expression is any clue, then she noticed them all.

NINE

I'm in trouble. And I don't know what to do.

Last night, not even Bob Marley could sing me to sleep. Instead, I listened for every creak in the hallway, any potential rattle of my doorknob. I played everything over in my mind until the sun came up and the morning bell rang.

And now here I am, dead on my feet. Just me and this lump in my throat. Wondering who wants me gone and why they won't give up.

I get the kids settled in the basement theater to watch *The Lion King*. The pitch-black walls swallow all light. Luis picks a fine leather seat right up front, and I help Jada climb into the chair of her choice—next to her brother. She's petite for her age. A baby doll pretending she's a big kid.

Ninety minutes. I need ninety minutes. To shut my mind off. To sit in the dark and breathe.

"I want a snack," Luis demands as I dim the ceiling lights.

"And what would you like?" I sound as if someone's squeezing my throat. The pitch of barely contained anxiety.

"Something good," he gripes. Like he's upset I'm not already in the kitchen. "Just make it for me."

I trek upstairs and head for the kitchen, which is mercifully unoccupied in this brief lull between breakfast and lunch. I grab a few mangoes on the counter. Fresh off the huge tree out back—and Luis's favorite fruit. This should keep the kids calm for a little while. I bring the knife's edge to the mango's skin.

"Playing chef?" Aaron asks.

Jesus. I nearly nick myself. Aaron places an approved bouquet on the kitchen island—not a single white bloom in the bunch. Still don't know why that's a rule.

"Luis demanded a treat," I tell him.

"Yeah, little prince. Will rule your life and not feel bad, not one bit. Can you handle him?"

"Up for debate."

Aaron moves next to me and leans against the kitchen counter. I wish he wouldn't. I'm glad he does.

"You seem tired. He run you ragged already?"

I focus on the knife sliding through the golden-yellow flesh. Careful cuts, careful words. "Just didn't sleep well last night."

"Banquet no fun?"

Be calm. Be normal. "Very pretty. Elegant. Not my style, but the Halls know how to throw—"

"Where's the snack!?" Luis's shriek whips through the air like a lightning strike. I jump.

My hand slips.

The knife's edge slashes down my palm. Time stretches out.

Blood rises, pools, drips onto the granite countertop.

The sight turns my stomach. I can't handle blood. "Shit."

Then the gash starts to throb. My vision blurs, warps Luis's frowning face as he runs over. A shaky chuckle escapes me. "Your mom will kill me if I get this on the floor."

Aaron sucks his teeth, gently pulls my hand over the sink. "Stay. I find something for the bleeding. Luis, back downstairs, friend."

I barely notice when Aaron steps away. Don't know if Luis leaves. The blood gathers in the center of my hand before dripping into the sink. One drop after another, into the bone-white porcelain basin, then down the drain.

But one drop doesn't budge.

My eyes settle on it. And it grows.

Morphs.

Two crimson horns emerge.

Ready to crash through the ring, impale us with his horns.

It sort of has the shape of . . . a bull.

It charged right at us.

I swallow hard.

The silence that permeates Blackbead. The heat that scorches me from the inside out.

The clank and rattle of metal chains.

It charged . . . right . . . at . . .

I can't look away.

The bull pins me in place, a death grip without touching me. Hooves thud in my ears. I can't hear my heart pounding.

But I feel it.

A scream claws at my throat.

I need to go.

But it won't let me go.

It won't let me—

Then the blood slips down the drain.

Gone.

Like it was never there.

Aaron's hand sits on my shoulder. "Bambi? You still with me?" He wraps one of the dish towels around my hand, applies pressure. The sting brings me back to my body. Everything's buzzing.

I examine the drain again. Nausea sweeps through me.

"You in shock?" Aaron asks.

That crisp, sweet scent.

"Might be."

"Talk to me, then. And hold the towel." I keep it steady while he rummages for Wesley's first aid kit. Aaron comes back and starts cleansing the wound. "You okay?"

I want to lie. I want to say, "Yes, I'm fantastic. Nothing weird is happening at all."

But I'm so tired.

So when the words start to spill out, I don't stop them. "I was watching the blood, and the droplet just ... turned into a bull. The horns, the chains, all that shit." I laugh. Nothing is funny. Not the slice in my hand, or the phone, or the lipstick, or the sweltering heat of my room. None of it makes sense, and none of it is funny.

I inhale—citrus and honey again. "And now there's that fucking smell."

Aaron stops cleaning my cut. "You smell it?" he asks. "Sweet? Stays with you for hours?"

Oh, thank *god* it's not just me.

"I know it's the garden," I start, "but it's like every time I smell it, something bad happens ... I think I'm losing my mind."

"You been feeling hot lately? Out of nowhere?"

Yes. "Jamaica's always hot. What are you saying?"

Aaron's attention is unwavering. His silence—his seriousness—gives me pause. "Bambi," he says slowly, "that smell? Honeysuckle. The Halls don't have honeysuckle on the property."

There's something wedged into the spaces between his words. "What does that mean?"

Aaron hesitates. "What do you know 'bout duppy?"

He's joking. "You think a ghost did this?" Warmth rises to my cheeks. If I'd known he'd mock me, I never would have said anything.

Aaron says, "The others would laugh if they heard this ... and Ora might send me straight to the church but ... some say if you smell honeysuckle, feel the heat, it mean a duppy nearby. Always thought Blackbead have 'em." He's got this sheepish face, but his words are stable, like he really believes what he's telling me. "When people pass on, we give 'em dead yard. For nine nights, we remember them, celebrate them, then cast 'em out this world. If they don't get a proper dead yard, they can linger. Or if they angry, can fight to stay here to even the score. Break an arm, take a life—all the same to them. Duppy cause trouble when they can't move on."

My vision goes dark at the edges, tunnels into a pinhole. Aaron's words fade.

My skin crawls like I'm covered in spiders. Like I can feel someone's stare piercing the back of my skull.

I try to breathe. A gasp breaks through instead.

Careful.

The only thing worse than the living trying to ruin me?

A ghost.

If they angry, can fight to stay here to even the score.

And if someone from the other side wants revenge?

I know who it is.

I know it's Joy.

Evening descends on Blackbead House. The chaotic playroom sprawls before me, toys and art supplies scattered across every surface. With my bandaged hand, I pick up a storybook with a glittery cover. This room is the brightest place in Blackbead, a mix of primary colors and too many games.

It doesn't match what I've felt the last two days.

For a few nights after Joy died, I would lie in bed, staring at the ceiling as if she were somehow on the other side of it. I begged her to come back. Because if disappearing was all part of some scheme to make me regret hurting her, then I got the message, loud and clear. But to be gone—to die—was a step too far. Make me grovel. Make me plead. But come back.

She never did.

And with each passing day, my denial loosened and reality settled. I lived in a world without Joy, and it was because of me. Her mischievous smirk was no more. We'd never again gossip in the middle of the night, curled up in her massive bed. Our memories were only mine.

Now she's here. Just like I'd asked. And I'm petrified.

Because Joy is angry. She deserves to be. And I deserve whatever else is coming.

That doesn't make me fear it any less.

"The Halls like everything a certain way, you know." Ora appears at my side and slides the storybook from my hand. Today, she wears tiny yellow-gold hoops that bring out the warmth in her deep skin. "Can I help out?" she asks, gesturing toward the mess from a day's worth of play. "Will go faster."

I nod my thanks. The kids have only an hour of quiet time before we sit for dinner, and I've already wasted ten minutes lost in my own head. I follow Ora's lead. She gathers everything meant for the bookshelf and I create piles for other items. Stuffed animals here, art supplies there, action figures by the window.

Ora reminds me a little of Joy. Givers, both of them. If they can lend a hand somehow, they do. I never had to ask Joy for anything, and Ora's just the same. Naturally helpful. I watch Ora arrange the kids' books by height and spine color. The Halls are lucky to have her helping them, even with little nitpicky stuff like this.

Then it occurs to me: What if Ora could help me with the duppy? At the rum bar, she briefly mentioned losing her brother. And she doesn't seem haunted in the same way I am. So maybe she has some experience, then, with helping to send off the dead peacefully. Knows something about closure.

My stomach twists. Using a new friend to get rid of an old one . . . I'm not proud. Still, I need some guidance. And maybe some self-defense.

But how do I even broach this big topic with Ora?

Toys, I guess.

I pick up a plastic bull, long separated from its set of shiny ranch animals. "Damn. Luis has not let up on this Rolling Calf bit. He spent half the morning chasing Jada with this thing."

Ora eyes the toy and laughs. "Serves him right. Someone was trying to tell him he was being naughty."

"Give him the benefit of the doubt," I say, my tone light. "Maybe he's being bothered by some spirit, and that's why he acts so . . . Luis-y."

Ora chuckles more, finishes organizing the books so she can tidy up another corner of the playroom. "He does have a way about him, yeah? But don't let him blame it on some duppy. He's just spoiled."

"Maybe not. Mrs. Hall talks about him sometimes like he used to be such a good boy." I shrug. "Couldn't a ghost or something affect how he acts?"

"Imagine if a man tried to tell you that he cheat on you because a duppy possessed him. Would you believe him?"

"No."

"Of course not. You'd burn his things and break his nose. And I'd help you do it." Ora tosses a stuffed animal in a labeled bin. "Duppies are not real. People just don't want to take responsibility for any bad they do. And that starts when they're young, like Luis."

She isn't wrong. But she has such a different take on duppies than Aaron. Or even my mom.

The fading sunlight bounces off the gold chain around Ora's neck; its cross lies tucked away in her work uniform. That's the piece I'm forgetting. The other day, Aaron said Ora would ship him to church if he mentioned duppies around her. So she doesn't believe in ghosts. But I know what I've experienced. I know it's not all in my head now. Could Ora ever consider the possibility?

"If duppies aren't real," I wonder quietly, "then where do you think your brother is right now? He's not still with you as a spirit?"

Ora silently places the last stuffed animal into a basket and slides it into the appropriate cubby. Long seconds pass. She doesn't speak—not like her. I regret opening my big mouth. "I'm sorry," I say. "You don't have to answer that. That was rude."

"It's good. Glad you asked. I miss talking about Omari." Ora grabs a cloth to wipe down some toys. "No, don't think he's a spirit. He's in heaven, for sure." She digs her rag into the crevices of a plastic car. Her forehead creases as she focuses. It's too intense. Like she's distracting herself from something else. "It's not fair, how he died. Because now, nobody but me and Mama believes he made it to the Kingdom. But know he did. Was a good person. Best brother."

Ora's voice is steady and melancholy. Her sadness is pure. It doesn't matter how Omari passed; she loves and misses him anyway. I miss Joy with everything in me, but it's not the same as what Ora feels. The night Joy died, I jumped back and forth between rage and grief, and even now, I can't always keep it straight.

That night, I wanted Joy to get hurt.

So what right do I have to miss her in such a messed-up way?

"Could I ask what happened to him?"

She sighs. "He was running in a bad crowd. Gang stuff." I wait for more detail, but she busies herself with dumping all the plastic blocks into a bin instead. So I fill in the rest of the sad story myself.

"Now everyone talk about Omari like he was some heartless man. But he only did all that stuff to look out for me and Mama. He deserved more than the world. Deserved heaven."

Ora's wrong. Omari deserved more than heaven. He deserved to live.

Joy deserved to live.

"How did you handle it? Losing him?" My best friend died and I couldn't function. I didn't know how. Still don't.

Ora adjusts her gold chain. "Prayed." She lowers her voice. "Then my mother and I decide to visit an obeahman. Wanted to make sure Omari's soul was protected as he move into eternal life." She leans in and says, "Don't tell anyone, though. Not trying to go to jail." She's joking, but her heart doesn't seem in it.

"What did the obeahman do?" I whisper back.

"His work," she replies vaguely. Yeah, Mom didn't like talking about Obeah either. I couldn't tell if it spooked her or she just didn't know how best to explain it to me. Maybe two things can be true at once. "Then he gave us a ring. As long as Mama wear it, Omari's okay. Or so the man say."

"Why not see a pastor?" I ask. "I know you go to church and everything. So why go to some obeahman you don't totally trust?"

Ora hums in thought. "It's complicated. It can be hard to tell one belief from another. Can't agree on what is what, what's good or bad. Say I get crazy again and decide to go see a 'mother' this time. Say she prays to the same God as me. Is that Obeah or Revival? White magic or black?" She kisses her teeth. "Don't know what we're messing with. That's why I never dabble in it."

"Until you lost Omari," I murmur.

"That was new," she admits. "And difficult. But I did what felt right at the time. Wouldn't do it again."

I straighten a stack of construction paper on Jada's activity table. It was already straight, but I need something to do with my hands. "I don't blame you, though."

"Well, the Lord might." Ora shrugs. "I repented, but I don't regret going. Don't think it's a sin to want my brother to be okay. After all, demons ferocious as hell."

"How can you tell a duppy from a demon?"

"Be serious! Demon actually real!" Ora laughs.

I chuckle along. But inside, my heart hurts. For Ora and her loss. For me and mine. For realizing that Ora can't help me with the duppy because she doesn't believe it even exists. Maybe I could convince her if she knew everything, if she knew why I ran to Jamaica. But that sacrifice feels too big. My truth is ugly, a poison that will kill a friendship that's only just been born.

I am on my own.

I will have to make it work.

TEN

Today's agenda:

- Do my job.
- Do it well.
- Please the Halls.

I'm barely managing the first item.

The backyard fills with Jada's screeches as Luis chases her. Another sleepless night, but Thomas may have gotten a jump start on surveilling me for "Blackbead standards," so I try to be attentive. It's not easy, though, handling this duppy shit by myself. Last night, I snuck into the theater and curled up in one of the seats to sleep. It felt like a good idea; my room seemed like the epicenter of paranormal activity, so the less time I spent there, the better. But I only rested for a couple hours before dragging myself back to my own bed. I didn't know what would happen if Thomas or the Halls caught me snoozing outside of my quarters, and I didn't want to risk it.

Two or three hours of sleep isn't enough, and I'm feeling it.

I'm in pieces. But unease and dread hold my eyes open. If the kids fell in the pool under my care, I'd never forgive myself for failing to protect them. Never mind that I'd be terminated faster than a half-baked Netflix show.

Except losing this job feels like the least of my problems now. In fact, it seems unavoidable. Joy won't let me stay here, happy and healthy. So either I leave on my own, or she finds a way to force me out.

And she's always been stronger than me.

Gregory and Aaron work close by, pruning slightly overgrown bushes. Gregory snipes at Aaron to work quicker; Aaron focuses on one area, trying to perfect it. Their usual dynamic.

A reminder to be normal. To hold it together. To not scare the kids by acting like a weirdo zombie.

"You thirsty out here?" Chef Wesley asks. He comes bearing a platter of glasses, each cup full of ginger beer. The kids cheer, grab their drinks, and sit on the poolside chairs, pretending to be little adults. "Got drink for you too," Wesley adds. He rotates the tray so I can pick up the glass with the pineapple wedge. In a blink, his soft smile shifts into some awful shark-toothed sneer. Before I can scream, it snaps itself back into his familiar kind face.

I'm tripping.

The sight of the drink makes my gut churn. I graciously accept it anyway.

Wesley hands Aaron a cup of water. There were only three glasses of ginger beer—for me and the kids. It bugs me, but Aaron doesn't seem to mind the rules about what he can and can't drink while working. Wesley hurries back inside, leaving Aaron and me alone.

"Still not sleeping?" he asks. I squint at him, confused. He motions to my eyes. "Little dark under there. I hope is not rude to say." I didn't bother applying concealer; here, my makeup melts right off.

"I could use a nap," I admit. After the endless phone calls from a few nights ago, and the blood bull... "And maybe, like, an exorcist?"

I tell Aaron everything that's happened since I moved into Blackbead. He listens well.

He places his water glass on the patio table. "Definitely duppy work," he concludes. "And it nah like you at Blackbead. Want you gone." He shrugs. "Might be the safest thing."

He's not wrong. Even without Joy terrorizing me, I legally shouldn't be in the Halls' home. Any way you slice it, it's dangerous to stay in Blackbead. But the wild thing? I still feel like I'm supposed to be in Jamaica. I'm meant to be here so I can figure out my life and be a better me. I'm closer to doing that than ever before. Yet it still might be out of my reach.

Justice is a bitch.

This disturbed, haunted life is what I'll have now, probably until the day I die. But no matter what happens to me, Aaron doesn't need to worry about it.

"Maybe you're right about leaving," I tell him coolly. "But I don't think my work contract will release me due to ghostly activity. So I'm locked in."

"Brave thing," Aaron says. "Need to brew you a bush tea to try keep the duppy off you. If you're staying, that is."

"I am." For now.

"A warning, then. Because the spirit seem like it on a real mission. And ghost them can be a beast if you not careful. You gotta move with caution around the Blackbead duppy."

The Blackbead duppy . . .

"Hold up. The other day," I begin, "you said you felt like Blackbead has always had duppies, right?"

His energy lifts at the question. He doesn't have anyone to discuss ghost stuff with, does he? "I'll be honest: I haven't seen anything too, too serious. But the day I start work here, I smelled honeysuckle right away, strong. The scent usually only that intense at night, so I figure the Halls must have a lot of honeysuckle here for it to be so . . . in your face."

"And you said they don't have *any*?"

"I asked Gregory. The Halls don't care for it, so none here. Not then, not now. So where the smell come from? I started to wonder."

"Anything else?"

Aaron's posture contracts a little. "Well, I once saw Wesley toss rice out the kitchen window. Said a spirit bother him while him try cook, so he make it count the grains one by one. Keep it busy until he could see Mother Maud and get a wash to protect himself."

No, Aaron's evidence isn't strong. Or definitive. But he believes in it. And I know what I've seen, what I've felt. There's a presence here. And at this rate, it's going to kill me. Or melt my brain. Whichever comes first.

"So you think some random ghost moved in to Blackbead and started going wild?"

"Nah, not random at all." Aaron takes a seat next to me, leans his forearms on his knees. "After a while, the valet told me about the legend of the Blackbead duppy."

Josh has mentioned the Blackbead duppy in passing, but nobody's explained its backstory to me.

"Don't know how true this is, but you gotta hold it down, okay? Don't spread this around." Don't have to tell me twice. "Some people say Mr. Hall have an ancestor way back named Solomon. Work 'pon the sugar plantation that used to be near here. Him close with the master's nanny—she a wet nurse. And she trust Solomon." He bounces a knee like telling a ghost story literally gives him life. "One day, she tell him she plan to escape with her little ones. She want to join the Maroons, live free with 'em. She even ask him to come with her."

I see where this is going. "She didn't make it."

"Worse. Solomon told their master. To gain favor." It's always betrayal that destroys everything. "The nanny didn't get far. She kept running. So the master kill her. And the children them."

"And then Solomon felt like a piece of shit and atoned, right?"

"If he did, maybe the duppy wouldn't be so mad." Good point. "Nah, for his loyalty, the man got his freedom, tiny plot of land, and the master's last name. But nobody trust him. What Solomon did follow him for generations."

"So the legend is that the wet nurse is the one haunting the Halls now?"

Aaron nods. "Solomon was Mr. Hall's great-great-great grandfather. So they say the nanny haunt Solomon's entire bloodline to this day. Because the Halls are successful, but the success born through deception. She lost everything because of him, and she nah stop until his family lose everything too."

A tiny spark comes to life. So small, so delicate.

If all that Aaron says is even slightly true, then the ghost might have been at Blackbead long before Joy became a ghost herself.

So, could the duppy . . . not be Joy?

Of course. Why not? If the ghost were Joy, why show up now instead of haunting my lonely-ass New York bedroom right after she died? It makes more sense that whatever's troubling me has been here longer than I have.

Or maybe I just want it to make more sense than what I've been believing. Is that so wrong? When Aaron said a duppy was tormenting me, my mind crumbled at the mere idea of ever facing Joy and her anger again. I felt small, overwhelmed. Like if she didn't end me, I might do it myself someday, because witnessing her rage is too much. But that's not what I want. I want to take the best of Joy and the best of me and get away from my wreckage. I want to be better. I want to be new.

Taking pieces of Joy's identity opened a path to freedom. I could come to Jamaica and escape the worst of who I used to be. So what do I do if I can't get away?

If Joy is the duppy, everything ends. There's no reason for her to let me survive.

But if the duppy's the one from the myth, then I still have a chance. At happiness. At redemption. I just need to appease it, exorcise it, *something*. That possibility holds me up, strengthens me.

This ghost can't be Joy. It has to be tied to the legend. And I'll prove it. Somehow.

I'd puzzle this out alone. But I think I need help. From an expert. A believer.

Like Aaron.

Careful.

If I play this right, I solve this mystery and go back to my new normal. My new normal is all I have.

I take in Aaron's tall frame and broad shoulders. The grim expression on his face. Two sharp horns erupt from the top of his head. I don't blink until I come back to reality, and the horns fade away.

I'm slipping.

And staying close to Aaron might be what keeps me sane.

I'd never do anything to purposely hurt Ora. But Aaron is all I have, the only one who accepts this, no questions asked.

I look Aaron in the eye. "So how do we get rid of a duppy?"

Aaron grows still. "We see Mother Maud."

ELEVEN

Dusk falls on the three wooden crosses in Mother Maud's yard full of dead grass and fabric scraps.

It's finally a Sunday *and* a free day for Aaron. After a little over two weeks, this feels like my first serious foray into Jamaica since the rum bar. And I couldn't just go to Dunn's River Falls or something.

I follow Aaron through Mother Maud's front door, and I'm immediately smooshed into his back. He has nowhere to walk. Wall-to-wall people, packed into the main room, shuffling nervously.

Aaron grabs my hand and threads us through the crowd, ignores the curses strangers lob at him. By a closed door stands a young girl in a white apron with pink stripes.

"Sister, could we speak to Mother Maud?" Aaron asks. "Is very important. Urgent."

The girl points back to the horde we just escaped. "Everyone think that. Gotta wait, no different than them. Mother Maud soon come."

"And then what?" I ask.

"Maybe she choose you." She scans the room. "But we busy tonight."

Meaning, don't get your hopes up.

Aaron leads us back outside to avoid the stuffiness of the little house. We loiter at the bottom of the front steps and watch the sun begin to lower itself back to Earth. A white flag attached to the shack stirs in the evening winds.

"I didn't think there'd be anyone here," I admit. Maybe that's my fault for not knowing better. I figured we'd walk in and Mother Maud would tell us the duppy is the wet nurse from the legend. Then she'd explain how to put that soul to rest, and I could get on with my life.

"Way I understand it," Aaron starts, "Mother Maud offer her service to whoever need it. Churchgoing or not, businessman or gang, she try help. Hard job." Aaron taps his feet. Anxious energy, maybe. "Guess lot of people goin' through it right now."

A massive billboard across the road stares down at us. It eats up the skyline.

SERVICE AND HONOR

IAN HALL IS HERE FOR YOU, JAMAICA!

His face is larger than life, grinning at a world that can't help but notice him. A world he's trying to make better for everyone going through it right now.

Still, I can't imagine Mr. Hall driving past this place, let alone stopping for a chat and a blessing. But I could be wrong. I don't have much in common with a struggling businessman or an at-risk gang member, yet somehow, we're all here. The main difference seems to be what's in our bank accounts.

"You know so much about ... everything ... Jamaican." Which sounds really ridiculous, but I'm embarrassed by all the stuff I know nothing about. Spiritual beliefs, societal issues, the culture itself. Now that I'm on the island, I feel the divide. People here know so much about America because they have no choice but to hear and learn about it. What do I understand about this country beyond some food and music? How do I not feel like an impostor?

"Know a lot, yeah," Aaron says. "Because this is my home. It's all I've ever known." A guy shoves himself through the space between Aaron and me, tries to fight his way inside the house. Hopeless. "Must be nice, going places. Why did you leave New York?"

Careful.

"Just felt like it was time. I needed to." True.

"Brave girl. Explorer." His feet keep tapping. So nervous. What for? "After you finish with the Halls, where will you go next?"

Don't have to lie about that either. "No idea."

"Well. Wherever you end up . . . how 'bout I visit you?"

His tone is so light, I'm not sure if he's being serious. His first time leaving the country, and he wants to see me? "You sure you can handle that?"

"I—"

Shouts rise from the shack.

"You want test me?" a man yells. No response. "Said you want test me, boy?"

"Me nuh 'fraid a you," someone finally replies, a quiver in his voice. "Never will be."

Something scrapes across the floor, crashes. Inside, people gasp and clamor.

"Pull 'im off!" a lady calls out.

"What's happening?" I ask.

Aaron steps back, grimacing. "Sound like a brawl."

The noise climbs. A woman wails. Glass breaks.

"If you don't calm yourselves right now—"

Then the front door swings open, bangs into the broken-down bench on the front porch. A flood of people try to scramble through the doorway, arms reaching and pushing, tall builds and short frames crushing each other. Like demons struggling to crawl out of hell.

"Shit." Aaron's voice cuts through the uproar. "We gotta go."

My gut clenches. Go where?

Aaron points to his motorcycle—our ride to Mother Maud's. He grabs my hand, and I stumble after him. Don't know where we're headed, but I'm not staying here. I hop on the rear seat.

As we peel away, visitors topple into the yard, shove each other on the porch. I hold tight to Aaron as he maneuvers us through long, empty streets.

"What even was that?" I shout over the engine's thrum.

"People get desperate," Aaron says. "Then they get stressed. Then fights happen."

The mood in that place was tense to start with, that's true. I'm used to some chaos, but not like that. "My mother would not let me behave that way in someone else's house."

"Can't expect people in pain to always act how you want them to."

Minutes later, we stop in front of a stone fence with an ivy-green double gate. We hop off the bike and Aaron parks it by the rock wall.

"So, respectfully, are we not seeing Mother Maud tonight?" I ask. That's the only reason I'm out here instead of at home, scheduling more texts for my parents. Duppy or not, I have shit to do, or else the whole operation falls apart.

Aaron shrugs. "Won't lie to you. It sounded bad. We'll head back in a while, see if everyone calm down. Or if Mother toss us all out for the night."

Why can't anything be quick and easy?

"Come on," he says, gesturing toward the fence. "We chill."

I follow him through the unmarked gate, even though every instinct in my body is telling me, I don't know, not to walk onto random properties. But I trust Aaron and the confidence he has when he strolls right in.

I hope trusting him isn't a mistake.

Inside is almost nothing but plants. It's like nature reclaiming the world, a jungle taking back what belongs to it. Purple flowers drape overhead, creating two shady tunnels that split east and west. Wide trees stretch tall, leaves filtering twilight over the floor of soil and stone. Red bird feeders filled with sugar water dangle from stakes all across the area.

"What is this?"

"Hummingbird garden," Aaron says. His eyes soften, follow the dense tapestry of trees and vines and blooms. "Almost everything planted here? Meant to attract the birds."

Except there isn't a single bird. Still a gorgeous spot. But it's more of a flower garden than a hummingbird one.

"Government runs this?"

"Nah. If it did, would have named the place after King Charles or the dead queen." He probably isn't wrong. Commonwealth things: almost everything's named after deceased white colonizers. "Never seen anyone when I come. But feeders always full and clean. Little mystery."

I sit on the hard edge of a small water fountain built in the center of the garden. It's peaceful here, a little oasis. A far cry from the chaos back at Mother Maud's.

"How'd you find this place?"

Aaron sits on my right side. His knee brushes mine. I forget what I asked.

"Come here once as a child, with my parents. Made me curious about plants and things." He peers around the garden, on the lookout for any flying guests. It's still just us. "One night, few months back, had a dream 'bout it. So tried to find the place again. Got lost for hours."

I dip my fingers into the fountain. Cool water flows across my hand. "Thought Rush was supposed to be the one with no sense."

He laughs. "For true, for true. But we all act foolish sometimes." Aaron's gaze catches on something behind me. "Can't regret this, though." He points over my shoulder. "Look there. Quietly."

I spin around slowly. Two birds float at a nearby feeder.

Never mind what I said. This is absolutely a hummingbird garden.

I can't even see their wings, they're beating so quickly. Long tail feathers trail behind them. Their heads shimmer in the sunset glow, reflect it in shades of mint and plum. Aaron presses close behind me, dips his face near mine and observes the birds hovering. His breath tickles the hairs on my neck. I don't want to startle him by moving. So I don't. I sit, breathe with him. I enjoy him enjoying the now.

Minutes pass that feel like hours. And still, I could sit here forever.

"This is gorgeous," I murmur.

"Of course," Aaron says matter-of-factly. "This my paradise."

And he shared it with me.

When he should be sharing it with Ora.

Fuck me.

I keep falling into moments not meant for me. Moments that feel so good, so real. But a hollowness dwells, plants itself in my heart like a microscopic black hole.

Joy wouldn't be here with Aaron. That would be the right choice.

But it's hard to say no.

And I never could say no.

Finally, Aaron stands, stretches his long arms. His shirt lifts a little. "Okay. Been long enough. Let's see what goes on."

I'm stressed on the drive back to Mother Maud, and it has nothing to do with the fist fight earlier, either.

We pull up to the little house. Nobody's rolling around on that lifeless grass out front anymore. But I can see through the windows. There's still a commotion inside, a wave of bodies crashing against each other.

"Damn, they're still throwing hands?" I wonder.

"Maybe . . ." Aaron squints. Then his eyes widen. "Mother. See her. Come on!"

We rush in, muscle our way through a crowd that keeps pressing forward, trying to lay itself before Mother Maud's feet.

I can barely tell my arm from the arm of the guy next to me. I can't be out all night, waiting to see if Mother will grace me with her presence, to see if she's even capable of what they say she is. But I fight my way to the front of the crowd anyway and reach out my hand, try to get her attention.

Mother Maud stands, a gaunt woman in a red plaid dress with navy-and-white stripes. Her hair's wrapped in a matching turban, white-gray wisps peeking out. Eyes like homing missiles, with darkness underneath, as if she's not slept in years.

She finds me. Points. "You. Come." Just like that. Do I actually have some good luck for once?

I stumble out of the groaning crowd. Moments later, Aaron pushes through too.

"No," Mother warns. "Just the girl." Guess luck ran out.

I grab Aaron's hand, like he did when he led me in earlier. "We go together."

Mother Maud huffs. "Suit yourself." She steps aside so we can enter the back of the house.

There's a single overhead light throwing a yellow glow across a small corridor. The floor lies narrow; the walls press in, cramped even with only us three here. Mother Maud leads us to another door at the end of the hallway. Her hand rests on the knob, but she doesn't move.

"Dress down first."

"I'm sorry?" The words sputter out, fueled by the fear that I'm misunderstanding her, that I'm an annoyance for misunderstanding.

"The clothes, girl. Remove them before you enter." She inspects Aaron standing behind me. "My work, my rules."

She isn't serious. Right?

Mother Maud seems to notice our hesitation. "You ask to come together. Suffer consequence now." But I didn't realize she'd be asking us to get naked. Maybe I should have known. Maybe this is more proof that I'm an outsider, that I don't understand this culture I've barged into and hoped to claim. "You come here for my help," she asks, "yet what you fear is your own body?"

Yes. And if she knew me, she'd see why. My body hungers. She devours. She can't be trusted.

Mother huffs. "Can go to your underthings, then, if you shy. But hurry on." She points toward the front room, full of people. "I have work to do." She finally twists the doorknob and slips into her inner chamber. And waits for Aaron and me to undress. I guess.

This is nuts.

"Swear, Bambi, didn't know about this," Aaron asserts. He rubs a hand across his chin. "We don't have to."

I want to sprint out of this ramshackle house, so fast that even the memory of its wooden crosses and white flags can't catch me. Run all the way back to the hummingbirds and the flowers and the trees. I'm not ready to be seen like this. I'm not ready for Aaron to see me like this, and he shouldn't—ever. If Ora finds out, it'll break everything I've made so far. And it's all so fragile as is. I will have to keep more secrets, lie more.

But these are Mother Maud's rules. And I need the duppy identified and handled. I need that ghost to quit sabotaging what I'm trying to create.

"How else can we get rid of the duppy?" I ask Aaron.

He stays silent. Because he doesn't know. And neither do I.

"Just . . . face the wall, maybe. So I can . . ."

"Yeah, of course." I feel him shift. "Go ahead," he says. His voice sounds farther away, proof he really turned.

It's pointless to hide. We'll be staring at each other, half naked, soon enough. But I stall. I try not to think as I remove my tank top, my shorts, my necklace, my shoes. My bra and panties don't match. If Aaron dares to look, he'll see the tattoo following the curve under my left breast, *soul on fire* in a swirling script. I ball up my clothes and set them on a chair in the tight hallway. It's humid but I have goose bumps all over.

Mom will end me if she ever hears of this.

"You ready?" Aaron asks.

No.

"Yeah, let's go. Before she changes her mind." I head toward the back room, try not to worry about what Aaron can see, what he's thinking, if he's as nervous as I am.

I open Mother Maud's door.

It's quiet in here. Partial light, warm and diffused. The room is full of potted plants I don't recognize, half-melted candles, herbs in containers and bags. Mother Maud stands behind a long wood table covered in the apparent tools of her trade. Mortar and pestle. Several sheets of blank paper with a stubby dull pencil. Vessels filled to the rim with a maroon liquid that I pray isn't animal blood because I'll scream if it is.

The young girl from the front of the house stands in the corner, hands clasped. Oh good, an audience. I fold my arms across my chest. Aaron shuts the door behind us, stands as far from me as possible. But I still feel him, know exactly where he is in the space.

Mother Maud doesn't even acknowledge that we're in our underwear. "Tellin' you now," says Mother as she organizes her items, "if you want me kill someone, no room in the schedule tonight."

Oh, I'm gonna die here.

"We're not here for that," I whisper. It feels like a mistake, speaking.

Mother places two large-jarred candles on her already jam-packed table. She strikes a match, lights one. The wick burns bright. "Tell me about you."

"Thank you, Mother," Aaron says. He's shaking a bit; I can hear it. He steps forward, right beside me. Even in my periphery, I notice the bare chest, the black boxers. "We here for her, Carina. She work with me in Blackbead House."

Mother Maud grumbles as she holds the glowing matchstick. Hangs her head. "Ian and Ruth."

"Yes. Thinking there's a duppy in Blackbead, and it seem to be bothering Carina from time to time. Wonder if it's an old spirit."

Mother hums to herself. Sets the second candle aflame. She leers over the flickering fire. Its light brings out the paleness of her right eye—nothing like the rich earthy brown of her left. Her pupil flashes—or I imagine it does. "And what would you like, Carina?"

Everything.

"I just want to know who it is, and then send it away." I swallow. "Please."

Mother Maud sighs, blows out the match, glances around like she's figuring out what she'll need to get this ghost off my back. She returns to the candles. What does she see in them? Maybe it's good I don't know. "All right," she says, finally taking a seat. "Me try speak to it."

She closes her eyes. Leans back, presses her palms onto the tabletop. Her fingertips whiten from the pressure. Mother's lips part, move, but whatever she's saying is inaudible.

Aaron sucks in a gulp of air, as if he's been holding his breath all this time. I want to hold his hand. I don't.

The moment of truth.

"Ah, there it is," Mother says. A smile flutters on her lips. "Hear a flute made of bone when this one talk."

No way. No way she's communicating with the duppy.

"Who is it?" I ask. "Are they old?"

Mother Maud's grin drops. Her forehead creases. "It's clear, you know."

"What is?"

"That this a young woman. Get struck down not long ago. Now they with you."

A young woman could still be the wet nurse.

But if the ghost is someone who died recently, then that doesn't work. This isn't the spirit from the legend.

"You and this duppy been connected before Blackbead," Mother Maud murmurs. "Bond deeper than that house. Tie of love and pain."

My body sways. Love. Pain.

I'm going to be sick.

"What does it want?" Aaron asks. "How we lay it to rest?"

"Duppy nah rest while Blackbead stands," Mother replies. Her eyes snap open and watch me. "So you will do what it wants, but what it cannot."

"Why me?"

"Because you're here," she says simply. "Because you stay."

It has to be Joy. Of course she would punish me for living this new life, birthed from her old one.

"Besides," Mother Maud continues, "you did bring a seed of destruction with you . . . yes?"

My mouth goes dry. I think of my bedroom, the lockbox stashed under my bed, the hateful screenshots packed into my phone . . .

Could Mother Maud be telling the truth? I want to be here, so I'm now forced to be a pawn to do the ghost's bidding.

Joy's bidding?

No. I won't accept that.

Mother Maud is wrong. Maybe the duppy isn't the wet nurse exacting revenge on Solomon. But it can't be Joy. Something else can explain this, I know it.

Mother stands from her chair, clears her throat. Her shoulders drop, as if the "spirit" has finally released her. We just made it into her presence, but it feels like the session's done. All that waiting just for her to make stuff up? Because she has to be bullshitting.

"What do we owe you?" I ask. I'm pissed and skeptical, but a service was still rendered, and I'm not a stingy bitch.

"You paying more than enough, promise you. Oh, and one more thing." She peers at Aaron. He immediately straightens his back. "No matter how pretty and perfect she seem, you know not to trust a lying woman. Don't you now?"

Aaron says nothing, merely bows his head in acknowledgment. He avoids me, deep in his own thoughts.

"Can't send the duppy away," Mother says, "but I can still give you a wash. No trouble for you after." Mother Maud and her helper stand before us. "Kneel." Aaron gets down first. I let my knees hit the floor and dig into the wood grain. Fold my hands together like I'm going to pray. Maybe I should. I've never done it before.

Mother pours oil into her open palms then glides them over my bare skin. She's tender but firm. As if she's working her will into my muscles. Her assistant handles Aaron, quiet, focused. Our skin shines in the candlelight. Mother whispers words that I can't understand, perhaps Bible verses meant to protect us. It makes my stomach clench.

The helper picks two big leafy branches from one of the potted plants. She passes one to Mother Maud, and together, they gently brush and pat our bodies. The humidity weighs on me, just as the branches do, just as my fears do.

"Will this really protect me?" I ask in a whisper.

Mother does not answer.

Do rituals work even when you don't understand them? Will the God that Mother Maud prays to give me the time of day? Shield me?

I don't know what to believe anymore.

From the corner of my eye, I peek at Aaron.

He is by my side and still so far away.

I take back everything I said about Mother Maud. She might be the real deal.

Ora and I refold the shirts and shorts Luis thinks he folded correctly, replace them in their appropriate drawers. Only days ago, this would have felt like one of the hardest tasks possible. That's why I used to need Ora's help to get the chore done at all. Everything's ten times more impossible to do when sleep-deprived.

But this afternoon, I'm refreshed. Awake. I'm not even annoyed by all the noise coming up from the never-ending basement work.

It's been three days since Mother blessed me. Three nights of peace. No duppy fuckery. No anxiety. I'm hoping we've come to an understanding, whoever the ghost was. But the "who" doesn't matter now. Thank god.

"You seem different today, Bambi," Ora muses.

"Different how?"

"Like . . . lighter. Like your real name finally fit you." If I could laugh without Ora looking at me crazy, I would, because that's hilarious.

"Just glad supervision is over. Not being stalked by Thomas anymore. Could fully enjoy my day off."

"Seem like it. Texted you Sunday evening and didn't hear back." Ora bumps a drawer closed with her hip. "So, what fun you have without me?"

Careful.

"Fun? Without you, Rush? Not possible."

"That's what I want to hear," Ora says with a grin. "Texted Aaron on Sunday too. Nothing from him either." She fusses with one of her earrings. "I thought, I don't know, you two might be spending time." Ora mentions this lightly, but "acting casual" doesn't suit her.

She wants to know if I was with Aaron. And I can't answer that honestly.

If I had any other path forward with the duppy besides poaching Aaron for a night, I would have taken it. I bet Ora would understand that, too, even though she thinks ghosts are bullshit. And if I could have kept my clothes on? Even better.

But still, I keep Sunday to myself. And if I won't tell her, then my conscience knows what I did crossed a line.

I won't cross it again.

Deflect. Now. "Don't worry," I tell her. "I didn't tell him about... what you shared."

Ora lets out a huge breath. "Good. Real good. Thank you." She grabs one of my hands and squeezes it. "Like a safe."

Ora moves on to meet Simone in Jada's bedroom, and I head down to the sunroom. Jada and Luis are, surprisingly, right where I left them: drawing on the floor under the big, bright windows, crinkling construction paper and abusing crayons.

"Miss Rina, see what I drew," Luis shouts.

"Show me, show me." He holds up his masterpiece: a rudimentary portrait of Mrs. Hall standing on top of Mr. Hall's head. I can tell because Cartoon Mrs. Hall is in a pencil skirt, and Cartoon Mr. Hall wears an oversized wristwatch. But are they acrobats or something?

"Wow, that's so cool. And so creative." Luis beams at the compliment. "How about you add me in the corner there?"

He tilts his head and studies the picture, assessing. "Don't know if I like that, but I'll try."

"And Jada, what are you drawing?"

She doesn't respond. Jada sits cross-legged, one hand methodically rubbing a crayon back and forth on her paper. There's something weird about her face. She's got that thousand-yard stare Joy had after she took a hit of something new—and potent. Like she wasn't in her body, at least for a little while.

"Jada? You feeling okay, honey?"

Jada doesn't look up.

My pulse quickens. I grab Jada by her shoulders and gently jostle her. "Hey, that's enough. Come on." Her hand never stops drawing. She never meets my eye.

Something's wrong with Jada.

I let her go and reach for her paper instead. Slowly slide it out from under her crayon. Her arm continues to arc erratically over the tiled floor.

What is going on? What did this kid draw?

It's a girl surrounded by darkness, an exaggerated tear falling from her huge eye. She is alone. The shadows close in. There's no way out, nowhere to run. The girl seems to know this.

There's a wobbly arrow scrawled into the bottom right corner of the paper. I flip it over.

A bull.

There's its misshapen body, large and dominating. It's frowning. Angry eyebrows drawn with firm strokes of a black crayon.

The tips of its horns colored red. Like they've been dipped in blood.

My eye twitches.

The bull.

Painted in red lipstick on the canvas of my bathroom mirror.

Dripping from my sliced palm like a blood sacrifice, barreling down the drain.

"What . . . is this?" A tremble leaks into my voice. "What made you draw these?"

"Hm?" Jada blinks a few times, peers up at me. Soft and friendly. Normal. She focuses on the backside of the paper, and her brows furrow. "Miss Rina, what's that?"

"It's what you dr—"

Stop.

"It's nothing, Jada. Don't mind me." I fold the sheet and hold it behind my back. "I need to run to my room. When I'm back, we'll talk to Josh and figure out our snack, okay?"

They don't question me. The kids busy themselves with poking at their little cacti while they wait.

I speed walk to my quarters, don't breathe until I've shut the bedroom door and laid out the paper on my half-made bed.

Maybe the bull's a coincidence. Luis knows about that stupid Rolling Calf myth. He probably told Jada. But Jada's never drawn anything better than a stick figure with curly "girl" hair and a triangle skirt. And the crying girl . . .

Is the crying girl supposed to be me?

I fixate on the pictures until the lines blend together.

Mother Maud took care of me. If she was for real, then the duppy isn't supposed to bother me anymore. Case closed.

But these images are so unsettling . . . Jada didn't even know what these were, that she'd etched them, where they came from.

I do, though.

I throw the paper away, bury it as deep into the trash can as possible.

The duppy remains. And even Mother Maud can't stop it.

Who are you?

It will torment me. It will addle my brain until I can't tell truth from lie. It'll turn the kids into playthings, dolls in a dollhouse of its own making. They don't deserve that. They're innocent.

What do you want?

Can I live with more of this ghost haunting me?

Don't take all of this from me.

I look at my bed. Remember the lockbox.

Maybe I should leave.

I *want* to stay, but this isn't working. I didn't steal a whole identity so I could suffer. And what about everyone around me? Are they in danger now too? I can't put them at risk because of me.

I reach beneath the bed frame, pull out the box. Pop it open. I hold each item inside, one at a time.

Passport, driver's license, some documents. Regular stuff.

Then, the extra ID. Joy's smiling, laminated photo. The light areas of her face overexposed, the highlights blown out. The other smartphone. Copies of paperwork that'd seem suspicious if one looked too closely.

Together, it seems like so little. But it's everything. It's right here.

Maybe this is what the seed of destruction is. A bunch of random papers, phones, and IDs. A nervous bitch clutching it all in sweaty, trembling hands.

The past really doesn't go away.

Okay, I struck out in Jamaica. My savings are still light from having to buy my plane ticket here, and my au pair wages are modest. Using Joy's identity begins and ends at Blackbead; wherever I run next, I'll have to be me. So where could I go until summer's over and my "road trip" is done? Because I'm not ready to go home. Even if I reinvent myself *here*, everyone *there* still hates me. Half of my senior class is probably going to the same local college as me. How could I show my face there? How could I walk back through the fire?

A one-way ticket to Toronto might work for now, but I can't afford to stay there long-term. Maybe I lie low in the Bahamas? But I need cash . . . Panama City might make more sense. My Spanish sucks, but I bet I could do housekeeping at the resorts and get paid under the table.

My hands steady. I can figure everything out when I reach the airport. First? I need to pack.

I need to leave.

A gust of wind forces its way through the room. Everything in the lockbox blows around like it's trapped in a tornado. And just like that, any sense of safety disappears. Mother Maud's hushed prayers over me dissolve as my bed drags across the floor from the strength of the vortex. My body buckles under a blast of air coming from every direction, toppling me to the ground in a heap. A nightstand lamp soars through the air at breakneck speed, crashes into a window and cracks the glass until it spiderwebs out. There's nowhere to run.

Until the duppy releases me.

The wind stops. All my stuff clatters to the ground. I scramble, gathering everything and tossing it back in the lockbox. Back where it's all safe. It was so easy for everything to escape me. It would be so easy for me to get exposed.

Run. Leave.

I need to leave.

My passport lies in a far-flung corner of the bedroom, face down. I reach for it.

Honeysuckle.

No. "Just let me go. That's what you wanted, right?"

I pick up the passport, hiss, drop it. I suck on my fingertips.

The booklet is scalding.

It's open to my photo now. Tiny flames scorch across the page, engulfing words, erasing my face.

When the fire dies, everything appears the same.

Except I'm no longer CARINA MARSHALL.

My name's singed. Impossible to read.

I no longer belong to THE UNITED STATES OF AMERICA. My nationality gets the same treatment: charred.

The photo survived, reflecting my deadpan face. But my eyes . . . the duppy's burned out my eyes. Two dark vacuums gape at me, soulless.

I can't travel with this.

I can't catch my breath. Dark spots take over my vision. What do I do? I can't take a half day to rush to an embassy without explaining myself. But how do I explain to the Halls without sounding crazy? And I can't—won't—tell my parents that I'm here. But what if I need their help to get back to the States? My muscles twitch, but there's nowhere good to run.

Leaving is no longer an option.

Do I deserve this?

Mother Maud said the duppy wants me. Chose me. And until it's satisfied, it will mock me, strip me, kill me, before it'll simply let me go.

I'm trapped.

TWELVE

Two days later, Ora whispers as she passes me in a hallway.
"Josh said let's meet in the old nanny suite later."

"You mean the creepy one in the basement?"

Ora kisses her teeth. "Just a messy room. Don't act like a duppy in there or something." She smacks my shoulder, playful. "We'll have fun. And we need some privacy. That room is where we'll get it."

It's the bane of Mrs. Hall's existence, and it's right at the end of a lengthy and poorly lit basement corridor. The door to the suite sports scratched-up white paint and nothing else. Inside isn't much better. Peeling shreds of floral wallpaper and naked plaster. Cold concrete floor. The damp air smells of sawdust. There's an ancient mattress propped against one wall, and a single velvet armchair in the corner, frayed and worn-out.

Nobody has rested here in a long time. But if you're quiet, and if you're careful, you can try.

The whole Hall family is in Kingston tonight. So Josh suggested we take advantage. "You mopin'," he told me while he filled up a garbage bag of expired canned foods from the pantry. "You need cheer up." Of course I'm moping. I'm tired. I'm scared. I'm hardly eating. My passport is destroyed. My mind swirls: *It's Joy. It can't be Joy. I need to get out.*

There's no way to leave. I have to accept this reality. This reality will ruin me if I accept it. I don't know what to think, and everything I think sends me down a blind alley.

But Josh doesn't know what I'm going through. I want to keep it that way. "Come have a laugh with us," he said.

I moved all my furniture back where it belonged, and I blamed the contractors working all over the house for my shattered bedroom window. On the surface, everything was fine. But glaring at that ugly blue tarp on my wall only reminded me of how it got there in the first place. What was fucking up my life. So maybe against my better judgment, I took Josh up on his offer. I'd try to have a laugh.

The Young Birds hid in Aaron's cottage until lights out so they could chill after curfew. The rest of the live-in staff is in bed. For once, we sort of have the house to ourselves.

The others are truly enjoying it.

Quiet chuckles float through the suite. Everyone but me squeezes together on the old, bare mattress that we laid on the ground. I take the armchair.

Simone gasps, throws a hand over her mouth. "Scoob, stop, no you didn't!"

"Of course I did," Josh says, proud. "Old man thought I was stealing anyway. So I deliver. Found the allspice and the sardines. Pick 'em up. Run for my life." Josh mimes the whole scenario, walking two fingers slowly across the back of his hand, then making them bolt once they've grabbed their loot.

"Only you stupid enough to be so reckless," Ora says, wiping her tears. "And for what? What you try prove?"

Josh shrugs. "Don't mess with me 'cause I mess back."

"Only mess you can handle is in the kitchen," Aaron jokes. Josh sucks his teeth while the others fall over themselves. I hush them a bit; if Thomas catches us in here, I'll be back on supervision in a snap, and I hope the others would get that same mercy. But Josh is probably one serious infraction away from getting fired. I'd miss him. I'd miss all the Young Birds. Even Simone, in a strange way.

My thoughts want to drift, but the Young Birds ground me. If I have to be stuck in Jamaica, at least I'm stuck with them.

"You laugh at me," Josh begins, "but you need me! All of Blackbead need me, the way people quit 'round here."

"The people probably quit to get far from you," Ora says. "Far as we concerned, you're a criminal."

"Nah, I know you all done wicked things too."

"Not like that," Simone replies. Aaron and Ora agree. Clean consciences for them both.

Josh turns to me while I try to get comfortable in the old armchair. "Bambi, know you been up to wild stuff."

My heart races. "How do you know?"

"You from New York. All kinds of trouble you get into."

He doesn't know anything about New York, or me. I can brush this off. "Oh sure, lots of trouble. Worked part-time as a babysitter and a jewel thief."

"Heard all about your fancy life back home. Know you have no need for jewels, Miss Cash Money." Ora points a judgy finger my way. "And me know this innocent girl act is, in fact, an act. You fake quiet. Still looking for that tattoo you a hide."

"Tattoo?" Aaron asks. He sits back, pondering. Like he's trying to remember something. Maybe he did see my ink at Mother Maud's.

"So you don't have to pretend with us," Ora goes on. "Tell me: What you take? Sweetie from the candy dish?"

"All Luis's mangoes?"

"Little Jada's thumb? So she stop suck it all the time."

They devolve into riffing off each other, a spiral of jokes.

I can't think. Words run on repeat in my head.

Can't believe you'd do this to me, Joy had said, tears streaked down her face. *You're just a greedy, shady slut.*

A greedy girl who steals. That's me. Even now.

The Young Birds are still going. What else have I taken?

"Dante's sense of humor."

"That fat ass do not belong to you, not at all."

"She keep all her loot in her room, see."

I think of the lockbox. My wrecked passport. Two different IDs, two different faces, two different names. Pressure builds in my skull.

"I'm serious," I say. "I've never taken anything, never needed to. Just let it go." I sound muffled, like I'm buried under the bass of a song I used to know. I'm going under. I need a minute. Just a minute to slow down, to think.

"You must have take something, Bambi," Ora says. Her red lipstick melts, mutates into blood running from the corner of her mouth. *It's not real. Breathe.* "Everybody get a little greedy."

Greedy, shady slut.

Greedy slut.

Greedy.

"I fucking said back off."

The words come out clipped and forceful. They echo against the walls. I'm a dog caged in its kennel, scared and ready to bite.

The Young Birds fall silent.

I'm supposed to keep things cool and fun and classy. This isn't that. This is heavy and loud and desperate. They were never meant to see this part of me.

She's supposed to be dead.

"You heard Miss Cash Money," Simone says quietly. "Let she have her secrets. We all got them."

Simone's the last person I thought might come to my rescue. But I'm thankful.

"Girls always stick together," Josh moans. "But if is me, all a you gang up on me. I see, I see."

"We like Bambi more. Simple as that. And speak of 'like'..." Ora risks a glimpse at Aaron. "How you doing? You ready to get back out there, date a little?"

Embarrassment levels me. Aaron and I have definitely spent some more time together trying to solve the duppy issue. Even though I know Ora wants him. Has she noticed?

Josh's eyes dart to me, then away.

Someone definitely has.

Careful.

Aaron shakes his head. "Nah, don't think so. Casual stuff, maybe. Fun. But that's all."

Oh.

An ache runs through my chest. Something wrings me dry, squeezes until it's hard to breathe.

All the talking and hanging out. Him showing me the hummingbird garden. It's been fun for him. Just fun. I should be grateful. He should be with Ora, so this should be good news. But then, why do I feel so bruised?

"Monique hurt you," Simone says to Aaron. It's a statement and a question in one. Who's Monique?

Aaron runs a hand over his chin. Whenever he's thinking or nervous, that's his tell. "No loyalty, no honesty until she already caught... Could've just told me she was done, you know?" Josh pats Aaron's shoulder in support. "Cheating don't make sense to me. Just leave."

Of course. Mother Maud's words are clear now.

A lying woman.

Like his ex.

Like me.

I retreat into myself. Keep my eyes trained to the wall beside my chair.

And to my right, between peeling layers of wallpaper, a flower blooms.

Layers of ivory petals that curl at the edges. At the center, slender yellow threads stretching out like tiny fingers. A real flower amidst the faded motifs. The only white flower in all of Blackbead.

It stinks of honeysuckle. I'm not surprised. I've been haunted by more than this duppy, whoever it is.

After I met Mother Maud, a dream kept coming to me. A dream where I move on from Blackbead when I'm ready, and wherever I go next, Aaron meets me there. We play tourist together, try every food, visit every attraction. Maybe we hold hands, and nobody gets mad about it. Maybe we kiss and act like we didn't, like that's something friends do. When our time runs out, we promise to meet soon. New country, new city, new adventure. And then we do it again. Follow each other across the globe. Run until our legs give out.

It was a stupid dream. But it soothed me.

Now, nothing soothes. Hopelessness lingers. Just like the strange flower's scent. It's an omen from a ghost who delights in reminding me of who I was. She reminds me that good things might happen, but not for long. Not while I'm still destruction given breath.

The truth is staring me in the face: Aaron won't be traveling to meet me in New York. Or anywhere else.

Because one day, he'll know I'm just the kind of person he hates.

Still, I have a job to do. The following morning brought absurd heat, even for Jamaica, so I shuffled the kids to the basement's sport court so we didn't pass out on the patio. In here, I see the clear vision that the Halls have for Blackbead House once renovations are complete: smooth shiny floors, plenty of lighting, not a hint of the old and musty left behind.

Luis is tall and gangly for his age, so even though all his free throws miss, they get pretty close. "Good effort, Luis. Just keep your eyes on the hoop, not the ball. You're getting it." Like I know anything about basketball.

His frustration gets the better of him, though, and he switches to practicing his dribbles. "More fun," he says. So I focus on helping Jada have her time at the net. I lift her by her waist while she holds a basketball in her tiny palms. She tries to throw it, but it gets almost no air time. Instead, it drops to the floor and pathetically rolls away. Jada pouts.

"We can try again. Come on." We reset the shot, and I heave her back into the air. "You have to throw with all your might, okay?"

Jada does her best to grasp the ball. She bends her elbows, prepares to toss it, hard.

Crash!

My arms wobble at the sound, at the rumble that vibrates through the concrete beneath the court floor. I pull Jada close to my chest, and her basketball falls from her hands. "What was that?" she asks.

"I'll check it out," Luis says. He makes a beeline for the door.

"Nope," I say, blocking his way. I plop Jada down beside him. "Stay here with your sister, please. I will take a look."

"But that's *boring*."

"Maybe. But I trust you with Jada. And I know you can keep her safe, right?"

Several seconds pass before he grumbles "okay," and takes his sister's hand. He has good-big-brother potential. We'll keep working on it.

I slip out of the sport court and into the dark corridors of the basement. Where did that crash come from? A rush of footsteps echoes from some other hall. Then voices. Urgent whispers that I can't make out clearly. I follow them around the corner.

At the very end of the next hallway, there's Thomas in his usual dark suit. And the Halls, too dressed-up for this dank passageway. All three gather by the door of the old au pair suite. Shit. Wouldn't be surprised if that heavy-ass mattress fell over or something. I bet we didn't put it back up properly before we left last night.

Thomas is the first to spot me lurking.

"Yes, Miss Carter?" he asks, scowling. Mr. and Mrs. Hall pivot. He smiles. She doesn't. I already fear I've walked into my own trouble.

"The kids and I heard a loud sound," I explain. "They were worried about it. Just wanted to make sure everything was okay?"

"Everything is fine," Mr. Hall says breezily. "Nothing but some challenges with the room here."

"Again," Mrs. Hall adds through tight lips. "Carina, if you wouldn't mind bringing the kids upstairs, that'd be lovely. Don't want them getting into the mess right now."

And if Luis had the opportunity, he would. "Of course, ma'am. Right away." I speed back to the sport court and pray that whatever's gone awry in the suite this time has nothing to do with me.

Minutes later, I walk the kids up and out of the basement. I start leading them to the playroom, but we pass Clive clearing the table from breakfast. He carries an armful of plates and utensils. One bowl balances precariously on top of the pile. I see the disaster waiting to happen.

"Luis, Jada, you two go on and pull out the art supplies, okay? I'll be with you in a few."

"You promise?" Jada asks.

"Pinky promise." I give her my little finger, and she twines hers around. "Can't get rid of me that easily, Miss Jada. Now, get going."

I rush to help Clive in the kitchen, grab that teetering bowl and place it on the counter. No, clearing the table isn't in my job description, but Clive was struggling. And let's be honest: if the Halls are watching, it looks good for me to do.

"Getting a little old for this . . ." he grumbles. "Thank you for your help, sweetness." It's an apt nickname from the guy who prefers to go by Candyman. He's the one who fills the candy dish in the living room. A public service. He's been at Blackbead for ages, since before Chef Wesley. Candyman deposits the rest of his dishes into the sink and runs the faucet. "Glad you're here these days. Kids think so too."

"Jada, yes. Luis? Debatable. But they're good kids."

"You're good, too, young one. Give it a few more weeks, and you'll be the nanny the Halls have had the longest since I don't know when."

I carefully place some glasses under the running water. "Why's that?"

"Why's what?"

"Why don't the Halls keep nannies for long?"

"Well," he starts. He shuts the water off, presses his lips into a line. "Between us? Blackbead ask a lot of its people. Especially the nannies, because the Halls do not play about those children." Candyman shrugs. "Some people just could not handle it. Thinkin' of Amani, Kelly, Viviene—all nice, nice women. But . . . too hard for them. I don't know." He pulls an Icy Mint from his pocket and quickly pops it into his mouth.

Josh mentioned the employee problem yesterday, how people quit Blackbead constantly. But Candyman claims the lost staff is almost entirely nannies. Even knowing that the Halls are stricter with the caretakers, what are the odds of them being the only ones leaving this place en masse?

The au pair suite tucked away in the basement, unused. The endless renovations that seem to always go awry.

The white honeysuckle growing through the tattered wallpaper.

Maybe that was more than the ghost mocking me. Maybe it was a clue.

And there it is. That small spark of hope, alight again.

What if the duppy is a former Blackbead employee? Someone who'd cared for the children. Mother Maud claimed the spirit was lost in recent times. Nobody's mentioned any newly deceased workers, but "recent ghost" compared to "ghost from colonial Jamaica" could mean twenty or thirty years in the past. Dante's the oldest Hall kid and in his midtwenties. Timing-wise, it could make sense.

I need it to make sense.

"Dante and Luis probably scared all those ladies off," I say lightly. Candyman's shoulders relax, and he busies himself wiping finger smudges from the faucet handles, silently rolling the candy around in his mouth.

Mr. Hall emerges from the basement and joins Candyman and me in the kitchen. Candyman reverts back to being Clive; he polishes the faucet harder. "Ruth and the contractors will figure that suite out eventually," Mr. Hall mutters, more to himself than to either of us. He throws back a glass of water, leaves the cup on the island. I grab the glass before he's even left the kitchen.

The ground rumbles once more.

Pause.

A vibration travels up the walls.

"We get earthquake?" Candyman wonders. He grips the edge of the sink. "Not again."

The wrought iron pendant lights above me swing and clank. Uh oh. I shuffle back.

Two lights hit the floor. Shards of the bulbs scatter everywhere.

The rumbling stops.

Mr. Hall is long gone.

Candyman and I take in the mess. He lets go of a very controlled exhale. "These renovations . . . Can't wait for this house to finish . . ." He steps away from the counter to start cleaning up.

Renovations? Sure.

But I checked Thomas's schedule for the day. No contractors are coming until this afternoon. And those lights? Mr. Hall was just standing under them.

I know something is messing with Blackbead House.

And I'll prove that something is the Halls' punishment. Not mine.

THIRTEEN

AARON

AARON: so you wanna chat with old nannies?

CARINA: Well, it's weird that only nannies leave Blackbead. And that the au pair suite stays wrecked.

CARINA: In our case, weird is a good thing. We should explore weird.

AARON: explore weird huh.

AARON: i remember the woman who worked here before you. maybe can start with her.

CARINA: Yes, please! Thank you!

AARON: for sure.

AARON: you been doing what i said? to keep the duppy off you?

CARINA: No. That bush tea tastes like death. Death and dirt.

CARINA: And my mom used to say wearing red clothes is only for protecting babies.

AARON: yeah. but would appreciate if you try. doesn't hurt, you know?

CARINA: I don't have anything red, but I'll think about it. I'm just not sure it helps. We don't do all this stuff back home.

CARINA: Like what's the difference between your ghosts and ours?

AARON: maybe nothing. dead are dead. nice if they wanna be. mean if they wanna be.
AARON: but you guys play games with em.
AARON: we live with em. we respect em.
AARON: we fear em.

Finally. Sunday again. Our only day off, and the one day we can really investigate. We're free. From Dante's eternal candle, from Thomas's vigilant eyes, from kid toys and stiff postures and "of course, sir" and "whatever you need, ma'am." A pause. A breath.

Aaron and I ride his motorcycle to our first target: the lady who worked this nanny job before me. The red hair ribbon Jada let me borrow waves in the breeze.

Sun shines as we cruise down clear roads. Every now and then, we pass a hawker on the roadside, eager to share their goods. And we stop, and I pay up. I give some bills to an older woman with plastic bags full of green and orange June plums, pulled straight from the tree, she said. A man my dad's age promises we'll love his homemade gizzada, that it's never too early in the day for dessert. Aaron's practically drooling, so I buy two little pastries to eat before we get back on the road, even though I don't love coconut. Yeah, I make money busting my ass in Blackbead. But what good is the cash if I don't share it?

If I'd been a better person, Joy would be here too. In the flesh. We'd cruise these roads together, and I'd choke down coconut pastries with her while she explained the meaning behind the tarot card she pulled that day. Best friends, like we always should have been.

Lately, my mind obsesses over everything in my life that should have been.

I finish the least nutritious breakfast I've eaten in a while. Let the sun warm my skin. Fight the grief of imagining realities I don't get to have.

Even after everything I've fought since coming to Jamaica, all the mysteries I'm still trying to solve, I'm glad I'm here. But I wish Mom had felt comfortable enough to share her home with me herself. Yes, her worries made sense. But I drive by all these trees thick with leaves, and eat all these new-to-me foods, and feel all this wind on my face—and a part of my soul exhales. A part of me finally lets go. For years, she's feared me getting close to this place. I might never fully understand why.

I tighten my hold on Aaron's waist as we return to our drive. Even when everything hurts, being around him doesn't. It feels good.

But that's becoming a problem.

He's Ora's. When the sting of Monique's choices finally wears off, he'll see how much he didn't need her because Ora has always been right there. All as it should be.

And if he knew I've been lying to everyone all these weeks, it's not like he'd be interested in me anyway.

No more imagining realities I don't get to have.

After a long ride, we pull up to a little one-story house that's seen better days. The concrete blue walls fade into random white splotches. There's some patchy grass in the front yard that appears to have not felt rain in ages.

A woman with a vein of gray shot through her black hair comes through the front door, a bag slung over one shoulder. She hurriedly looks up, adjusts her polo shirt, then hops down the two steps. She stops when she sees Aaron and me standing at the edge of her yard.

"How you doing, Miss Viviene?" Aaron asks.

She goes, "I'll be better when you both get out of my way. Just let me go to work."

"We'll be quick," I reply. "You worked for the Halls about a month ago, right? Caring for the kids?"

Viviene stalls. "Why you need to know? And what for?"

"I'm Carina." Her expression doesn't change. I wipe my palms on my shorts. "I'm the Halls' current nanny. From the States."

"Yeah, a foreign. I can hear that." She straightens her back. "Why come to me?" She glares at Aaron while she asks. "If you stayin' over Blackbead, you know more than me by now."

"I wanted to ask if you remember"—God, this sounds so stupid—"feeling a . . . ghostly presence . . . while working for the Hall family?"

She's silent. Which is how any normal person would respond to my question.

Aaron clears his throat. "There's a young duppy at Blackbead," he explains, "and we curious if you know a thing about it, who it could be. If you knew anyone who might have . . ." Guess he doesn't have the heart to say "died recently."

Viviene looks me over. The obvious judgment makes my hands sweat, reminds me of the Halls sizing me up that first night I arrived.

"Nothing to say," she finally replies. "Don't want nothing to do with Blackbead. Or those people." She tries to walk around us.

I stop her.

"Ma'am, a yes or no is all we need. We came all this way."

"Well, child, I did not call for you." I shrink. "I left that place behind. Couldn't run fast enough. Duppy, no duppy, doesn't matter. Don't regret it. And you?" She shoves her pointed finger in my face. "Don't owe you not a damn thing." She readjusts her bag. "Whatever you're up to? I want no part. Bother Shantell Banks. She watch them kids before. She have time for you."

With that, she stomps off.

Okay, so, some folks have strong feelings—either about the Halls, about ghosts, or both. But I can work with strong feelings if people are willing to share why they have them.

"Shantell Banks ... I recall that name," Aaron mutters. "I think I know where she is. Come."

Her chocolate shop's a short ride away. This time, I let Aaron ask the questions; maybe people will be more open to talking to him than to me, who come from "foreign." Or maybe I'm just too forward.

Doesn't matter either way, though.

"Yes, I did leave after watch the pickney," Shantell says. She chooses her words thoughtfully. "The energy at Blackbead was strange. Uncomfortable. Plenty rumors and such, but I can't speak much more on that." She puts final touches on some custom gift basket, furrows her eyebrows like she's annoyed we interrupted her work day. Guess Viviene was wrong; Shantell does *not* have time for us. "Heard Amani Ford came up before me, though. Know where the market is?"

Amani: "Don't know if it was duppy. But I left 'cause I could feel I was not wanted in that house. I was not meant to be there. Nothing else to say. The Hall them business none of mine."

She gives us another name and sends us on our way.

On and on, like the most annoying game of Telephone.

On and on with no actual answers.

The Halls are all over the news broadcasts, mentioned in every other article online, but privately? Nobody wants to speak about them. Nobody says they remember a ghost. But nobody denies one either.

Aaron and I amble back to his motorcycle. I grit my teeth so I don't curse anyone out. Lift my braids off my neck and pray for some wind.

Aaron wipes his brow. "You know, maybe this not a nanny after all." He half smiles, amused by his own jokey tone. The grin pisses me off. "Sure you didn't bring a spirit with you from New York?"

"Of course not."

The words come out quick, sharp. Aaron pauses. This feels night-and-day from my little dreams where he'd hold my hand and run across the world with me.

"Sorry," I mutter. He doesn't deserve my frustration; he's the one toting me around and helping in the first place.

"S'okay. Long day." He squints down the road. "One more stop, all right?"

And the last stop is more unhelpful than all the others. The lady just slams the door in our faces.

Dead end.

"Sorry for dragging you all over for nothing," I say when we get back to the motorcycle.

"Not *nothing*."

"It was nothing." I squat by the roadside, exhausted. The sun begins to dip toward the horizon; the long light gets me right in the eyes. "What else can we do? Interrogate Candyman? Break into Thomas's office for employment files? That all sounds crazy."

Aaron's shadow moves into my line of sight, blocking the sun for me. "Thomas wouldn't take kindly to us prying," Aaron agrees. And seeing how antsy Candyman was just alluding to the nanny situation, I doubt I'll get him to discuss it a second time.

I needed today to crack this thing open.

Every night, I've waited up for the duppy. I don't know if or when it's coming, what it will do, or even who it might be. I'm so drained from keeping my guard up, I sometimes see stuff that, deep down, I know isn't real. Even though it feels like it is.

Today was supposed to give me some peace. Give me the answer and save me. But I have nothing.

I can't prove the duppy used to work at Blackbead. Which means I'm back to square one. Back to fearing that I'm wasting time running from a truth I don't want to believe.

A reality I can't accept.

JOSH

JOSH: yo u up

CARINA: I don't like you that way.

JOSH: wtf r u talkin about

CARINA: "u up"? It's almost midnight. Sneaky link shit.

JOSH: u women r mad. make up crazy things

JOSH: just wanna talk. bout wut I shuld do

CARINA: Oh. Give me like thirty minutes. Have to do something.

CARINA: But you know what I'm going to say.

JOSH: not that ez. ppl rely on me. dont have $$$ like u. cant jus quit.

CARINA: You won't get the chance to quit if you let the Halls fire you. Everyone will know you got termed. You'll never get another job anywhere.

CARINA: I say this with love: you can stay or you can go. But you have to choose.

CARINA: It's not easy. But it's simple.

CARINA: Be back soon.

I never wanted to break into Thomas's office.

In fact, I just told Aaron that doing so would be too risky.

And yet, days after that conversation, in the dead of night, here I am. Slowly shutting my bedroom door and inching to the stairs. After curfew, the house is silent but wound up, like I'm walking through the moment right before the beat drops in a song. Like something is coming.

Do I want to snoop through folders upon folders of paperwork? No. I stay out of Thomas's way, and he doesn't get me deported. But if the duppy could be a former employee, someone that recent nannies don't know or haven't heard of, then raiding Thomas's records might be my one way to get some answers. To prove the duppy isn't Joy. It can't be Joy.

I'll keep fanning my little flame of hope until I can't. Maybe I won't stop even then.

So I'm using my strengths to get somewhere. And for better or worse, when it comes to sneaking around at night, I've had a lot of practice.

Don't tell Aaron.

I tiptoe down the spiral stairs. Everyone should be knocked out, so I have time to dig for ... anything. I pass through the west-side gallery, a hallway decorated with abstract paintings, framed articles about Mr. Hall, years' worth of awards, and exclusive private photos of the family. Each frame is lit by its own cool white light. I slither between the displays, conceal myself in the sooty darkness.

On the left is the door to Thomas's office. The right side has the long corridor that leads to Mr. Hall's work space. I hear my breath and the indoor fountain near the front door, trickling water into itself.

Then, the footsteps.

The duppy's toying with me. Because it would. But the closer the steps come, the more I realize this is no ghost.

It's definitely a person.

Someone leaving through a well-hidden door, one of the exits that staff uses to move around Blackbead unseen. Someone walking briskly across the marble floors, their shoes squeaking. Someone around my height. Slight build.

There's no way.

Simone ... ?

I press myself against the gallery wall, try to blend into it. I hold my breath as Simone creeps through the hall.

Please don't see me. You can't see me.

Simone swings down the passageway opposite me. Toward Mr. Hall's office.

Why would Simone be here after curfew? Yeah, she, Ora, and Josh hung out the other night, but the Halls were away. Calculated risk. Skulking around now, when our bosses are home, is suicide. Ask me how I know.

Heart pounding, I snake my way across the gallery and look down the corridor. I'm soundless. Slow.

"Simone, wait."

I didn't speak. That wasn't me.

That's a deep voice, like a man's voice. I can't tell where it's come from until Simone turns in the speaker's direction.

This wing of Blackbead is getting crowded. I'm out.

I book it back up the stairs. This was a mistake. Trying to go through Thomas's shit, trying to prowl around. Like, when has sneaking ever done me any good?

And what was Simone doing here? And that voice... rich, warm...

Was she meeting Mr. Hall?

No. No, that's stupid. She's always lecturing everyone about damn near everything, the moral compass she is. So why would she lie to all of us and fool around with our *boss*? And Mr. Hall loves his wife. I've seen it myself. The doting way he presses his hand to her lower back when they walk together. The calm tone he uses when she's worried. How happy he seems when she talks to their kids.

But that person I heard sounded just like him. I can't deny that. And that was definitely Simone.

What she said the other night was true. Everybody has secrets.

Once I get back into my room, I reach for my lockbox. One check to calm me before I head to sleep. I flip it open, shuffle through everything. It's all here, as it should be. I grab my messed-up passport, open it to the photo page. And there I am.

Eyes intact.

Name and country replaced.

Like nothing happened.

Like I shouldn't ever trust what I think I've seen.

FOURTEEN

YOUNG BIRDS

ORA: danger!! VOJ is out!! halls mad as hell!!

CARINA: ?

SIMONE: Voice of Jamaica. Gossip magazine.

AARON: yeah, did see a copy in the foyer. not good.

JOSH: no big deal. so mr hall illuminati. who care

ORA: they accuse mrs. hall of bleaching her skin again!!

CARINA: . . . Does she?

ORA: maybe?? they say she do it because her husband like his women light!! scandal!!

AARON: don't think mrs. hall would do that for any man. those writers full of lies.

SIMONE: You know VOJ say Bambi from Trinidad and getting herself beat by the Hall children

CARINA: Where did Trinidad even come from? And how does anyone even know me?

JOSH: halls got eyes on em evrywhere. now u 2. Need 2 watch urself

Mrs. Hall is a masterful actress. I see that now.

She puts up a good front at dinner, our first complete family gathering in a while. She flashes her white teeth at everyone while the kitchen staff sets down plates and platters, while the housekeepers draw all the curtains.

"Carina said the children did well in tutoring today," Mrs. Hall tells her husband as she fusses with the purple and yellow flowers on the table. "Seems Luis reads above his grade level."

"That's good," Mr. Hall replies, his tone controlled. "Very good."

"And you?" Mrs. Hall adds, to Dante now. Her grin never falters. "Are you enjoying Wesley's meal? He knows you love curry, and we haven't had any in a long while."

"It's fine." Short, almost annoyed.

Mrs. Hall is trying, she really is. When she's stressed, she tends to hole up with a pot of tea in the sitting room. She'll stay there for hours, won't come out until she's composed again. And her time in contemplation seems to have worked today. This is as close to housewife vibes as I've ever seen her. But I can't get around the nausea sweeping through me, the strange tension in the room as I refill Luis's glass with fresh juice.

And Mr. Hall is feeling it too. He's reserved, mechanically shoveling forkfuls of curry chicken and white rice into his mouth. He and Dante are two moody peas in a pod. And for Dante, that's normal, but Mr. Hall has been nothing but jolly and charming to me since I joined Blackbead. It's unsettling.

Let's think this through.

They're definitely not happy about the *Voice of Jamaica* crap.

And then there's Dante's recent crisis: He held a town hall–type event at a local church, and from what I could gather, it sounds like Badrick crashed the affair. The guy wasn't violent or aggressive, but the same can't be said for some of his more ardent supporters. I don't think Dante knew how to handle that as calmly as he should have, so everything escalated. Yelling, fighting, accusing. The situation became so unstable, Dante had to end his appearance early so he could get out safely. And all of it was caught on camera. The public might respect, or fear, Mr. Hall, but that doesn't seem to extend to his son.

And the Halls don't like to be embarrassed.

My napkin shifts on my lap. I want to figure this out, put the pieces together and pinpoint exactly what's bothering everyone. But my mind's busy. Why was Simone in Blackbead so late? Could she really have been meeting Mr. Hall? Right under his wife's nose? It doesn't make sense.

But some of it does.

What if Simone stayed behind after work and hunkered down in the servant passageways? In the evening, it's the perfect hiding spot because there's so little foot traffic.

And that man clearly planned to meet Simone. If they're getting together in the middle of the night, they must have wanted to keep the meeting secret.

Mr. Hall couldn't be cheating on his wife with a literal employee. Upright Simone wouldn't put out for her boss, of all people. But I don't know what else to think.

"My love, when are the contractors coming tomorrow?" Mrs. Hall asks.

Mr. Hall chews his food. I don't know if he can taste it. "I'm not sure."

"Well, will you check? I need the basement finished."

"Oh. Yes. Of course."

It's so *awkward*.

Maybe the weird mood and what I saw that night are more connected than I think. I need more information.

Except I know Simone isn't going to offer it to me. She's distant when we speak, and it feels like it's purposeful on her part.

Imagine she's been worried this whole time that I'd discover the truth and uncover her secret. She knows how to keep things from the other Young Birds. But I live in the house, work closely with Mr. and Mrs. Hall. If I knew something, I could ruin the both of them. In Simone's mind, anyway.

Figuring this out could clear the air between us. Maybe I could prove that I'm not bent on spilling her personal life to the world. How could I tell on her when I'm keeping a dead girl's phone under my bed? I just want Simone to be safe in whatever she's doing. And, shit, if I'm wrong and she hates me regardless, she still needs someone to protect her.

I mix the golden curry and white rice in a corner of my plate, busying my hand. "Mr. Hall, you seem a bit tired."

He nods like he's a song playing at half speed. But still, he smiles at me. "Work never ends, Carina."

"Must be stressful, right? Pulling all those late nights."

Mr. Hall looks at me a little strangely, as if he's considering what I've said, what I mean. Did he clock me already? He picks at his food. An oily yellow stain soaks into the white tablecloth in front of him. "I'm not sure what you mean."

He won't like being questioned. Maybe it's stupid to put my employer under a microscope like this. What would stop him from kicking me out for insubordination? Or just for being nosy and annoying?

But I need to know if Simone is okay. That alone feels worth the risk.

"Just, the other night, I came downstairs after curfew because I needed a drink, and I thought I heard you going into your off—"

The table floods with liquid. Glass clinks against the surface. Dante's water splashes everywhere. I jerk back, but some of his drink still spills on my pants.

"For the love of God, you don't know how to hold a cup?" Mr. Hall spits. His wide nostrils flare. "Children know how to do it. Jada can do it." Jada's little body trembles at the sound of her name.

"Sorry," Dante mumbles.

"Don't apologize to me," Mr. Hall says. "Apologize to everyone who has to clean up after you, mess after mess." On cue, the servers swoop in, heads down, and begin moving dinnerware out of the way.

Mrs. Hall attends to her husband, speaks softly while stroking his face. "A breath, my love," she says. She's focused on calming him down. She almost seems relieved that he's come alive. The kids keep their eyes on their laps.

I have to get them out of here.

"Luis, Jada, let's get ready to sleep, okay?" I escort them from the room, weaving through staff as they zip around the cluttered table. The kids stick close. Upstairs, we can still hear Mr. Hall losing his head. I rush to clean up Jada and put her in her room—door closed tight.

Luis is quick to turn down for bed.

"How are you feeling?" I ask.

He pulls his blanket over his head, stays buried until I leave.

I get it.

Even for the kid who never shuts up, it's hard to know what to say. Before I leave, I make sure his night-light is on.

I check on Jada one more time before I go to my quarters. She's barely visible in the dark, but when I get a step closer, it's clear she's wide-awake, thumb in her mouth. I sit on the edge of her mattress. "Can't sleep?"

She shakes her head.

"Was dinner scary?"

Her shadow hesitates. "Daddy gets mad sometimes."

She says it so simply. It's a fact of life to her, her whole five years of experience. Sometimes, her father snaps. Sometimes, she witnesses that rage.

"Mum says everybody gets angry, though."

Sure. I know I do. But I'm not proud of how that anger comes out, the intensity of it, the way I sometimes can't control it. That's how innocent people get hurt.

I pat Jada's cheek. "Everyone gets mad. But I'm sorry you saw that. That wasn't kind." I tuck her in again, then notice her stuffed elephant is missing. "Let me find Ellie, and then you'll fall asleep easy, okay?"

"Thank you, Miss Rina."

I look through all the usual places: the hallways, the playroom downstairs, the sunroom. I even poke my head into the library, because if there's anywhere the kids shouldn't be, they've probably been there at least once without me realizing. I steal into the reading room connected to the library, a cozy space with a dark-brown leather couch and matching armchair, a super-low coffee table, a few artsy-looking lamps. It's one of the "family use only" rooms, so I've never been here. But it's worth checking for Jada.

There's one chunky stuffed elephant leg peeking out behind the couch.

Score.

And then people arguing.

Someone's coming. Of course someone is coming. And of course I'm not supposed to be here.

I dive behind the couch and still my whole body. Grab the toy carefully. If I squeeze it too hard, I'll trigger the sound chip, and they'll find me.

The door creaks open, then shut.

"You and Patrick lied to me," Dante seethes. "I spoke to him today, and I know he's lying."

"You question my integrity," Mr. Hall replies, "and that of my board chair. I won't tolerate this disrespect."

I don't think they're arguing over spilled water anymore.

"I've known Mr. Clarke my entire life. I thought he was a good man. Now I see how he's stomached being around you all these years. You're the same. You move the same." Heavy footsteps tread across the floor, make it vibrate. What if they walk over here? I curl into a ball, make sure I'm as close to the sofa as possible. I focus on the bookcase across from me, read the inscription on one of the shelves: *Servitium et Honorem*.

"Don't speak on situations you don't understand," Mr. Hall warns.

"Or you'll send Patrick after me?" There's more passion in his voice than I've heard since the banquet. "Have him deal with me, like you have him deal with everything else you fuck up?"

Smack.

Flesh against flesh.

I freeze.

"Do not speak to me like we are equals. Do not speak." There's a whimper. "You have nerve, boy. Peed up the bed till age twelve, but turn twenty-four and suddenly grown enough to cuss me out, in my face."

I grip Ellie's ears. I can't believe Mr. Hall fucking hit him.

"Want to act like a big man? Okay. But when you get hurt, you will realize that you are nothing. Just soft. Too opinionated for your own good."

Dante sniffles.

"You think I'm hard on you? Try dealing with what I deal with. Your mother babies you. That's why you stand here and cry when I put you in your place." He sneers. "Grow up. Quickly."

Silence. The slam of the door. More silence.

I wait behind the couch for several long minutes. Because I can't handle another ambush. Because I don't know if I can stand without my legs becoming jelly. Because that was crazy. What Mr. Hall did—what he's capable of, how he spoke—is crazy, and I don't want to get my ass beaten too. I'm heading back to Jada's room, dropping off Ellie, and going to bed before anyone can catch me.

I finally get up.

But I'm not alone.

Dante's in the middle of the reading room, half focused on nothing. He slowly notices me. The floor lamp highlights his left cheek, swollen from the blow of his father's hand. A welt appears where Mr. Hall's wide wedding band made contact.

I drop the toy. It hits the floor. Ellie's hidden speaker plays a tinny giggle.

"I'm . . . I didn't—"

Dante pivots and leaves. Shuts the door behind him.

He knows. That I overheard everything, that I have information I'm not supposed to have. He knows I was in a place I shouldn't have been.

Ellie keeps laughing.

Like this is funny.

The next morning, I wait for Dante by his usual spot: the garden. The kids are inside with their tutor, and with how busy Dante is with his father's campaign, this might be the sole opportunity I have to catch him. This is the second time he's seen me blatantly come short of "Blackbead standards." I don't know what he's thinking after last night.

And I need to know.

The ghost left me be. But nightmares found me anyway. I dreamed of loud insults and silent tears, insecurity posing as bravado. A father and son in a standoff with no clear winner.

Dad said growing up, he was the only son, and he had four younger sisters. Every day, his father gave the same refrain: "You have to be a man." And that had a narrow definition. Play the appropriate sports, protect the girls, but don't cry and be a little bitch like them.

Sometimes, Dad would fall out of that tiny box, and he'd be punished. A thump to the back of the head, forced push-ups, no dinner. "You need to learn," his father said, "how to toughen up. That's my job. To make sure you learn."

Dad grew up and became a man. Dad also grew up to never lay a hand on me.

"I'm lucky I have a daughter," Dad told me one night when I was up late, weeping, missing Joy and feeling guilty about missing her. He held me while I sobbed. Kissed the top of my head. "Don't be tough. Stay soft."

My mind plays back the tape. Mr. Hall—charming and composed, proud representative of friendly, welcoming Jamaica—striking his son across the face. Driving Dante to tears. Basically calling him a spineless pile of garbage.

Another father hurting another son and thinking they've done him a favor.

Just as I expected, Dante eventually rolls up, hands deep in the pockets of his slacks. His cheek is less swollen. He spies me right away.

But he doesn't seem pissed. Doesn't even seem surprised that I'm there.

"Sir, sorry to bother you," I start. "I just wanted to address—"

"Last night was a disaster, I know."

"Pardon?"

He ambles about, picks a leaf off the big mango tree. "No point in pretending. You see my face. Seemed to hear everything yesterday." He crushes the leaf in his hand.

"I didn't mean to eavesdrop, sir. I mean that. I was there for Jada's toy."

He laughs, and it seems he laughs mostly to himself. "It's a good thing you heard. I'm glad you saw a glimpse of who my father actually is. A true family man, isn't he?"

I know not to answer that.

"What, do good fathers not hit their children?" he asks. "Do good fathers not value appearances over everything? Not insult the people they bring into the world?" Dante peers into the distance, past the cliffside edge of the property, to the mild rise and fall of the ocean.

"I'm sorry. For . . . whatever happened last night." My words are tentative, meager. But I'm serious. As much as I'm trying to cover my ass, I want him to be okay too.

"Don't be sorry. He's being who he is. Who he's always been."

Dante doesn't seem mad at all. At least not at me. Maybe he has no plan to terminate me or relinquish me to the au pair agency.

And maybe, just maybe, he trusts me. Just a little bit.

Just enough.

If I could get one of my bosses to see me as an ally, as someone who understands him, this could be key to staying at Blackbead and protecting myself. Just like that, I become valuable.

That's a dangerous move. But it has to be the right one.

"At the banquet," I say, "you said something similar. That your dad is sort of . . . not real."

"The banquet was proof of everything wrong with my father. The excess, the fake kindness, the blind devotion."

"But you work for him. And people believe Mr. Hall cares about the people in this parish, and in the country."

"The only things my father cares about are this prison of a house and himself. What Ian Hall wants, he gets. Even when it's immoral. Even when people get hurt, he—" Dante's breath catches. His eyes dart across my face, searching for something.

Someone.

Trust me. Let me help you so you can help me.

The walls are down. "I'm listening . . . Dante."

We share a look. Static covers his face. I can't blink it away.

Then he sighs. "Get back to work, Miss Carter."

Yeah. Back to work.

"Yes, sir."

YOUNG BIRDS

JOSH: so the rumor tru? mr hall box dante upside the head? he break 1 of his mother rules?

CARINA: It's not funny, Scoob.

JOSH: didnt say it was.

JOSH: but not worry 4 him either. right woman will get him feelin better fr. ez 4 him 2 find

ORA: you know. saw him chat with juney today.

CARINA: 👀

SIMONE: Just told me to polish his shoes and check on the candle

SIMONE: Would not date Dante anyway. Not my type

AARON: thought money is everybody type.

ORA: not mine!! and what are some dollars to bambi?? we classy women!!

CARINA: OK, fun fact. I've dated so many rich guys, I could start a basketball team. And truthfully?

CARINA: Almost all of them were massive assholes. Like their bank account was their personality. Couldn't even remember my birthday if I asked.

CARINA: So no, money really doesn't matter to me.

JOSH: so all the rich men no good POS? y am i not surprised?

SIMONE: Scoob stop putting all your feelings in writing before you get yourself in trouble we can't get you out of

---

Time might not heal all wounds, but maybe it dulls them.

The weekend came and went, and it brought some calm with it. The Halls started acting like levelheaded adults again. No violence, no insults. And that's a relief because the staff has been jittery as hell. It's been damn near psychologically distressing, what with everyone wondering if—or when—Mr. Hall might blow his top again. All the nervous cleaning has Blackbead gleaming.

So, no more yelling. Fortunately, no duppy nonsense. And Gregory has graduated from glowering at me for daring to exist in the same world as him. Now he just ignores me. A fragile peace.

Peace bolstered by the fact that, tonight, the Halls are away. I thought I would be too. Plans change.

The schedule said they were aiming for a six o'clock departure to some renowned charity gala, so I made the best use of my time. I dressed Jada in her preferred purple ensemble. Laid out Luis's button-down and pants for him to put on himself. Then I ran to my quarters to make myself presentable according to "Blackbead standards."

I could only leave Luis unsupervised for so long before he'd wreak havoc, so I slid into the white-and-gold banquet dress and pinned my braids into an updo I thought was acceptable—and pretty. I was still carrying one of my heels in my hand when I led the kids down to load into the car.

Mrs. Hall stopped me at the bottom of the staircase. Her sapphire-blue shawl draped across her shoulders and chest in an elegant sweep I could never replicate. "Carina, dear, a thought: you should enjoy a night off."

"I'm sorry?"

Mrs. Hall gave this dewy-eyed look I couldn't translate. "My husband and I were discussing our plans for this evening, and we realized we won't be needing you tonight. You understand how these things go, yes?" She rested a hand on my shoulder. Her acrylics dug into my bare skin. "Please wipe down the children's bathroom counter before you turn in."

Stay here? Clean counters?

You understand how these things go.

I should. I didn't. They needed me; they'd told me so. Luis was a handful by himself. Why not let the au pair deal with wrangling him and Jada?

But as I stood in front of the massive window, watching the BMW drive away, the puzzle pieces came together.

They wanted to look "normal." A "normal" family. And most "normal" people don't have live-in childcare following them everywhere. So if you want to seem relatable yet unattainable, well, drop the au pair and keep the Fendi.

I was an accessory best left at home. Yes, now I understand how these things go.

The physical space is probably a good idea. After Dante brushed me off, I don't want to be around him anyway.

At least I have free rein of Blackbead for a few hours. And I have the Young Birds.

When we're not forced to uphold the Halls' appearances, we keep things simple. Like letting Wesley cook whatever he wants for dinner—and him letting us have the food since nobody's going to tattle. He worked his magic with the brick jerk pit the Halls have in the backyard. "They never want use it," Wesley said, disappointed. "Decoration for them. Don't even like jerk. Can you believe?" So when Wesley lit the pimento wood, placed the grill grate atop the raised pit, and cooked his jerk chicken, he did it with glee.

We stuffed our faces. Josh moaned and rolled over once he was done.

Josh, Simone, Ora, and Aaron settle in the grass and covertly pass around a blunt. Simone doesn't partake, scrunches her nose a little at the scent. She acts so proper. It's hard to imagine she's getting dicked down here at Blackbead, by Hall, shittiest man alive.

I might be weak on boys and booze, but I do resist the weed. A few weeks ago, I wanted nothing else than to smoke and get out of my own head. Now, I'm so mired in my thoughts, it's not worth trying to escape them.

I wait for the duppy everywhere. In the shower, by the pool, with the kids while they're getting tutored. It's almost all I think about.

When it's coming back. What it wants. Who it might be. Who I pray it isn't. I'm consumed by questions, by waiting.

I'm struggling to even keep up with the Young Birds chat. I've stopped knowing what to say. I don't know how to fit in when there's so much pushing me out. I'm not connecting like I once was.

But it's still hard to sit with the group and not join the fun. I'm not strong like Simone. And honestly, I can barely look at her. So I stay by the jerk pit, walk around it to fight the sleepiness from a full belly. White smoke still rises from the pimento wood coal, twisting and twirling.

The longer I watch the haze, the more it seems to evolve. It becomes like a curtain or sheet, like I'm somehow viewing shadow puppets against a backdrop of embers.

This is a contact high or something.

The image quickly fills with details, and the smoke paints a scene. A semirealistic portrait. The impressions of a world.

A jutting cliff. Craggy rocks at the bottom.

A slim woman lying on the ground. Sprawled. Motionless.

Her skull crushed on one side.

My heart climbs into my throat.

Honeysuckle wafts around me. Something hot builds in my gut.

Her face is covered by long braids. Some strands splay across the stone. The vision blurs, distorts in the haze, but I make out the woman's mouth, lips stretched wide as if midscream.

Body like mine. Braids like mine. Lips like mine.

I tremble and muscle back a cry.

She looks just like me.

I think she is me.

Crash!

"The hell?" Aaron asks.

I spin toward the house. A window splattered in crimson, cracked at the point of impact.

"Lord Jesus . . ." Simone goes.

On the ground lies a small bird. Blue feathers all over, with a shock of orange at its throat. Blood on the gray pavement, on its pocket-size body. Its head doesn't appear the way it should.

One leg twitches. Still alive.

Gregory steps out of the guesthouse, probably hearing the commotion. He follows our gazes, catches sight of the bird writhing on the concrete patio. He paces toward it, evaluates the creature.

"Can you—" I start.

He snaps the bird's neck before I can finish. Its crushed skull bobs at an unnatural angle.

Gregory collects its body and stalks away.

Acid burns my throat. I fight the urge to vomit.

"One smoke for the young bird," Josh mutters before taking another hit of his blunt.

"Share," Ora demands. "Now."

The others fall back into conversation, though more subdued than before.

One smoke for the young bird.

Young bird. Crushed skull. The woman at the bottom of the cliff.

Aaron raises his eyebrow as if to ask why I don't join the rest of the group. But I'm stuck.

I'm the only one who saw the smoke. The only one who saw that girl—saw myself—frozen in a moment of pain, of loss. I'm the only one who knows that young bird's death was no accident.

It was a threat.

What am I supposed to do?

Do I risk Thomas's office again, search for former Blackbead staff like I'd planned? But if Thomas caught me, he'd throw me out immediately. And if I run into Hall while he's sneaking around with his secret lover? I could have his breakneck fury flipped on me.

If Thomas's files are the one thread I have, and I won't pull it, then I'm out of leads. Again.

So do I take my fixed passport and run to Panama? Will it still be in one piece by the time I reach the airport? If the duppy's vandalized my stuff before, it could do it again.

I press the heels of my palms onto my eyelids. I sit, unmoving. If I move, I'll scream. A few feet away, Ora cackles. Her voice grates my nerves, more than hearing Ellie the Elephant's robotic laugh the other night.

Wait.

The other night.

The other night, I heard more than Ellie's laugh. More than Hall's outrage, more than his abuse.

I also heard a name. A name Dante uttered.

Patrick Clarke.

I've still got one thread left.

And I'm pulling it.

FIFTEEN

After I got Aaron up to speed on what I heard during the Hall Brawl, he tracked down Patrick Clarke's residence himself. A public figure, Clarke was well-known for being Hall's charity board chair—which doesn't sound like a real job. And, apparently, he's less known for some way more interesting side work.

Always room for more secrets.

According to Dante, Patrick Clarke's been around him for at least twenty-four years. Mr. Clarke worked so closely with Hall, he probably spent plenty of time at Blackbead, acquainting himself with the staff. Which means he should remember if one of Blackbead's old nannies died while working for the Halls.

I'm so close to the truth, I can taste it.

We pull up to Mr. Clarke's place. And he clearly does well for himself. He has a big house, like a scaled-down Blackbead. The colors are softer, creams and browns instead of the Halls' stark black and white. The scent of freshly cut grass tickles my nose.

A masculine voice crackles over the intercom at the front gate. "Name and business, please."

Which name do I give? What if it gets back to the Halls that I came here? But it sounded like there was a rift between Mr. Clarke and the Halls—or at least Dante. They might not even be speaking right now.

"Tiana Thompson." What's another false name to me? Better safe than arrested. "I'm here with my colleague to speak to Mr. Clarke."

"Appointment?"

"It's urgent," I say, adding some tension. "The Honorable Ian Hall sent us. It's about the charity."

Aaron looks at me sideways, but he doesn't say anything.

The front gate opens, and Aaron cruises us through. At the door, an older man waits to escort us into the house. The butler, maybe. He gives us the once-over. Fair enough. We don't seem like much, though we both tried to dress up a little—me in a dress, Aaron in a too-tight baby-blue button-down. And yes, we rode in on a motorcycle because neither of us has a car, let alone a fancy one.

We have a lot of convincing to do.

"Miss Thompson, was it?" the butler asks as he closes the door behind us. "You aren't from here, are you?"

"That's correct, sir. I'm from the States."

I don't like how he's studying me, but if Joy could handle all eyes on her 24/7, I can stomach the stare down for a minute or two. Still, my skin crawls. "Could I see identification, please, Miss Thompson?"

"Excuse me?"

"Some work ID. For Blackbead House."

We don't have IDs. And if we did, they'd just out us as an au pair and a gardener.

"Sir," Aaron starts, "we're sorry, but—"

He's going to ruin this.

"—but we don't have IDs *yet*." I smile as if I'm embarrassed to say this. "We're new hires."

Aaron shuts up.

"Is that so?" the butler says.

"Yes, and we apologize for the oversight, sir. Mr. Hall just needed this issue handled immediately." It's a fine line to walk between too pressing and not pressing enough, but I'm trying. "He might have called ahead already, told Mr. Clarke to expect us."

The man straightens his vest, fidgets where he stands. Uncertain. We're losing him.

"We understand and appreciate your commitment to protecting Mr. Clarke," Aaron says. "He's lucky to have staff like you."

After a moment, the butler beams. "Thank you, young man." He glances down the hall. "Let me show you to Mr. Clarke's office. Follow me, please."

We allow the man to lead the way. I give Aaron a thumbs-up behind the guy's back. Aaron sends it back. I know he's got damage around lying, but he's catching on to it real quick. I'm weirdly proud.

Now we just have to fool the man that Hall hires to fool everyone else.

I hope that's easier than it sounds.

"Go in," says the butler before leaving us alone in the hallway. Aaron knocks, then opens the door.

The office of Patrick Clarke.

He's a tidy older man with a neatly trimmed salt-and-pepper beard. When he looks up from his desk, he seems almost bored. "I'm sorry. I don't think I have any appointments right now." His gaze lingers, like he's trying to place me. "You seem familiar. Have we met?"

Uh, I hope not.

"We apologize for interrupting, sir," I say. "But we're new workers at Blackbead House. Tiana Thompson and . . ."

"And Andre Grant," Aaron chimes in. "Here on important matters."

"Blackbead?" Mr. Clarke asks. Now he seriously checks us out. "Ian sent you?" The question feels like a challenge.

"Of course," I reply. "You sound surprised."

"As I'm sure you know," he says in a way that suggests I have no idea, "things are a bit . . . complicated . . . with the Halls at this time." He sits back in his chair. "Dante even canceled our bimonthly dinner. I get the sense the family isn't too pleased with me right now."

Regular meals with Dante? They must have been close. No wonder Dante was so pissed that night. Imagine learning that the person you spent so much time with wasn't who you thought they were.

"Funny you mention him," I say. "Dante was the one who actually sent us here. He asked us to speak with you, sir."

Aaron's watching me again. There's a smattering of guilt right there in my stomach, and I ignore it, push it down. I need data. Answers. I didn't do all this for nothing.

"I see," Mr. Clarke mutters, definitely not seeing anything but my bullshit.

"Dante was surprised by what he learned about you and your past. But he wants the truth so you two can . . . clear the air." Clarke's past might be the key to my future. To my sanity.

Clarke clicks his pen a few times, thinking. "Yet he's not here. And you two are."

"He was . . . nervous," Aaron adds. "About being seen here with you, sir." He pauses. "And about seeing you. The situation has been difficult, you know."

And just as I hoped, Mr. Clarke takes it upon himself to fill in all the blanks that we can't. He visibly softens.

"I do. I do." He sighs. "What does Dante want to know?"

"For starters," I answer, "what you do."

"Preside over meetings, fundraise, strategize charity activities."

"I mean, what you really do, sir." I make my request. "What you've done for Mr. Hall, for how long . . . anything you can share will rebuild his *trust*."

Clarke's lips press into a thin line. "Dante is a smart man. He must have the gist already." He laces his hands together. "I've worked with his father a long time, since he first became serious about government. Anything he needed help with, I helped. Politics, charity, even personal life, when that went awry. And it often did." He sighs again. "Ian is like my brother. His family is mine. Dante stuck to me like glue, always has."

I believe him. He talks about Dante like a father should talk about his children. With love. With care. Maybe that's why Dante gravitated to him—because his own father isn't who he appears to be. But neither is the dad that Dante chose.

"What types of things did you help with?" Aaron asks.

Mr. Clarke shrugs. "Anything. Someone needs a small loan from the charity, I make it happen. Details on an opponent's past? I know some people. Ian has to send flowers to Ruth so she'll forget whoever she caught him sleeping with? Her preferred florist is on speed dial."

I'm sorry, what?

"You're saying Mr. Hall cheats on his wife," I state flatly. I think of Simone again, hanging around his office after midnight. "And Mrs. Hall knows?"

"I suppose you truly must be new," says Mr. Clarke, smirking. "Everyone knows. He finds a pretty girl at home or away, she's wowed by the money, and so it goes. Open secret. And when he's done with them, or they threaten him, I settle those situations. Quietly."

So, Hall has a whole system for infidelity? A process for messing with girls like Simone?

Was the duppy once one of those girls?

"I get why Dante took some of this news . . . poorly," I say. "Seemed like they'd just be rumors, his father sleeping around."

Clarke clicks his pen more, each beat loud in the quiet office. "Well. Sometimes, rumors are true."

"And everyone Mr. Hall has been with," Aaron probes, "you've . . . taken care of?" It feels silly to be speaking in code about paying people off. But he's asking the right question.

"I've taken care of just about everyone," Mr. Clarke says. "All but one."

Bingo.

"Someone slipped through the cracks?" I ask. "Mr. Hall must have been upset about that."

"No," Clarke says with some edge. "I know how to do my job. The girl just handled herself for me." He places the pen on his desk. "She worked at Blackbead as Dante's nanny for a couple of years, left for months, returned to the position for a good while. Then she suddenly went abroad. Never heard from her again, hasn't extorted Ian for funds. She was a nonissue. After some time, we just . . . moved on."

"Do you remember her name?"

"Kelly. Kelly Rowe. R-O-W-E."

Kelly? Didn't Candyman mention a Kelly? Someone he said left because she couldn't handle the pressures of Blackbead.

I turn to Aaron; he shakes his head ever so slightly. He doesn't recognize the name.

"Are you sure of this?" Aaron asks.

"Dante sent you to clear the air, not question my memory. Yes, I'm sure." He stands from his huge leather chair. "I appreciate you both coming to patch things up, but I have work to do. Tell Dante to call me when he's ready."

On the way outside, I wonder how I can convince Dante to speak to Mr. Clarke without revealing that I, maybe, possibly, also stalked Mr. Clarke. But that's a problem for Future Carina.

Problem for Current Carina?

"What do we know about Kelly Rowe?" I ask Aaron as we hustle down the front steps. We still need to leave the property without seeming suspicious. But I feel suspicious as shit, for more than the usual reasons.

"Not a thing. Didn't even know Mr. Hall run around like that."

"But someone must know something, about the cheating or about Kelly." A new name is progress but not enough. Dante might know more if she used to care for him, but talking to him is out of the question. Candyman remembers her, but he clammed up when we spoke. "All we've got is that she left suddenly." I don't say "disappeared" because that's not what Mr. Clarke claimed. But her exit is unusual. People don't typically leave without warning.

I'm an exception, not a rule.

"It's strange," Aaron says. He rubs a hand over his chin. "Lemme try something. Got a guy I know, owe me a favor. His parents were friendly with mine. Now I hear he just join the police force." Aaron meets my eye, and there's this spark, like he's excited. "We got a name now, a fresh one. Someone missing. Maybe he find something about Kelly, some document from when she work here."

"We're betting on Kelly running into the cops at least once while she worked for the Halls?" That's such a long shot. In the spirit of privacy, Blackbead isn't near the bigger cities. Josh told me cops hardly bother coming out that way to patrol, rarely respond to emergency calls because they don't have the resources. That's how he gets away with stealing shit—like the sea-glass anklets he so kindly gifted Simone, Ora, and me a couple days ago. So even if this Kelly wanted to report something, she might not have thought it was worth the hassle of going all the way to the station. Especially with no guarantees that the cops would take her seriously.

"I didn't say it was a for-sure thing," Aaron admits. He deflates a little. "But we out of options—at Blackbead and with Clarke. Unless you want to try Thomas still?"

Glad he doesn't know how that attempt went.

So I agree. Any details about Kelly could help me prove what I need to be true: that the duppy isn't Joy. That there's a chance I could be free once the spirit's appeased. But waiting for those details might be the end of me.

Aaron gives me a helmet, a bell-pepper red spare that he dug up because we were spending so much time on his bike. "You smooth in there, you know."

"What do you mean?"

"The lie to see Clarke. The thing about Dante. On the spot, you come up with the little fibs them." He smirks a little. "Clever, you know?" He searches me a little ... like he's hoping cleverness is what he sees in me. Cleverness rather than dishonesty.

A lying woman.

My back stiffens.

"You're being so weird. They were just conversations." I throw my braids back, away from my face, lift my chin a little as I put on the helmet. "You were there. You saw."

"Yeah, saw you play everyone."

"I just talked to them," I push back. "And so did you. And it worked. Got a name, didn't we?" A name that tells me there's still hope of getting rid of this duppy. A relief.

Aaron pauses, confused. But he lets it pass. Like he always does with me. Slowly gets his own helmet on. "Sure did."

We ride back to Blackbead. My arms wind around Aaron's torso. His abs tense as he steers.

I don't want to lie to him again. I don't want to treat him like I treated Mr. Clarke.

But maybe I already am.

I button Luis's gray vest for the third time. And if the photographer doesn't hurry up, I'll probably have to do it a fourth.

The kids stomp around the concrete patio, tired of waiting. Mrs. Hall hired someone to come take outdoor pictures for this lifestyle magazine called *Vision*. Why? Because, frankly, Hall's campaign isn't going well. Though Mrs. Hall would never claim it was tanking, not at all. *The world is bleak*, I heard her say a couple days ago. *We have to give the people something positive to look toward.* She said the upcoming benefit concert she's nearly done organizing will be one such positive. This magazine feature will be another.

And if there's one thing the Halls are going to do, it's sell happiness. The two of them pose in front of the camera, make kissy faces at each other, pretend the photographer they requested isn't even there.

With Aaron's bright flowers thriving in the gardens nearby, with the ocean waves lapping the rocky shore behind the Halls, with their big smiles pushing wrinkles into the corners of their eyes... They seem perfect. Giddy, even.

Mr. Hall cups Mrs. Hall's chin, and something inside me aches. Someone once touched me in that same loving way, though love wasn't really part of the equation. I still miss it sometimes. I imagine Aaron holding me like that, wanting me, and I cheer inside, and I fall apart.

But my fantasies of Aaron aren't real. And the Halls aren't real either. Hall regards his wife with longing, but he does the same to others. Everyone knows he's stepping out on the woman holding him down. Including Mrs. Hall herself. *Open secret*, Clarke had said.

Jada yanks on my pants, jerking me to the left. Luis is on the other side, trying to grab her. They run around me, and Jada screeches when Luis's fingers catch her elbow. A migraine grows in my temples, fueled by heat and sleepless nights and all this loud, loud whining.

"Settle down, please," I beg.

"He's chasing me," Jada shouts while dodging Luis.

"Leave her be," I say. Sweat drips down my forehead. There's a knot in my throat, something building.

"Gotta tag her," Luis replies, "so she can be it."

"I don't wanna be it!"

"Stop it, now!" The words shoot out. Frustration rises in me, fills every cell in my body. "God, why can't you listen?"

It's like I hit pause in real life. The Halls' heads swivel in my direction; I look away immediately.

The kids halt. Afraid.

Of me.

For the love of God, you don't know how to hold a cup?

I'm just as bad as their dad.

I kneel, get on their level. Luis takes two big steps back. I remember how he huddled under the sheets the night of Hall's first blowup, how he chose his own solitude to get him through that scary moment. To protect himself.

I'd never, ever hurt them.

"Hey, I'm so sorry." Jada was right: we all get pissed sometimes. I used to rage out a lot. But that's why I understand how destructive anger can be. I've fucked up enough to know.

Jada's bottom lip does a quick wobble, as if she might sob.

Simone quickly races over. "Take care of this, Bambi," she mutters. "Or we all have problems."

Anxious thoughts tumble together until I can't tell what's possible from what's likely. It all feels big. Like if the kids cry, everything falls apart. The Halls will worry I'm hurting their children. I'll be pulled off duty and questioned. Then they'll try to file a complaint, and everyone will realize the truth and how far down it goes. Catastrophe right here, in Jada's tears.

"Juney, could you get three glasses of ginger beer?" She rolls her eyes a little, but she still rushes away.

"Mama said we aren't supposed to drink that today," Jada whispers.

"But would you like some?"

They both nod furiously.

"Then you can tell Mama to blame me."

Sly grins creep onto their faces. One crisis averted.

I view the set, pray that it's nearly time for the complete family shots. Off to the side, just out of frame, Dante stands. Hands stuffed in the pockets of his dress pants. The fabric pulls where he's made a fist.

A few camera flashes later, I lead Jada and Luis to their parents. Mr. Hall raises an eyebrow at me, and I already know I'm getting reprimanded once all these strangers are off-property. Fingers crossed the punishment is supervision with Thomas again and not a request to spend the night in Mr. Hall's office.

I fall back to the patio.

"Can we have the kids come forward a little?" the photographer asks as he fusses with his camera. I check the nearby monitor. On the screen, they're a gorgeous, happy family. But when I really look, I see the tension around Mr. Hall's smile, the way Mrs. Hall nervously fixes her gold necklaces, the barely contained discomfort on the kids' faces. The details tell the truth. I can't ignore the truth.

The Halls group up, the water at their backs. My stomach rolls a little. Like I've seen this scene.

Someone taps my elbow. It's Simone, holding a glass of ginger beer. "I put the kids' drinks down over there," she says, pointing to the patio table. She studies me for a while. Like she's crafting a unique insult that I will obsessively think about until the day I die. But instead, she whispers, "You good?"

"Lightheaded." I lift the drink. "This'll help." She pauses for a moment before heading off.

I'm acting weird. Jittery. Yeah, I've felt off since I entered Blackbead. But this is the first time it's spilling out in front of the Halls. People are noticing.

Pull it together.

I sip from the glass. Bubbles burst on my lips, and the dark-orange liquid catches the light.

There.

Through the bubbles.

A bull's head, swirling in the drink.

That citrus and floral scent. I'm not alone.

The drink thickens. The bubbles go flat, and the ginger beer moves more like beet juice. It darkens, from honey gold to rust. Then the color completely shifts.

Reddens.

As if it were blood.

I am drinking blood.

I drop the cup. It splinters on the patio pavement.

"Cheese!"

The photographer brings me back to reality, to the photo shoot, to the monitor. I observe the family. The waves crash noisily behind them.

I do know this place. I've seen it before. That evening at the jerk pit.

The Halls are posed in front of the cliff I saw in the smoke. The cliff that overshadowed my dead body, my smashed head.

It's a real place. And it's right here, in the Halls' backyard.

If I can't pacify the duppy, I will die here. It wants me to know this.

Saliva floods my mouth. I can't vomit here or now, not in front of everyone. I've caused enough issues as it is. I bend down, panic at the muddle of glass and drink I need to clean before the kids come back and hurt themselves. I slowly let my fingers graze a small pool of fluid.

Red. Syrupy.

"Cut yourself on the glass?" Simone asks plainly.

I didn't cut myself. I didn't. But the blood . . . I can't stand the blood. On my lips, on my tongue, all over my hands . . .

I heave bile into the grass.

"She's sick," a man's voice calls out. "Give her room."

Dante.

"I'm sorry," I babble, "I'll get up. Just let me get—"

"Enough. Bring some water for her, please." And that's all he says as he stands guard, blocking everyone from seeing tears and snot run down my face. I try to catch my breath. My body quivers.

I look up, my stomach tight. The photographer's still shooting pictures of the family.

And Dante's not in any of them.

SIXTEEN

The family didn't punish me for "being sick." I'm grateful.

But I'm still tasting blood when *Vision* publishes the Hall puff piece a few days later.

Ora stole a copy while cleaning the living room, held on to it until after curfew, when the Halls are gone for another event and everyone in the house is fast asleep. We sit by the pool. The water has this eerie glow from the lights at the bottom.

"Think he got a chip tooth," Ora says, squinting at the slick pages, holding the magazine close to her face. "Can't tell."

I robotically spray my bare arms and legs with insect repellent, try to be present and agreeable. But staying in my body is hard these days. Pretending I am present and agreeable is hard. "You mean Luis?" I ask Ora.

"No. Mr. Hall." She cackles her witch cackle, passes *Vision* to me. I don't want it. "He lose charm with age."

"What you mean?" Josh asks. "Me tooth chip, and plenty charming."

"Oh man," Aaron says. "The way your mother must lie to you."

"Pity," Simone adds.

I force a laugh and have my moment with the magazine. I can't focus on the text right now, so I check out the pictures instead. The main spread is gorgeous: a stunning portrait of Mr. and Mrs. Hall in front of their mango tree. Its leaves envelop and shade them. Fruit hangs from the branches, and a few mangoes pepper the grass. Mr. Hall holds his wife close. She melts into his side, one hand on his chest, beaming. A woman in love.

What bullshit.

Simone pulls blades of grass from around the pool, lines them up by length. "What's the whole thing about anyway?" she asks, gesturing at the glossy cover. "The benefit concert?" She sneers a little at the mere mention of it.

"A little," I reply, skimming the pages for keywords. The mansion's felt livelier than normal because of all the preparation . . . and invitations. The Halls decided to let staff join as guests. Probably to make attendance numbers seem high compared to Badrick's functions. Not sure why else you'd ask—no, demand—all your housekeepers and cooks and valets to accompany you and your high-status acquaintances.

It's going to be a whole thing. I don't feel up to it, but I still had Ora rebraid my hair on my last half day. Almost everyone's said they're going . . . except Simone. She's been tight-lipped. Or she just doesn't like me asking her literally anything. It's a toss-up. "The writer mostly talks about the Halls' love story. Family values. Happy home. That stuff."

"Need Mr. Hall to feel like a family man," Simone murmurs. She yanks out another piece of grass. "Bad press lately."

I've kept an eye on the media play, and it hasn't been super positive. But bad? Not sure about that. Then again, I get the feeling Hall tells Simone way more than she lets on, and if they're spending so much time together, she might know what's actually up.

"What do 'family values' have to do with the prime minister job?" Aaron wonders, plopping his bare feet into the pool. Droplets of water splash onto his rolled-up pants. "People struggling. Can't afford food at the markets anymore. No money for the schools he have his name on. Got people trying to live off cleaning windshields." Aaron sucks his teeth.

Jamaica seemed so different when I first arrived. But some things keep cropping up, feeling familiar. Like people fighting to survive. What's more American than that?

Ora crawls over and roughly rubs Aaron's head. Little-brother energy when I know she does not feel sisterly. She doesn't know how to act with him. "You and Scoob hang out behind my back?" she teases. "He turn your brain?"

Aaron leans forward on his knees, away from her. "Maybe Scoob know what he chat about. That's all."

"That I do, Chicken," Josh says with a cheeky smile. "The article pure cheese."

And he's not wrong. I finally read a quote from the piece aloud. "Mrs. Hall revealed that she gifted the mango tree to her husband on their tenth wedding anniversary. Now, they stand before it, proud and pleased. Mrs. Hall explained, 'The mango tree is the perfect representation of a solid marriage. Tend it, water it, give it loving attention, and it will bear the sweetest fruit.'"

Josh fake gags. The sound almost makes me want to puke again.

But everyone else chuckles. The whole article is silly, mostly a series of vibrant family photos and "you wish this were you" shots of the property. But it looks good. And it makes the family look good. Hall is lucky to have his wife in his corner, fixing things, smoothing over his bumps and lumps.

"What we know anyway?" Ora asks, pointing at the magazine. "Me always say: what you see is what you get."

"You would never say that," I argue. I set the magazine aside. "And that's not always true."

"We shouldn't trust what we see?" Simone asks. She has a lot of nerve asking that, given her situation. But I don't dog her for it, not in front of everyone.

"I just mean people hide stuff all the time. Like, freshman year, I started talking to this guy. We texted all the time, he liked everything I liked, the whole thing. So finally, I ask him out, and we start dating. But it was like the real him suddenly showed up. Come to find out, he didn't like any of the shit I was into. He'd just google stuff to keep the conversation going. In front of me, even."

"No . . ." Aaron groans.

"Yes! I was with a dude who thought Beyoncé was overrated. I was livid."

"So why he even date you?" Ora asks.

"I asked him the same thing. And you know what? He admitted that he lied so he could get closer to my best friend, who he *actually* wanted a chance with."

Josh sucks his teeth. "Bumbaclot . . ."

"I didn't date another guy until senior year, I was so traumatized. I'm telling you, people will lie about anything."

The group goes quiet. And I get it because that story is so rage-inducing that it still pisses me off today, and it's been years.

"You say different a while ago," Josh says quietly.

"Huh?"

"Before, you say you date whole heap. Now you say you date almost nobody."

Shit. "No, I didn't say that."

"I can pull up the text," Simone presses. "Said all those rich boys them were dogs."

"They're right . . . seem shaky, yeah?" says Ora. "What that 'bout?"

My stomach drops. They're right. I've been jumping back and forth between Joy and Carina, and I finally tripped. Joy was bait for well-off dudes who couldn't recall that her favorite color was periwinkle. But me? My truth is what I said to the Young Birds just now. Why'd I tell them the truth?

Suddenly, I'm wishing I had my own squad to save me from myself. A Mrs. Hall to swoop in and smooth this over for me. A Mr. Clarke to fix my mistakes, make them go away.

I pick at the skin on my thumb. Pull my tank top away from my sweat-covered stomach. From nowhere I can name, a chorus crows. Voices layered atop each other, tickled by how dumb I am. I can't think.

Aaron waits.

Say something. Say anything.

"Right, what I meant to say was that I didn't date anyone again *seriously* until twelfth grade. But I was casual with a lot of guys, and they sucked. That's what I meant."

Everyone stares. Hard.

Then Aaron: "Careful with your words."

"Pickney them rattle your brain," Josh adds.

Ora snickers. "Yeah, there's dating, and then there's *dating*. Need to be clear."

And with that, "misspeaking" saves the day. One by one, the Young Birds slowly let my slipup go. Though I think I feel eyes flitting to me for the rest of the night. I focus on my hand like it's the only interesting thing around. A tiny red bead sits where I dug my nail into my thumb. I gulp.

Red like a bull made of blood.

Red like the blood on my hands.

I'm at the mercy of my own lies. And if I don't get it together, it's only a matter of time before I take myself out.

But then everyone but Ora heads home. She, Aaron, and I sit at the pool's edge. I make sure there's a full foot of space between him and me, but her lingering tells me that maybe that isn't enough. When she finally hauls herself off the property, I breathe, and immediately feel guilty for my relief. But I shove all the worries—and voices—out of my head. The world falls quiet.

I put up my fresh braids even though the teeth of the claw clip dig into my tender scalp. My "On Repeat" playlist streams through my phone's speaker and switches to a remix of Marley's "Is This Love." I'm not trying to set the mood. I'm just cringe.

The moon sits high and full. If the sun's rays make Aaron's skin glow, the moonlight shows the depth of his color, the shadows and highlights across his face.

He looks how music feels to me. Sad eyes in a minor key, more blues than rhythm. Summertime nostalgia with a bass drum heartbeat.

"Excited for the concert," Aaron admits, his words backed by the song of cicadas. "Lots of rah-rah, busyness, should help us pull everything off." And by *everything*, he means me running back to Blackbead to *finally* search Thomas's files—and maybe the rest of the mansion—for anything about Kelly Rowe. With everyone out of the house, this might be my one opportunity to freely roam.

"Luis will probably forget something for real. I won't even have to lie about having to go to Blackbead to get it for him."

"Reckless child."

"Hard head," I agree. Aaron chuckles; the phrase sounds totally normal when he and the other Young Birds say it, but it feels put-on and jokey when I try. Some things don't change.

"We can work on the patois some more," he says, and I smile even though I know I'm too deep in my New York accent to ever convincingly talk around it. He and Josh try with me, but it's hopeless, and that's okay. "You know, I glad you come here. Must have been tough, being alone, struggling to train your ear to hear."

"At this point, the duppy has been harder to deal with than the language barrier." And that's only half a joke. "I like it here. Visiting made my world twice as big."

"First time you travel by yourself?"

"Yep."

"And it didn't scare you to go?"

"No, it did." I've never gone anywhere without my parents, or Joy. And Mom's had years to load me up with fears about Jamaica. She'd shove US travel advisories in my face, talk about how much she wished she knew what happened to that one family member of hers. "But I needed to go."

Aaron leans back on his elbows, watches the lit-up pool. "You've really never left Jamaica?" I ask.

"Monique—my ex-girl—did. Left with her new man." Yikes. The disdain's obvious. "My parents too."

I'm not touching the ex-girlfriend thing. But he's mentioned his folks a few times. I've never met them, seen pictures, nothing. And he lives at Blackbead with Gregory, of all people. "Can I ask . . . where your parents are?"

Aaron's silent. Maybe I pissed him off. Is there anyone who doesn't consider their parents to be a sensitive subject?

"When I was fifteen," he starts, "they both went to the States. Said they'd get their papers right, then come back for me. So them left me with my aunt." He picks up a small twig, tosses it into the pool. "Auntie fell into trouble after some time, so then I stay with an uncle. Then he drink, get loud, kick me out. I bounce around for a while."

I let my feet slip into the water. So before Blackbead, Aaron was couch surfing? For who knows how long? "Why not stay with Ora?" Ora and Aaron have known each other for so long, she would definitely help him through any struggle he was having. Even if she was suffering herself.

"I decide that was not a good option" is all he offers. So if he didn't want his closest friend to know, or he didn't want to stay with her . . . maybe he just felt weird living with Ora and her mom. Or he didn't want to be a burden.

Or he didn't want to give Ora the wrong idea.

Aaron clears his throat and continues. "So move from place to place, look for work, until Gregory catch wind. He and Father went way back. So he got me an interview with Mrs. Hall, and rest is history. Been here almost a year now."

As much as we probably annoy Aaron, he doesn't have anyone else. The Young Birds and Blackbead. We're his whole world.

"Do you miss them?" I ask.

"Nah, Monique not worth missing." He sucks his teeth.

"And your parents?"

"You know, they started out sending shipping barrels full a shoes and bagged rice. Kept me clothed, belly full. But after six months? Nothing." He sniffs. "Good riddance to dem."

Aaron's gone to some world I can't see. But I know that face well. He's lost.

And why shouldn't he feel that way? It's like everyone lies to him and then leaves.

"It's okay to wish they were here."

"I don't wish that."

"I don't believe you."

Aaron frowns. "I not proud to miss people who choose to go." He presses his lips tight. "But maybe I do. Sorry for that."

"Don't apologize. You're just telling the truth. I like that."

My music changes. Another track about love. I guess there's a reason almost every artist sings about it.

"Okay, so they're away. What about you? Don't you want to see the world?" Aaron opens his mouth to answer, freezes, stays frozen. It's like he's never considered it before. "Let's just pretend," I add. "If you left Jamaica, what would you want to do?"

He sniffs, makes quick work of composing himself. "Um . . . see the Grand Canyon."

Of everything there is to do and see on this planet, that's what he picks? Weird but sure. "Okay. I'll book the trip and take you someday."

"That's a good dream."

"Could be real. Could do it in a few months, maybe, if you save up. If the Halls pay you okay, I mean."

"But my parents—"

"—are gone. They're probably living their lives, and you should live yours." Aaron moves like he can't get comfortable. A boy still waiting for his parents to come home, even though he'd never reveal that. "You deserve to do what makes you happy. Think about your own future."

"And what if they need me?" he asks. "After all this time. They could be in trouble. Could need my help."

Maybe. But I shrug and say, "You need you more than they do."

That's why I came here. My mom wanted me locked up at home, safe and sound, but I needed to escape. She wasn't wrong, but neither was I.

Aaron sits all the way up. "You an independent thing, Bambi."

"Like, lonely?"

"Like . . . you do what you want, always. You live your life." He passes a palm across his chin. Then he reaches out and places his hand over mine. Warm. A little rough. "I like that," he says. "Admire that."

The sincere way he speaks makes me blush. The way he always seeks something good in me makes me blush. The way I want to close the foot of space between us makes me blush. Moonlight hits his face again, the curve of his shoulder, the length of his arm. He is so beautiful, and I want to be beautiful with him.

Aaron is my friend, but I shouldn't want to touch my friends the way I want to touch him. I pretend, like Ora does. I pretend I don't imagine us wrapped together. I pretend I don't daydream about sneaking him into my suite at night, where nobody can hear us. I pretend my body doesn't come alive every time we're alone, ready to swallow him whole.

Fireflies drift through the air, dots of light floating past. The air's sticky. Weighty with tension I can't keep ignoring. This constant pull.

Most of my time in Jamaica has been me faking. Pretending I'm this normal girl with a normal past. A jumble of who I was and who I try to be, cherry-picking between what's me and what's Joy. And by now, I've proven I suck at maintaining the act. So maybe I should pretend something else.

What if?

What if I really were Joy? What if I could have who I wanted? No qualifying my desires. No squashing them to spare someone else's feelings.

What if Aaron could want me, and have me, and choose me without it being the end of the world?

And I could want him. Have him.

Relish him.

Aaron's thumb traces circles along the inside of my wrist. My breath catches.

What if I lived without shame, without fear, without regret?

I should say no.

But I could never say no.

I slide off the side of the pool, sink into the water. My tank top clings, my denim shorts pull on my hips, and my feet barely graze the tiled floor.

"It's hot," I call out. "Come cool off."

Maybe Aaron won't join me. Maybe he's not living in the same desperate dream that I am. That invisible line separating us could be one he's willing to toy with but not cross.

But then he pulls his shirt over his head and slips into the pool. Wades until he's standing right in front of me, gaze locked with mine. His Adam's apple bobs.

Aaron whispers, "You out of your mind, Bambi."

"Complaint or compliment?"

"Compliment." He takes my hand, lifts it, and presses a blood-hot kiss to my inner wrist.

My knees buckle a little. I dip in the water, and Aaron grasps my waist to steady me. Even over my clothes, his touch is lightning.

Something within is wide-awake.

Hungry.

A flicker of uncertainty crosses his face. "Can I—"

I don't let him finish.

My lips are on his.

Finally.

Aaron lifts me, his hands on my ass, my arms coiled around his neck. His mouth is soft, gentle—too cautious. More. Deeper. My mind tumbles over itself, heady with excitement and freedom and *finally*.

Ora seeing me dig my nails into Aaron's back.

He pushes my back against the pool wall. The more I feed, the more ravenous I become. Feeling him is like listening to music high, becoming one with a song you can't stop humming. Replay, replay, replay.

Joy's face, twisted in rage, screaming.

Aaron trails his lips down my neck. Goose bumps. Everywhere.

Joy staring dead-eyed from her driver's license, tucked away in the lockbox.

I start to shake.

You're just a greedy, shady slut.

"You not goin' nowhere," Aaron murmurs.

My burned-out passport photo, eyes smoldered.

I put my hands on Aaron's chest and push him back.

He blinks, confused. Can't catch my breath. "I'm sorry. Did I—"

"No, I just . . ." I want to tell him. I want to tell him how badly I've wanted this, how much I think I care about him, how hard it's been to pretend like I could be the kind of girl he deserves when Ora's right there, waiting for him.

But I can't. I can't tell him any of that without telling the rest of the truth. Why I'm wrong for him. Why I forced myself into Blackbead. Why I lie.

I don't want to lose Aaron. I don't want to lose Ora's trust. And if I take this any further, I'll lose both.

"I'm sorry" is all I say. Whether or not he understands why I'm apologizing, he accepts it.

He lets me down to stand, quickly exits the pool. I'm slow to get out. When I pull myself onto the side, Aaron's waiting with a towel.

"See you at the concert," he mutters.

"Sure."

"Good night, Carina."

Carina.

He walks to the guesthouse. He takes the moonlight with him. My head's buzzing.

Don't scream.

But I want to scream.

I dry off, pick up the leftover mess so Gregory and Thomas don't complain tomorrow. Autopilot. No thinking. If I think, I'll throw myself back in the fucking pool to drown. I move to grab the *Vision* magazine. It's still open to the photo of the Halls standing in front of their magnificent mango tree.

But the image has changed.

Mr. and Mrs. Hall grin without eyes. They're burnt out. Just like on my passport.

And at their feet, in between them, the singed mark of an *X*.

SEVENTEEN

YOUNG BIRDS

ORA: see you all tonight?? lookin hot??

JOSH: after pantry clean-up. and only no how 2 look good btw

SIMONE: Surprise you get an invite Scoob

JOSH: act like the halls is ez. light the candle. ring the bell. smile n lie. can do fr.

ORA: not responding to that!!

ORA: bambi if you wear white tonight have to box you in your face!! your dress better have some color!!

CARINA: 😬

AARON: juney, you be there?

SIMONE: No

SIMONE: Not for me

CARINA: I have an extra dress since the Halls gave me one to wear tonight. We probably wear the same size. You would look nice in white, too.

SIMONE: No thank you

CARINA: Seriously. I won't miss it.

SIMONE: Seriously no thank you

SIMONE: Charity not needed

SIMONE: Have fun tonight

Nothing can go wrong tonight.

The chauffeur drops me at the concert hall with the kids. I straighten my white dress, ensure my train hasn't caught on anything, then check that Jada and Luis are still presentable. They're not loving their frilly clothes, but they don't complain. It's like they know tonight's important for their parents.

Or how important it is for me.

The outside of the concert hall is dripped out, starting with the red carpet running straight to the glass double doors. Colorful spotlights surround the building, alongside torches that cast a warm glow on the ground. Green vines wind across the face of the venue and up the white columns framing the entrance. Nearby, there's a sign announcing the event in giant, hard-to-read script font:

The Honorable Ian Hall Presents

Melody of Hope

A Benefit Concert for Education Excellence

Through the glass doors, guests mingle in the lobby. Cocktail dresses and floor-length gowns, everyone chatting while holding copper mugs and martini glasses. Mrs. Hall insisted on rum-based cocktails for the bar since this is Jamaica and rum is what we do best. Seems like they're a hit.

I wish I could drink, but I'm on the job. And even if I weren't, I need to stay sharp.

I walk the kids inside.

And it's beautiful.

Every surface gleams with polish, from the staircase banisters to the bar top where Gregory awkwardly stands next to a flirty—and curvy—brown-skinned woman. Maybe those rumors about him *were* true.

A sweeping mural adorns the walls, painted portraits of some of Jamaica's iconic musicians. Peter Tosh. Jimmy Cliff. Dennis Brown. Big Youth. And Bob Marley—of course. A small plaque hangs nearby:

> IN GRATEFUL RECOGNITION
> IAN AND RUTH HALL
> *Servitium et Honorem*

The Halls invested in this place. Figures. They're everywhere.

The speakers play some popular dancehall, which feels like the opposite of the family's vibe. But that's probably the point. Appeal to the people. Do the song and dance folks expect.

"Hey." Aaron sidles up beside me. The heat of his body is frustrating. I've never seen him in such classy clothes. A two-piece navy suit, white collared shirt, a light-gray tie. The pants are a little short, but Aaron models his outfit so well, nobody would notice. And he's checking me out too. Looking at my shoes, my dress, the single silver necklace I packed.

"It's all really nice . . . Bambi."

My whole body loosens.

"You clean up good too, Chicken."

He smiles stiffly, adjusts his jacket. He's a little distant, but that's on me too. I made things awkward. But maybe the friendship part of us is salvageable. And maybe I can be okay with friendship by itself. Didn't I spend weeks desperate to talk to . . . anyone?

"You ready?" Aaron asks.

"Have to be." I monitor the room, hoping to avoid the other Young Birds for now. The Halls circle the lobby in their color-coordinated suit and dress. Thomas trails them, humorless and vigilant. "Anything I need to know?"

"Just keep your phone close in case. If anything go wrong, will text or call. Then you can hurry back." The weight of this plan finally settles on me. An evening in Blackbead, alone. A chance for some answers.

"Watch the kids." I slip Luis's inhaler out of my purse and pass it to Aaron. "I need them safe."

Aaron drops the inhaler into his jacket, pats his pocket. "I got you." He's got worry all over his face. "Careful, please."

"I got *you*."

I find the driver still sitting in the car near the entrance. Knock on the passenger-side window until he winds it down. "I am so sorry. I need to run back to Blackbead. Luis forgot his inhaler; his asthma is crazy right now."

Eventually, we pull up to the house. No light from inside, all curtains closed. Deep breath. The kids are safe with Aaron. Everyone's about to be engrossed in the evening's performances.

It's just me and Blackbead now.

Inside, I kick off my heels and dash for Thomas's office. Twist the doorknob and pull. Unlocked. Can't believe that worked. I peel off the piece of tape I placed over the latch. I don't even close his door behind me.

Time to hunt.

I riffle through manila folders, drawers, cabinets, all kinds of boring shit. Rotate methodically through every scrap of paper, trying to inspect without disturbing anything in a way Thomas might notice tomorrow when he's tired and cranky. I search for any hint of Kelly. But nothing. Not a stray receipt or pay stub or anything.

The hunt sucks.

Was Mr. Clarke screwing with us? Or am I missing something?

I check the time on my phone. Six minutes gone. How long can I be here "getting Luis's inhaler" before the chauffeur starts getting pissy?

"I don't have time for this," I mutter.

Then darkness swarms me.

I stand in the gloom. My breath traps itself in my chest.

A dim light flickers down the hall outside.

On. Off. On. Off.

I listen for footsteps. I don't hear any.

Am I still alone? I hope so.

I tiptoe into the hallway and creep toward the light, an elegant wall sconce. The moment I reach it, it shuts down. Blackbead plunges into night again, hiding her secrets.

Then the chandelier flashes to life in the foyer. The dazzle of light shimmers against the wall. Honeysuckle tickles my nose.

I get it. This is the duppy. Leading me somewhere.

This could be a trick, a way to march me to that final resting place the ghost keeps teasing. I pivot back to Thomas's office and try to convince myself to give everything another once-over. But when I stare into the void of the room, I know that what I need isn't there. It's a dead end.

I need to try something else.

"If this is a trap, and I die," I warn, "I will find you."

The lights are the sole response.

So I close Thomas's office. And I follow the lights.

I walk through the foyer, let my iridescent dress catch the gleam of the chandelier. Halfway across, the fixture turns off.

Then a light in the second gallery hall flickers on.

Then one more at the very end of the corridor.

I track each one until I'm right next to a small, average-looking door.

Should I . . . ?

Yeah, I should. I pop it open. Flip a switch.

Linen closet. Floor-to-ceiling shelves of starchy bedsheets and soft towels in white and light blue. Nothing of note. Great.

The bulb above the top shelf burns out, fizzles.

"There's gotta be a better way to communicate..." If the duppy agrees, it doesn't tell me. But I get the message: check the shelf.

I step a foot onto a lower ledge and reach. My hand grazes the flat surface, feeling for anything. And it's nothing. So much nothing.

Until it's something.

The corner of a box, shoved in the back. I get my fingers on it, pull it down. Modestly sized and cardboard, it's unassuming. And inside?

A key. Small. Brass.

All the lights from Thomas's office to this closet surge on, then off. Definitely a sign. This is what the duppy wanted me to find. But what does this key open? I imagine all the drawers in Thomas's room or in his desk, trying to mentally match the key with any of them.

Then it hits me.

This can't be for some random drawer. It's too fancy, too weighty.

This is the key to a door.

A door to a room that's always supposed to be locked.

Mr. Hall's office.

I sprint through the hallways, fly down the corridor that leads to his workspace. Shove the key into the heavy lock and twist.

It's so dark in that office. I can sort of see the outline of his window, a wall of bookshelves, a scented candle smoldering on the edge of his desk. But when I enter, it's the smell of stale coffee that bowls me over.

The office lights switch on.

"Back to the hunt."

I rampage, seeking anything about Kelly Rowe. I check Ian's alphabetized financial records, rummage through the drawers in his cherrywood desk, pull out any suspicious-seeming books from the bookcase in case something's hidden between the covers.

There's nothing. Again. There's no sign that a Kelly Rowe ever existed. And besides the lights, there are no more clues as to what the hell I'm doing here. If there's something I'm supposed to see, I'm missing it. But what is it?

I crash, drop onto Mr. Hall's pebbled leather sofa.

There's a strange sound. Like a crinkling.

"The hell . . . ?"

I stand, pull up the cushion. Just crumbs underneath. But what about inside? I grab the zipper. My fingers slip off the pull from my sweat. I push a hand inside and feel around.

I grab a stiff piece of paper before realizing it isn't just paper. It's a photograph. A very faded one featuring a young woman. The colors are worn, the image distorted with age. But based on how she holds herself and the softness in her face, she seems like she'd be around my age, eighteen or nineteen. She's got a blowout styled half up and half down. A long hair ribbon flutters in a time-stop breeze.

Her dress hugs the curve of her breasts, her hips. I can't tell the colors, but it looks similar to my white-and-gold banquet outfit. The one Mr. Hall gave to me. This looks exactly like it.

Around the woman's neck is a chain with a hanging pendant. I draw the picture closer. The charm seems like an instrument, maybe. Something skinny. Like a flute.

Hear a flute made of bone when this one talk.

Mother Maud mentioned a bone flute ages ago.

No way.

My trembling fingers trace the subject's face. "Are you the duppy?" I ask her, voice hushed. Not Joy. Kelly. The flute can't be that big of a coincidence. And if the duppy led me here? If the duppy helped me break into Ian's office to find *this* photo?

Then the duppy must be Kelly Rowe.

I could cry. An unsteady laugh fights its way out of me, and I can't help it. This ghost isn't my fault. This isn't my sin.

And all this time, I've been running from someone who isn't that different from me. In fact, we both made the same dumb mistake.

We became side chicks.

I wish I could talk to someone who finally understands me. But that won't be possible. Because I'm still alive to suffer some of the consequences of my bullshit. Kelly isn't.

Mr. Clarke claimed she "moved abroad," that he had no part in how she vanished. Except she didn't vanish. She died. And I'm not sure Mr. Clarke knows that.

If he's being honest, if Kelly didn't leave Blackbead on her own, if she's so angry that she's still here, waging war against the house and everyone within it . . . then what really happened?

Who killed Kelly Rowe?

I lose grip of the seat cushion. When it hits the floor, it makes a little crackling sound.

I reach into it again and pull out another slip of paper, well crumpled. Unfold it. Scribbled handwriting covers the scrap. The ink wavers on the downstrokes, smears on one side where the writer's hand must have grazed the letters.

I'm so sorry for what I did to you, Kelly.
I'm sorry I'm sorry I'm sorry I'm sorry
And I'll never be able to tell you.
I so very much wish that I could.

—I.H.

I.H.
Ian Hall.
Holy shit.
My head swims, and I stiffen to keep myself upright.

A confession?

The overhead lights crackle and pop. A shower of sparks cascades from the ceiling, touching the rug, the curtains, the long train of my dress.

Everything catches fire.

My mouth goes dry. Sweat breaks across my skin. I drop to the ground, try to kick and roll to put out the flames before they burn me. But the blaze moves quick—too quick—tearing across the carpet, consuming the skirt of my dress.

I keep turning. The temperature rises, licks at my skin.

I've faced this heat before. I roasted in my bedroom, weeks before I knew of any ghost besides my past, besides Joy.

There's nothing but amber flames and sinister shadows thrown across the walls. Smoke chokes me. Nothing I do stops the fire.

I don't understand.

My heart's racing.

I thought we were the same.

I'm so tired.

I'm so tired.

But no.

I didn't come this close to freedom to fucking fall apart.

With the last of my energy, I grab the couch cushion and slam it onto the blaze. I grunt and pant and shriek as I beat back the inferno. Each swing harder than the last.

"Not! Done! Yet!"

And finally, *finally*, the flames die down.

I sit on the brown rug, stunned. Surprised I didn't burn to ash. A sob roars through my body, and I wipe away tears, probably smudge my eyeliner and mascara. My braids fell out of their updo while I was writhing on the floor. And my dress?

Oh, the dress is fucked.

The fire devoured my train, consumed the fabric all the way to my knees. I run my fingers across the gown. The new "hem" sits charred; white crumbles fall to the floor.

I move to push myself up, and my hand brushes something powdery. More remnants of my dress, maybe. Then I realize it doesn't look right. It's more brittle, like paper.

Mr. Hall's letter to Kelly. Now a pile of dust.

I didn't get a photo, didn't transcribe it in my notes app. No proof this existed.

And next to it, Kelly's picture. Miraculously untouched.

I take in the rest of the office. Half the carpet is charred. The pearl-white walls sport a dense layer of soot. The bottoms of the curtains sit in a singed heap on the floor. And Hall's scented candle lies top-down on the rug. The label is too wrecked for me to read.

But I smell honeysuckle.

EIGHTEEN

The photo was returned to the sofa. Both offices got locked up. The key was thrown back into its hidden box.

It's as if I were never there.

And when everyone finds the damage in Hall's office, that's the story I'll stick to, for everybody but Aaron. Him? I have to tell him what happened and hope he doesn't think I've lost my mind.

The car stops at the concert hall. I stumble in my heels as I make my way to the entrance, royal palms waving overhead. My bare legs catch a cool breeze that I couldn't feel back when I still had a full gown. The fire got me good.

Inside, the lobby's devoid of anyone but venue staff. Music floats through the closed auditorium doors; everyone's in the theater. I stick close to the walls. With my clothes ruined, I need to text Aaron so he'll meet me out here instead. I pull my phone from my purse. *Now now now—*

"Miss Carter."

"Dante—Mr. Hall—hi."

Of course he shows up while I'm looking completely deranged. That's like his thing.

"Are you feeling sick again?"

"I'm sorry?"

"You weren't with Luis and Jada, so I watched them until performances began. Figured you'd run to the restroom."

Sure. "Absolutely, yes, thank you for that. My apologies for leaving my post, sir."

"It would turn my stomach too if I had to observe . . . that." He grimaces at the theater. I peer through the panes in the doors and straight to the stage. There's Ian, hands wrapped around a microphone, doing a little two-step. He's become honorary lead vocal for one of the bands. The audience claps and hollers; they are feasting on this weirdness.

"He seems . . . jolly."

"That's one word for it," Dante mutters. He finally takes a good look at me—the smudged eye makeup I tried to fix in the car, the faded lipstick. He notices my dress. Very crispy.

"Right when we arrived, my train caught on one of the torches outside," I quickly lie. "The flame burned it right up. Scared me sick, actually."

Dante raises an eyebrow. If a pit could open beneath me right now, that'd be great. He says, "Well, you can't go into the theater like that."

"I didn't bring a spare dress, unfortunately."

Dante hums. "You still don't know my mother, do you?" He nods toward a simple side door, painted black. I follow him down several gray fluorescently lit hallways that snake backstage.

Finally, we reach one of the greenrooms.

It's lightly decorated with some sofas, refreshments, and lots of curtains to change behind. But most impressive, more than the beautiful porcelain-white vanity on one wall, is the rack of dresses on the other side. I immediately browse the outfits. The tags are *loud*.

Dior. Chanel. Versace.

"These were my mother's other options for tonight," Dante explains. "Most are new. Help yourself."

Just when I think the wealth of the Hall family has lost its sheen, I'm stunned again. I haven't seen this much designer shit since...

Since I was at Joy's place.

I freeze, gripping the length of an orchid-purple gown. She might not be the duppy, but she'll still find a way to haunt me. "I can't wear these."

"And why not?"

"I don't just take other people's things."

He gapes at me like I'm stupid. "I'm sorry, Miss Carter, let me see if I understand. You intend to walk into that auditorium—full capacity, by the way—with your hair undone and your dress singed?"

Okay, maybe I am stupid.

"What is my parents' money for if not making problems disappear?" Dante asks. "My mother will toss these in storage tomorrow. She only splurges to remind my father that he has to allow it. Happy wife, happy life." He sniffs, disgusted.

The image of the Halls in front of the mango tree, Mrs. Hall claiming they were thrilled to be in love... I know Ian's a piece of work, that his fondness for his wife is questionable at best. But I at least believed Mrs. Hall adored her husband, blissfully gave passes for his nonsense because she loved being with him more than being alone. I figured she thought they were more powerful together, however imperfectly.

Might be wrong about that too.

I reach for another dress, this one dyed a deep burgundy with small glass beads woven throughout. This gown is not mine, and I don't want to take it. So much of my past was *take take take*. But I have things to do, important things. So this is what has to happen.

"Thank you. For the dress, and for keeping the kids."

Dante makes his way to the door, stops. "You know, the torches outside?"

"Yes, sir?"

"They're electric."

A beat passes.

Oh.

He knows I didn't burn my dress out there.

It wasn't possible.

Dante smirks. "You're not as good a liar as you think."

By the time I've changed into the new gown and done something with my braids, the audience has trickled back into the lobby. It's intermission, and everyone's mingling. I blend into the crowd, let everyone loop around me as I search for Jada and Luis.

The concert doesn't feel remarkable anymore.

This could have been any fancy event in the States. Mostly non-Black attendees, most snobby and bored at the same time. Burdened by more wealth than anyone knows what to do with and spending more on tonight's outfit than regular folks can afford to put toward food in a week. So much money for people who don't need it, people who could help many more by giving rather than keeping.

And the Halls are fighting to stay relevant here. They've tried to fit into a space that was never meant to include them. A space I wanted to be part of too. Favor bought at any cost. Like Solomon from the Blackbead legend.

Was I wrong? Speeding to a country I didn't fully understand, assuming it'd be so different from the one I left because I thought it should be? Because that's what I wanted to believe. I wanted to believe that this world would be so much nicer than the one I left.

Of course I was wrong. I've been looking at Jamaica through a pinhole and fooling myself into thinking I saw the whole picture. I saw only what I wanted. What I hoped for.

Just an hour ago, I learned a young woman died in this country, her name lost to almost everyone but the man paid to pretend girls like her didn't exist. And the guy who might have been the cause of her death? He's cheating on his wife and trying to become prime minister on a platform of "service and honor." Is any of that so different from how things usually go back home?

At the fundraising banquet, Ian said that he worried Jamaica was losing its identity. Focusing on individualism over community, on status over mutual respect. He said Jamaica was becoming too much like America.

He was wrong. I don't think Jamaica's becoming like America. But if Ian and Patrick are any indication—if Kelly's death is any indication—then there are clearly people in both countries who are sick with something I'm not sure is curable.

And I don't want any part of it.

The kids sit at a special table designated for the Hall family. Luis and Jada are passed out on the gold tablecloth in front of plates of half-eaten hummingbird cake. Not even the sugar rush or the adrenaline of getting to stay up late could keep them awake. Mrs. Hall hovers near them. She deigns to grab a napkin and wipe the drool from Luis's mouth. She looks like a mom. A dedicated, loving mother.

It doesn't fit the reality I've seen. The one where she comforts her pissed-off, unfaithful husband but not her children. The one where she tolerates a man who screams around two kids who can't defend themselves or talk back.

But now's not the time to start a fight with her. She's a victim too, in her own way.

I approach the table, head bowed. I'll apologize for being away, for wearing her dress without permission. I pray she won't discipline me too badly for ditching the children if I find the right lie to keep her calm. Could I get away with playing the "I'm unwell" card again? "Mrs. Hall, I'm so sorry. I had to—"

"It's okay, dear. Take the night off. Enjoy the concert, will you?"

"But ma'am . . ."

"I insist." She gives a wink. "The children are safe with me."

Not sure about that.

But I take the out and rejoin the mob. My head's spinning. Didn't get yelled at by Dante, didn't get told off by Mrs. Hall—who didn't even seem to recognize the gown. This is the luckiest I've been in a while. And now, I have time.

I need to find Aaron.

I check my phone. No texts, no calls. Where is he? Still in the auditorium? I march in that direction, seeking Aaron's usual pulled-back bun.

And I spot Simone instead.

She's standing by the double doors to the theater. No dress. She's in a uniform like the rest of the venue staff, black pants and white shirt. Is she working the event? Even though she was invited as a guest? Why?

Her eyes remain steady on the stage, where Ian dallies, chatting with the upcoming act. She doesn't seem to feel me staring.

Simone waiting by Ian's office in the middle of the night.

His deep voice echoing in the hallway, calling for her.

Someone gently touches my waist. I jerk around.

"It *is* you," Aaron says. "When did you change? And your dress is . . ."

It's not white. He's never seen me in any other color.

"I'll explain later." We beeline to an empty corner of the lobby. Aaron presses his hand into the small of my back, guiding me.

"Was lookin' everywhere for you," he murmurs.

Me too. Me too.

"First thing: talked to that friend of mine, the cop. Met me here." Aaron checks the room, then leans in. "Found some stuff on Kelly."

Now I'm sweeping the area, a bundle of nerves about how what Aaron knows links with what I do. Nobody's looking at us.

Except Ora.

She stands in the center of the lobby, decked out in a short sunflower-yellow dress that sticks out amongst all the dark floor-length gowns. Josh is next to her, shirt half tucked, chatting her ear off. Their arms are twined. But they don't remotely read as a couple; there's too much space between them, a subtle leaning away from each other. Ora's gorgeous, as always. Her facial expression isn't one I'm used to, though. It's solemn, a little wooden. My heart drops, and I run through all the possibilities. Maybe she feels out of place. Maybe she had a rough day before the benefit.

Or maybe she saw Aaron and me talking. Standing so close.

And here I am . . . crossing the line. Hurting her.

All I do is repeat the past. But I want to change.

Aaron's voice brings me back to the matter at hand. Focus. "Clarke did not lie. Kelly work with the Halls for a long, long time. Then about fifteen years past, she disappear."

"Just . . . gone?"

"Her family file a report, say she missin'. Nothing turn up."

So she vanished and didn't tell *anyone* she was going *anywhere?* "Did the police talk to the Halls at all?"

"Questioned them, yeah. They said they heard Kelly move abroad. Said that's all they know."

"A woman went missing, the Halls were probably the last ones to see her, and the cops just . . . believed them when they said she moved?"

"Friend said it seem like the police investigate a little bit . . . but then it stop. Case closed." I must look frustrated, disappointed, or both, based on how Aaron's own face twists seeing mine. "He think some money might have change hands. Because that's what the wealthy do, you know? Make problems go away."

Only the ones they created themselves.

What is my parents' money for if not making problems disappear?

"You okay?" Aaron asks. No. "No color in your face. What happen back at Blackbead?"

I tell him everything. The pointless search through Thomas's archives. The lights leading the way to the key for Ian's office.

"You sure you don't just *think* you see something funny with the lights?"

"Oh, I'm sure."

I mention finding a woman's weathered photo, a bone flute necklace dangling from her neck. Reading Mr. Hall's pleading apology note to Kelly Rowe.

"And then that duppy lit the office on fire." I gesture to my new dress. "I had to change."

"A fire, for real? You hurt?" He tries to inspect me for wounds. But I brush him off, attempt to tell him I'm fine, attempt to keep the conversation on Kelly, on Ian, on this fucked-up hell house we're living in.

Aaron catches my hand.

There's a burn on the inside of my forearm. Where just last night, his thumb circled the delicate skin. Where his lips left their mark.

Didn't see the damage before. Didn't feel it.

The burn is in the shape of a bull.

Aaron traces its outline, makes sure not to touch. "Duppy really try to hurt you." And I deserve it. Because why did I even think the duppy and I could understand each other or be on the same side? It tried to kill me tonight. It tried so hard, it nearly burned down Blackbead, and I'm surprised it didn't.

Then I remember what Mother Maud said.

Duppy not rest while Blackbead stands.

So you will do what it wants.

But what it cannot.

You did bring a seed of destruction with you . . .

The irrepairable au pair suite. The fallen lights. Ian's burnt office. I shiver. Maybe tearing down Blackbead is exactly what the duppy wants me to do.

Aaron's touch distracts me. Soothes me. And I can't have it. Not anymore. I gently pull my arm back, cradle it near my chest. Can't think about what happened, what could have happened, what might still happen.

Across the lobby, Wesley sees us and waves. I don't want anyone to notice the burn and ask questions; I have no easy-to-believe answers. So Aaron fake smiles and points to the auditorium as if to say we'll meet him there. Wesley heads into the theater, and I can breathe again.

"So, Kelly's the duppy then?" I question.

Aaron takes off his jacket and throws it around me so I can hide the mark. "How it seem."

"And Kelly and Ian were having an affair before she disappeared."

"Very likely."

"So what if..." The words stick in my throat. I don't want to believe what I'm going to say. I don't want to even consider it. Because for all his faults, it's still hard to think Ian would cross this line. The Halls were supposed to be respectable people.

That might have been a trick.

"What if Ian killed Kelly?"

Aaron takes his time responding. When he does, his tone is grave. "Hope you wrong."

I close my eyes, slow the overwhelm for a few moments. I just need to think.

Kelly is the duppy. She must be. She practically told me herself.

But what she won't tell me is what she wants me to do with this information. Where do I go? How do I help, besides torching Ian's mansion to the ground?

Why me?

When I open my eyes, the lobby has thinned. Most have paraded back into the auditorium for the next performance. Aaron and I stroll toward the open doors. Ian is still onstage, joking with the audience.

I almost fail to spot the young woman standing inside the door.

Simone. Watching the show with full attention. As if Ian were a sun she orbited. Her long braids sway behind her.

Braids splayed against the rocks...

A vision made of haze and ember.

A woman with her skull fractured, crumpled at the bottom of a cliff.

What if I was wrong? What if the woman wasn't me?

Similar hair, similar height... another Young Bird at risk of flying straight into peril and breaking herself.

Simone finally sees me. Unreadable.

Maybe what I saw at the jerk pit wasn't a threat. It could have been a warning.

And just like that, it clicks. It makes sense, what Kelly has been trying to do, what she wants me to do.

She wasn't trying to kill me. She wanted me to understand how dangerous this is. That we are dealing with life and death, a situation that killed Kelly herself years ago.

Simone walks past Aaron and me, exits the theater. But I can't stop following her.

I ran to Jamaica to start over, to be better. Now Kelly's asking me to keep another girl from repeating the mistakes we've both made. I know what it's like to fuck up. I know how much it hurts, how wrong choices can kill. Somehow, Kelly figured me out. And she chose me to do what she can't.

Simone disappears through a side door. She never looked back, not once. She's in her own world. If she's not careful, that world could crumble.

I have to stop Simone.

And it has to be me. Because I am the one who understands.

The audience claps for Ian, for the band, for this night of patting one another on the back for being a "have" rather than a "have-not."

When I arrived in Jamaica, I told myself that I'd do almost anything for a second chance. Maybe what drew Kelly to me is what drew me to Jamaica.

Redemption.

This is how I earn it.

NINETEEN

MOM

MOM: Your photos tell me you're in Montana. Like you should be.

MOM: But you haven't answered any texts. You only send pictures.

MOM: Don't ignore me, Carina.

MOM: You're not answering your phone. Why?

MOM: This was my #1 rule. You have to let me know you're alive.

MOM: Don't make me regret letting you leave. Pick up your phone. Please.

Things feel too real in the daylight.

The Halls pack the house full of people handling the fire damage in Ian's office—apparently from a fallen candle that must not have been properly extinguished before we left for the concert. Ian's been screaming at Dante all morning, like it's his fault somehow.

If only they knew. Dante probably does. I'm lucky he hates his father too much to snitch on me over this.

The kids' tutor didn't bother to come because she thought they'd be too tired to focus on lessons after the benefit. And she was right. Luis and Jada are dead weight, exhausted.

So I set them up in the basement theater for a movie. They'll probably fall asleep within the first fifteen minutes.

Once I lower the lights, I sneak upstairs.

I need to find Simone.

My fingers toy with the bandage wrapped around my burn. I don't know for sure if this is what the duppy wants me to do. Sleep didn't clarify that. But even if I'm wrong, this feels right. Simone's responsible and smart, but she's also so obsessed with Ian that she's putting herself in danger—and under Mrs. Hall's nose too.

How could this end well?

Blackbead has been haunted for ages. But not by some half-baked legend. It's been haunted by Ian. His messy past, his egotistical behavior. Behavior that he'll repeat until someone gets hurt. He'll run until he can't.

Simone's in the library, wiping down a side table. I knock on the door. She slowly turns. Her under-eye bags are obvious today, and her lips are cracked. Allergies? Sickness?

Tired from an after-party with Ian?

"I thought you'd take today off," I start.

Simone shakes her head, gets back to cleaning. "Bills don't stop. So work don't stop."

"Can we talk?"

She wipes sweat from her forehead. "Can give you five minutes. What do you need?"

I hesitate. Simone hustles so hard, barely takes time off. She even gave up an invitation to the benefit and served at the event instead. It's like all she has is work, the Young Birds ... and Ian.

What if Simone's not in this for the sex or the thrill? Maybe Ian's cash gives her a chance to chill out. To have fun, be taken care of. If

I say something, am I taking that from her? Stealing something she needs to keep from losing her sanity?

"Got a lot to do," she drones.

I don't want to rob her of anything.

But I don't want Ian to rob her of everything.

I take a deep breath. "I just wanted you to know that I know."

"About?"

"About what's going on. What you've been doing." Her expression is unchanging. "And I'm not judging, honest. Like, I understand why. But it's so risky, and I'm worried about you."

Simone drops her rag on the table. "I don't get you. Speak up."

I don't know how to talk about this politely. "I know you can handle yourself, and if this were any other guy, I swear, I wouldn't bring this up." I lower to a whisper. "But this is our *boss*, Simone. You could get caught, fired. If Mrs. Hall catches you running around with Ian like you were a couple weeks ago, you're—"

"You got no idea what you're talking about," Simone says. She's stern, cutting. "You do not know who Mr. Hall really is, okay? And what you think you see? You don't. So mind your business, and hush your mouth."

"Do *you* think you know him? Be for real." The way she's protecting him—protecting them—makes me sick. But I see so much of me in her right now, in the delusion and denial. "You're playing with fire. Ian will eat you up and spit you out." I rest a hand on her shoulder. "Don't mess with him."

"You got a lot of nerve." Simone jolts out of my grasp. "And when you so close-lipped about yourself too. Talk a little, but almost never about you. That's your game, isn't it?"

I stay silent.

"You thought I forget those calls, your phone hot as hell in my hand?" she asks flatly. "Or how you jumpy when Scoob ask if you steal before."

"I wasn't feeling well that day."

"Weren't feeling good at the pool either, right? That's why you suddenly couldn't remember if you date no man or every man."

"Simone—"

"You're hiding. Don't know what, but it clear as day. So maybe, if you don't want to get caught ass out, stop putting your nose where it don't belong." She glares, and we're back in the rum bar where she stared as if I'd done something wrong, like she knew me. "I'm done here."

Simone gathers her cleaning supplies and leaves the library. And I stand there. Stock-still. If Simone hated me before, now she's leveled up. And everyone knows the more you push someone away from something, the faster they dash toward it.

Did I push Simone too far?

I hum Marley's "Sun Is Shining" until my heart stops racing.

I hum until Dante's heavy footsteps stop pacing the hallway outside.

I hum until things make sense.

By the time I return to the basement, I've made a decision.

I will save Simone. From Ian. From herself.

Maybe it's sleep deprivation or guilt about Joy or the fact that I've clearly cracked inside this madhouse. Doesn't matter.

Simone doesn't know what I do. She has no idea how devastating her choices could be. I don't know what it will take to get her to see reality. But I have to make her see it. Period.

I've protected myself all this time. Pretended to be someone else when it was too dangerous to be myself. Tried to be the right kinds of fun and appropriate whenever others were around. Fought ghosts past and present to get my chance at a future that'd be all about me, no matter how nobly I attempted to frame it.

But I can't choose myself again.

That's how I lost Joy. That's how I lost everything.

I will take care of Simone. I will help her. And I'll need help to do it.

It's time to let some secrets loose.

"You went to Mother Maud!?"

I found Josh and Ora in the butler's pantry, and Ora has no inside voice. I shush her, leer at Josh so he knows to keep it down too.

This is probably the most I've ever talked about myself at once. And maybe I could have saved face and skipped the duppy saga, jumped right to "the good stuff." But I need Ora and Josh to hear the whole story to get how I fell into this disaster waiting to happen. How the duppy helped me recognize what's really happening inside Blackbead.

And I know that, right now, they think I'm ridiculous. But I'm certain of what I've witnessed, what I've felt. Once Josh and Ora hear everything from me, they'll understand. They'll help me protect Simone. Maybe we could even work alongside the duppy, because I'm not sure breaking up this couple is a job that the living alone can manage.

"Yes, I saw Mother Maud. I didn't know what else to do."

Josh stacks a bunch of canned chickpeas. "Was Mother crazy?"

"What sort of question is that?"

"It's fair," he insists. "Only crazy people ask other crazy people for advice." Josh chuckles and slaps his knee. That shit isn't funny.

"Scoob, do you think I'd get half naked in front of an old woman for fun?"

"Well, you fake quiet," Ora says, smirking. "Still got that tattoo hidden somewhere. Maybe you like show it off to Mother."

Frustration starts bubbling up. Breathe.

"Look, I visited her because of all the weird shit that was happening to me. Not sleeping, seeing stuff, smelling honeysuckle everywhere."

"Told you was stress," Ora says. "The Halls them will do that to you."

"It's not *stress*. It's a duppy. Mother Maud confirmed it, and the damn thing's been trying to communicate with me for weeks."

"Thought duppy supposed to smell like sulfur," Josh says. His tone is light, amused. As if we're trading tall tales.

"Aaron said honeysuckle," I admit, "and I've smelled it every time she's appeared. She doesn't talk much, but she still has a lot of shit to say."

"She?" Ora asks.

Right. "Aaron and I talked to I don't know how many people. Finally figured out that the duppy used to work at Blackbead, and her name was Kelly Rowe."

The name clearly doesn't ring any bells for the two.

"She worked here for years. Kelly was one of Ian's girls back in the day."

Ora's eyes widen. "You mean all those little rumors true? Mr. Hall really been sleeping around all these years?"

"The night of the concert, I snuck back here to search the house, and her picture was stuffed in his couch cushions." Her short frame, her necklace hanging from her dainty neck. Hiding in a politician's sofa like a porno mag.

The weight of what I'm saying finally seems to land.

"Kelly disappeared ages ago. Her family searched for her, the Halls were questioned, and nothing happened. Until now. Because she's the duppy, and if that's true, then she probably died here."

Josh's face twists in confusion. "What you saying? You think someone here . . . kill her?"

"I found an apology letter Ian wrote to Kelly," I add, somber. "Said he was sorry for what he did to her. That's practically a confession." I tread carefully at what I explain next. "Ian is powerful. We know he's fooled around with staff. And I know who he's working on right now."

Ora and Josh look at each other. The worry is there. Fear. "Who?"

They'll listen. They always do.

I take a deep breath. Ready myself. "Simone."

Silence.

Ora does a double take. "What?"

Slowly. Clearly. "Simone and Ian are hooking up."

More silence.

Then they burst into laughter.

Something shatters in my mind.

"I'm not kidding. I saw her hanging around his office one night. And then Ian called out her name. She's seeing Ian. The duppy practically told me so."

They laugh harder. Rage builds in my skull. Why are they ganging up on me instead of being serious?

"What did Chicken get you into?" Ora asks, wiping away tears. "Even when we were little, he love to believe a bag of nonsense."

She doesn't get it. "Aaron's been helping me. He believes the duppy is real too."

Ora raises an eyebrow. "He visit Mother Maud with you?"

I can't answer that.

"If he believe," Josh wonders, "where is he? You come to us with this wild story. Why come alone?" He shrugs. "Maybe Chicken just look for excuse to spend time with you."

Perceptive Josh needs to shut up before he gets me in trouble.

Ora gives this pitying simper of a smile. "Chicken love to joke as much as Scoob. Think he pull your leg, Bambi." I try to steady my breath, try to keep it together so I don't cuss out Ora and Josh. "That's why he's not here to face us. Couldn't follow through." She pats my cheek like I'm some child.

I snap.

"Or maybe he's actually doing his job, unlike you two lazy fucks."

They stiffen.

Save this. I have to save this. "I'm sorry. I just . . . I need you guys to believe me. If you don't, something bad could happen to Simone. You have to help me."

Neither speaks.

"Please."

Ora scoffs. "Think we need to get back to our work, Scoob, yeah?" Ice-cold.

The two gather their stuff and scatter. I slam my hand against a silver serving tray on the counter.

No Simone. No Josh. No Ora.

Nobody's listening. Nobody's hearing me. Nobody will help.

All I have left is Aaron.

Aaron wouldn't play games with me. Even Ora said he's one of the honest guys. He wouldn't bullshit me just so we'd hang out, just to get me alone. Just to humor me.

But I've been wrong about people before.

Why would this time be any different, when the common denominator in all my screwups is me?

It's bedtime, and I'm spiraling.

I could be wrong about Aaron.

I could be wrong about Simone.

I could be wrong about Ian and Kelly too.

Brush teeth. Wash face. Change into pajamas. Go through the motions wordlessly and think and brood and rack my brain.

What do I know? Should I really feel so confident about everything I think I've figured out? Am I sure I'm still in my right mind?

I sit on the edge of my bed. Images and memories blend, a confusing mix of what is real and what feels real. I can't tell the difference.

Pop!

The light bulb in the ceiling fan blows. Darkness flickers across the room.

"Sure. Why not?"

I flip the light switch off, grab a fresh bulb from my closet, and pull out my desk chair so I can reach the fan. I grasp the used bulb, begin to unscrew it.

Something crackles. Sits in the air like a lightning storm.

Run.

Red-orange sparks rain from the socket. I stumble off the chair and sprint for the light switch. But it's already off.

Honeysuckle floods my nose. The duppy.

Repeating its newest trick: fucking with the lights.

The flares cascade and swirl above my head. Merging. Creating some kind of eerie work of midair art. I make out a distinct shape.

The letter *T*.

Then *R*.

Followed by *U*.

T-R-U-T-H.

Written in fire. Then fading away.

The room returns to darkness. To silence. I exhale.

Like always, I see what nobody else does. Maybe because I'm willing to see it. Everyone wants to keep the truth hidden; if it comes out, then they pretend it's a lie. And I get it. The truth is hard to face.

But the truth is all there is. It's the most powerful force I've ever known.

Clarity washes over me.

TRUTH.

A literal light in the darkness.

The truth in the light.

I know I don't have all the answers. But my gut is telling me I'm on the right path. The duppy—Kelly—is telling me I'm on the right path.

And that means Simone still needs help.

Shadows cling to the walls as I lie down. I listen to my breath. I am alone.

But that isn't true.

Kelly's here, watching. Waiting.

One way or another, we're on the same team. We have to be.

Tomorrow, I start again.

I must start again.

TWENTY

Come morning, I'm focused.

The gray clouds offer some shade while I take a broom to the patio, sweeping away the dirt the kids and I have kicked up in the last hour. I'm balancing au pair duties and reviewing everything Aaron and I have learned over the last few weeks. And I'm doing a great fucking job, thank you very much.

The patio's almost clean when my phone vibrates in my pocket. Since nobody's speaking to me right now, it's probably Aaron calling on WhatsApp. I discreetly pull out the phone to text him back. We'll chat later; I need his brainpower if we're going to save Simone from Ian.

But it's not Aaron.

Unsaved number: 876 area code.

Could be one of the nannies we spoke to weeks back. Maybe they have more information or finally want to talk. Some details about how Ian used to behave could help me convince the rest of the Young Birds. I answer.

"Hello. This is Lloyd Jones, senior staff reporter for the *Gleaner*. Is this Miss . . . Carina Carter?"

The *Gleaner*? That's like Jamaica's main newspaper. Why would they be reaching out to me? Do I lie to the press?

No, if he's a senior reporter, he's likely well-researched. If I lied, he'd probably know. I don't need that attention.

"Yes. This is her."

"And are you the current au pair for the Hall family?"

"Yes."

"Good, good, thank you. I wasn't sure if I had nailed down the right person. Cultural CareScapes couldn't provide a good contact number."

My heart rattles in my rib cage. I step away from the kids as they attempt to play hopscotch in the grass. Even breaths, slow breaths. But I'm choking. Did the reporter call the agency, then? Ask about me? Tip them off?

"Would you like to make a statement?"

"Excuse me?"

"About the Honorable Ian Hall? Would you like to make a statement regarding the latest allegations?"

Shit. Something's going on. And it has to be terrible. Especially if the media is calling me, some random babysitter with a fancier title. If I say anything, it'll be used against me.

So I hang up.

It's rude, and that's the point. I consider blocking the number, just in case.

"What's wrong?" Luis asks. Grass stains streak across his light-blue polo.

"Nothing," I reply with a smile. "Come on. Let's color for a little while. I have something important I need to finish up."

I get the kids settled at the patio table with two fresh coloring books, sing along with Jada as she pulls out all the green crayons for her picture. I'm on automatic.

And once they're busy, I start googling.

Query: *Ian Hall*

The first result? Breaking news from the *Voice of Jamaica*.

IAN HALL'S HIDDEN AFFAIRS EXPOSED!

Oh no.

I open the article.

> The Voice of Jamaica investigative team has obtained exclusive evidence of a truly jaw-dropping discovery. Our quality informants claim that politician Ian Hall has allegedly led a repulsive double life. By day, Hall portrays himself as an upstanding citizen of our beautiful country and as an advocate for our global expansion. But by night, the politician fills his time with disgraceful affairs, often with his own au pairs, nannies, and housekeepers. Is the Honorable Ian Hall truly honorable? Is he fit for public office? Is Ruth Hall too frigid to keep her man satisfied at home? The Jamaican people have a right to know.

Bolstered by anonymous sources, the article details years and years of Ian stepping out on Mrs. Hall. Blatantly.

And it isn't just hearsay. There's evidence—like a disturbing amount of it. Receipts for lingerie stores in Kingston, invoices for weekend stays at Treasure Beach, extravagant dinners in Montego Bay, photos of Ian canoodling with an East Asian woman near Emancipation Park, embracing an Indian girl on a yacht. How the hell did Patrick Clarke not burn this shit ages ago?

If the *Gleaner* is wanting to report on this, then the evidence must be solid. Even though the *Voice of Jamaica* broke the news—and everyone knows not to listen to them—nobody would touch this story if the proof wasn't damning.

"Miss Rina, color with us!" Luis calls out.

"Just a second," I mumble. I jump down the page.

But the real bombshell lies in the claim that Hall has harbored a closely guarded secret for years. Sources allege that the man who rose through the ranks of Jamaican politics has also fathered at least one secret child, likely born from his illicit liaisons with a member of his domestic staff. How far has Hall spread his seed? What other secrets are Hall and his associates keeping?

I stop scrolling.

The infidelity, I knew. Kelly's just one of many on Ian's roster.

But the kids? *Secret* kids?

That's new.

And that's possible. If someone's fooling around that much—and probably never wrapping it up—they're going to slip. At least one of his girls had to have gotten knocked up by now.

You do not know who Mr. Hall really is.

When Simone told me that, I thought she was saying she knew him better than I did, that I didn't understand the relationship they had or how good he was to her.

Maybe she was right.

What if Simone isn't Ian's latest side chick?

What if she's his child?

And what you think you see? You don't.

Could Ian have brought his own daughter to work in the mansion so he could keep tabs on her without tipping anyone off about who she actually is? Maybe that's how she gets so much work, too, like at the banquet and the benefit concert. Of course her father would make a way to provide for her without having to expose all his wrongdoings. And if Simone truly needs the money, of course she'd agree.

She's definitely been more defensive of the Halls than the other Young Birds. Like when Josh complained at the rum bar, she said we all need the Halls to survive. She listens, behaves, works hard, never gets into trouble.

The perfect daughter.

My hand wobbles as I lower the phone. This is nuts.

The kids color a few feet away. For once, Luis isn't being a menace. And Jada isn't sucking her thumb. They're comfortable. Peaceful.

And they have no idea how much of that peace is about to be ripped away.

YOUNG BIRDS

CARINA: Anyone want to hang out at Blackbead after work?

CARINA: If you say no, I understand. But . . .

CARINA: The Halls have a thing this evening.

AARON: sure! be by later.

CARINA: Thanks. Anyone else?

CARINA: Anyone . . . ?

CARINA: We could play pool or darts or something in the game room.

CARINA: And it would be good to see everyone.

CARINA: Seriously.

ORA: ok ok!! will try come.

JOSH: will h/o if u sneak me in. thomas fire me this morning

SIMONE: No way

AARON: you lie.

JOSH: caught me w/ bag of pantry things. been donating them in badrick name.

JOSH: will be eatin rice and bully beef 4 a month. but regret nothin.

JOSH: fuck the halls fr.

CARINA: Can't believe it . . . One last YB hangout at BB then. For Scoob.

ORA: juney??

ORA: you have to come!!

SIMONE: Fine

I spend my first evening in the abandoned game room losing. Badly.

I center my stick and aim for the solid red billiard ball.

Ora kisses her teeth. "Can't believe they just fire you like that." Josh stands beside her and sips the ice-cold pineapple soda I handed him as a paltry goodbye gift. He looks even more relaxed than usual. Didn't think that was possible. "And all over some food?"

"It gets better," Josh says. I lose focus on the game as Josh digs into his pants pocket and retrieves a crumpled sheet of paper. "Thomas gave me a bill. So I can pay the Halls back for what I took."

Aaron scoffs. "Don't pay that, man. If Thomas didn't catch you, bet they wouldn't even notice the food was gone."

"You get it now," Josh says, smirking. He drops the invoice on the ground and digs his shoe into every fold and crease. "Knew you'd all come around. Now I can leave happy."

"But who's going to piss me off if you're not here every day?" Ora whines.

Josh smirks. "Bet Aaron will bother you if you ask nice."

My hand slips. I tap the cue ball, and the red ball veers in a random direction. My turn's over. I put down the stick while Ora does a dance and cheer.

Losing a game is no big deal. I'd rather lose and have most of the Young Birds talking to me again than win and keep getting iced out for being a bitch.

Green and yellow wood masks stare with hollow eyes from their place on each wall. My mind drifts. I was desperate to get the kids to bed just to gather my thoughts in peace. But there are too many, scattered all over like the billiard balls.

Ora misses her shot, so Simone takes hers.

We're on the same team, but Simone and I have barely spoken. And if I was wrong about the Ian affair thing, I deserve the silent treatment. But I have to know how true the new rumors are. The bastard kid story was the one thing the *Voice of Jamaica* didn't provide any hard proof for. So is that lead bullshit? Or is it the next big scandal if Ian and Simone aren't careful?

"Got a weird call today from some reporter at the *Gleaner*," I say casually. "Dude was asking about Ian." Maybe teasing out the topic will get Simone to spill.

But instead, everyone else does.

"I got a call too," Aaron says.

"Same," Josh joins. Beside him, Ora nods. Her too.

Simone doesn't respond. Focuses on her shot.

"He asked you all about Ian?"

"No," Aaron replies. "He left a message asking about . . . you."

"Asked what you like, what type of person you are," Ora says.

Josh adds, "How you and Mr. Hall connect."

Aaron clears his throat. "He wanna know if the two of you were . . . very friendly."

Because after that article, everyone thinks the au pair must be sleeping with Ian. No wonder that reporter called. He wanted to see if I'd defend myself or lie or admit to it.

Simone shoots. Pockets the solid blue ball. She moves to a new target.

"Think only Scoob had nerve enough to call him back," Ora says. "Thought it was finally his chance to tell the paper how he honestly feel, yeah?"

"The Halls them not my boss anymore. Could have said anything." Josh sucks his teeth. "But just spoke truth. Don't know anything for certain, and I told him that." He looks at me. "And not say a word about you, Bambi."

Hearing that pet name is a relief. "Thanks," I tell him, and I mean it.

Josh shifts uncomfortably. "The man did say some weirdness, though," he admits. "Ask about Twitter, some hashtag."

My mouth dries out.

"Something about New York, something between you and this girl. Jan? Jay?"

He means Joy.

My stomach drops.

I did everything right. Did everything I could to cover my tracks and kill the version of me I no longer wanted to claim.

But still, that bitch lives.

The truth is out there. I can't erase or delete it. And I can't hide forever. One day, the Young Birds will know. One day, probably soon, Aaron will know. And I will lose them. I've had a taste of that already.

Isolation hurts. Loneliness hurts. Being misunderstood hurts. And I will suffer it all again.

I wouldn't have survived Blackbead without each of the Young Birds keeping me going, in their own way. I'm a hair's breadth away from being back in a bedroom, curled under the comforter, hiding. Or in a jail cell. Which would be worse?

"Very weird stuff," I mutter. "Not sure what that's about."

"So you don't know anything about none of that?" Simone asks. She scowls at me. And I get it.

But back the fuck up.

"No, I don't."

"But that's a lot to ask about. Specific too."

"It's strange. But I don't know anything more than you do."

"You know what funny to me?" Simone wonders. She slams down her cue stick. "Carina love love *love* to be in everyone else business. Did scold all of us on her first day because we share a rumor here and there, but run her mouth more than we. Right?"

Nobody speaks.

"Yet anything about her, nobody can know. Suddenly, *she* don't even know. Tight lip." She whips around to the rest of the group. "What we know about her? Truly?"

The question I asked her, about Ian. Here she goes, throwing it back in my face.

Why did I ever say anything?

"Juney, stop," Aaron murmurs. "Keep your voice down. We're chillin'. It's Josh's last day."

"No, you all let the girl act stupid 'cause she foreign, 'cause she pretty. She play dumb like the pickney them. Wake up." Simone points a shaky finger at me. "If the news 'bout Mr. Hall true," Simone spits, "Carina just as bad as him. Two-faced."

Simone never talks like this. And to hear her sling these words—about me—hurts like hell. I want to shout back, push back, fight back. She doesn't know me or anything I've gone through.

But is she wrong?

I'm expecting Simone to share everything, confess to sleeping with Ian or admit to being one of his secret kids. But when Ora asks me what my favorite color is or if I've ever ridden a roller coaster, I spend an extra five seconds debating the consequences of being honest versus telling Joy's truth instead of mine. I've curated myself so heavily, built a persona for everyone to accept, from Ian and Mrs. Hall to the children to the kitchen staff. I've built a pen for the monster within, thrown a muzzle on her, tried to tame her.

And who has the monster become? Do I recognize her?

Do I see me?

"Simone, enough," Aaron orders. "If *Voice of Jamaica* true, what we know is Mr. Hall a coward. People who lie like him? Cowards. Bambi, she nah like him, never has been, never will be."

Even faced with all my bullshit, Aaron imagines the most generous possibilities. He hears all my off-key notes and assumes they're simply part of the song. To him, I'm brave. Open.

What does he see in me?

Being in Jamaica, being with the Young Birds ... it hasn't been perfect, but I've felt more me than I have in a long time. Guarded, sure, but myself. I imagine the rum bar, me dancing with strangers and friends, or joking around in the group chat.

That was me. Not Joy. Me.

Listening to Ora's love for her dead brother. Giving honest advice to Josh about leaving Blackbead. Comforting Jada and Luis at night while their father's shouts echoed in their ears. Telling Aaron it's beautiful to feel. Trying to help Simone so she doesn't get hurt like I did.

Bits of me showed themselves, even when I tried to hide them. Pieces of myself felt safe here, with these friends I'd made.

The truth in the light.

No shadows to hide in. No secrets to keep.

If getting justice for Kelly means exposing everything, even about myself, will I do it?

Run.

My gut twists, and acid rises in my throat. I've worked so hard to cover it all. But that's what Ian does. Plays pretend, shows the photo-ready version of himself to the world.

I want to be better than him. I want to own all of me, show all of me.

I've faced loss before. Embarrassment before. Emptiness before. But I survived.

If the truth means losing my friends, so be it.

Because I can survive anything. Even heartbreak.

Especially that.

By sunrise, I make a choice.

After the morning bell, I get dressed, pad quietly out of the house, and sit underneath the big mango tree, cell phone in hand. The air's heavy with the promise of an incoming storm. A strong, cool gust rustles the leaves, races across my skin. The world is headstone gray.

Blackbead used to be so beautiful to me. It still is. But there's something rotten here.

And today, I root it out.

I open WhatsApp and dial Lloyd Jones.

"Miss Carter?" he answers. There's a smugness to him. Asshole. "Glad to hear from you. We were . . . disconnected yesterday."

"Yes. Apologies. Poor signal." My eyes flit to the kitchen window. I don't hear anyone in there yet for breakfast. And Dante could come out soon to sulk in the garden. I need to be quick. "I have some information about the Honorable Ian Hall."

"I'm all ears."

"It's not . . . I'm not fooling around with him."

"I understand why you would say that, Miss Carter."

"I'm not trying to protect him. It's the truth. But I have a story—a real one—that is way more important than who Mr. Hall is cheating with."

There's a long pause, as if now he's debating whether or not to hang up on me. Then: "Go on."

"One of Mr. Hall's girls was a young woman named Kelly Rowe. R-O-W-E. She worked at Blackbead as a nanny, and she was deep into it with Mr. Hall. Then, fifteen years ago, she vanished."

"She left?"

A cabinet slams in the kitchen. Blackbead's waking up. Shit. I whisper. "Allegedly. But it was very sudden. Her family reported her missing and got nowhere. The Halls claimed she went abroad. And then the police just dropped everything and gave up."

"So your theory is—"

"My theory," I say, attempting to hide where nobody can see me if they peer through the window, "is that Mr. Hall had something to do with Kelly Rowe's disappearance. And I'm pretty sure Kelly isn't missing. She's dead."

Saying this aloud to someone other than the Young Birds feels crazy. Like I've dropped a bomb. But as I say it, I feel the heft of my words. The duppy is Kelly. Something awful happened to her. Ian *must* be involved.

And finally, the truth is out there. I brought it to light. Kelly will have some justice.

"You'll need to provide evidence for this claim. You understand this, right?"

"Pardon?"

"The burden of proof rests on you, Miss Carter. As of now, what you've shared is mere speculation. The *Gleaner* is a prestigious publication, not TMZ. Without concrete support for your allegations, we could not, in good faith, run a story like this." Lloyd half chuckles. "I mean, if I'm hearing you correctly, you're accusing a party leader of murder."

"I know, but—"

"Then you can understand my hesitation to simply take you at your word."

Without proof, the press isn't interested. But I can't tell him that my source is a fucking ghost. So I shut my mouth. Exhale hard through my nose. Stay calm.

"I also admit," he goes on, "that I'm somewhat skeptical of you." His condescending tone grates me. It's like he can't imagine speaking to me about anything more serious than my presumed sex life with a married man. Gross.

"Just because I'm young doesn't make me untrustworthy."

"Oh, it's not your age, miss. It's you." On the other end of the phone, I hear the sound of papers shuffling. "Are you aware that there is an old picture circulating online of a now-deceased Joy Carter . . . and her close friend Carina Marshall?"

My throat closes.

"Seems a bit convenient that you wish to minimize your visibility in the press at this time. And that you'd do so with this narrative about . . . Mr. Hall killing a young woman."

"Bring me some more cornmeal, will you?" Wesley's request filters outside. Dante will walk by soon.

I'm out of time.

I can't control Lloyd. What he discovers, what he shares with the world—it's up to him. But I know what I *can* do.

"I'll get your evidence. Have a good day."

I hang up, wait for my hands to stop shaking.

One more time.

I will find the truth just one more time.

Because something is rotten here.

And I will root it out.

TWENTY-ONE

It works out perfectly.

It's the lull between lunch and dinner. Most nonessential staff has been dismissed because of the approaching storm. Every mirror is covered. The valet said it's to block any spirits that come with the rain and thunder. The house feels hollow.

Jada is on the edge of a tantrum. Luis has a stomachache. I put them both down for a nap.

I'm alone.

One hour to find some proof for the *Gleaner*.

I grab the key from the box in the closet and hide it in my bra. The brass is cold against my skin. I tiptoe through the hallways, the gallery, the corridor to Ian's office.

Ian is home, hiding in his bedroom upstairs, conferring with Thomas about how to handle the media blowback. Mrs. Hall, on the other hand, has retreated to the sitting room. She only just headed in, so she'll be out of the way for hours, hopefully. Normally, I'd never thumb through their stuff while they were home, but this felt like a necessary risk, considering they hadn't been leaving the house much since the island started digging into Ian's many misdeeds.

But Cultural CareScapes must know something's up. Reporter Lloyd suspects me too. I'm in a bind.

I get myself into the office and lock the door behind me. My memory reloads the spike of adrenaline, the searing heat, a fire ignited by a phantom. The flashbacks nearly stop me in place—as does the leftover damage. But I waste no time.

I push papers, move books around, open file cabinets. I pick through a room I've already combed, and—surprise!—there's nothing new. All I have access to is the photo of Kelly.

Why did the duppy burn Ian's letter? It was some of the only solid evidence I had that he'd done *something* potentially criminal.

And if there's more here, Kelly's not showing it to me.

"Can't blow another light bulb or something?" I groan, crawling on the floor around Ian's desk, searching the darkness for anything strange, for any clue I could be missing.

Wait. Darkness.

The best tool against darkness?

Light.

I whip out my phone and throw on the flashlight. Then I open every desk drawer, checking for something out of place, shiny, weird. This man has too much dirty laundry to not be hiding more stuff. What am I not seeing?

I pull out a middle drawer, extend it to the stop. Full of junk papers and half-filled manila envelopes. Then I point the light at the back. The rear of the drawer is a different color than the sides, a stain that doesn't quite match. The sides don't touch the back panel, either. Little gaps sit on its left and right.

There's something in the back of this desk. I grip the handle.

If I'm wrong, Ian is going to kill me.

I wrench the drawer past the stop.

And there is a small hidden compartment.

With a stack of white and yellowed envelopes tied together with fraying twine. I peep the top of the bundle.

Addressed to Ian.

Kelly Rowe's name in the top left corner.

No return address.

Jackpot.

I grab the stack, place it on Ian's desk. Untie the twine. I swipe the first weathered envelope and flip it over. It's been opened already. I slide out a few pages of paper.

Letters.

February 14, 2011

Ian love,

Miss me?

   Miss you.

   There is so much to say that I do not know how to say. You are good with words. Not me.

   You must be mad. Maybe you do not want to hear from me after everything. I would understand that.

   I'm sorry for leaving. I'm sorry for how I left. It was not easy. Please believe me. I was not sure how I would spend a night without you. But I had to do it. Maybe I can explain someday. Then you will understand why I had to go, and we can make up. For now, just trust me.

   I think about you all the time, Ian. I think about everything we had. Maybe it wasn't much, but it was ours. Maybe we can have it again. I hope so.

   One day, you can come visit. Guess where I went? You never will. But I think you would like it here. It's quiet. You like the quiet. Until then, hold on to this letter. Piece of me with you.

Give me some time. I will write again with better words. I love you. Always will.

—Kelly

What in the actual hell did I read?
I pick up the next letter.

May 23, 2011

My Ian,

I can't sleep. So I write.

Remember I said I think about you all the time? It's true. Loved your warm hands. Loved your deep voice. Loved your beautiful smile.

It is all past, but I feel it now. Do you? Do you still remember me?

Do you remember how I kissed you? You always said I tasted like guava. Have you had guava lately? Did you think of me?

Do you remember how I touched you? Did Ruth ever learn how you like to be touched?

I do not think she has. She never has.

Do you remember the night you took those pictures of me? Do you still look at them? Do you sneak a peek when Ruth is not around? I hope so.

Ian, I will not forget you. Please do not forget me.

I will write again soon so you cannot.

—Kelly

My skin crawls. I need a fucking shower.
I fly through five more. They're all like this. Simple but romantic. Sentimental. Sometimes filthy. And dated as recently as six months ago.

All written when Kelly is supposedly missing.

I don't get it.

What the hell does this mean, then? That she isn't missing? That she isn't dead? That she left *and* somebody knows she's okay?

If Kelly's in contact with Ian, maybe he doesn't have anything to do with her disappearance at all. She doesn't even sound upset. She sounds like she's still in love. She's straight-up saying she is. So Kelly could be fine. Maybe she needed a fresh start and ran away to get just that. Like I did by coming to Jamaica.

The tightness in my chest suffocates me. I sink onto Ian's sofa. I was so sure. I was so sure that I understood what was happening, that I got what the duppy was telling me.

And now?

If Kelly's alive, then the duppy isn't her. And the duppy isn't Joy because there's no reason why she'd show me that photograph of Kelly, or that vision of Simone at the bottom of the cliff—two people she didn't even know. And Mother Maud said the duppy isn't from that Solomon legend. Maybe Simone is Ian's lover or his daughter, I don't know. She won't tell me either way.

I have no leads. I have no evidence. I have no idea what's going on.

It's over. It's over, and I—

Footsteps.

In the hallway. Getting louder.

I throw the letters back into the compartment, close the desk drawers, tidy the desktop. Slide the key back into my bra. Then I fly out the door, closing it as I leave.

And there's Mrs. Hall. Rounding the corner.

"Good afternoon, ma'am," I force out. What's she doing out of the sitting room? Did she see me leaving the office?

"Hello, Carina." There's a sadness to her today. None of her typical poise and determination. Her complexion seems pale and washed-out, drained.

For the first time since I learned about Ian's escapades, I think about how Mrs. Hall must feel. Years of her husband's infidelity. And now, the public embarrassment. Not just from knowing he's cheated. But from everyone in the country knowing he cheated on *her*.

Does she know about those letters tucked away in Ian's office, or about the photos that Kelly teased? Has he ever hit her the way he's hit Dante?

Is this the life she dreamed she'd have?

"You seem tired, ma'am."

"I am, I am. Long, uncertain days."

"Must be dealing with a lot . . . because of everything in the news." I half expect her to fall apart at the mere mention of the media circus, because I would. But she doesn't. She simply sighs.

"Well, it's why we surround ourselves with people we hope we can trust." She holds her gaze on my face. Even now, after weeks together, she's a bit wary. I don't blame her. But then, she says, "It's been good to have you, Carina."

I turn away.

"Were you looking for something?" Mrs. Hall asks. Gently wondering why I'm here. And why I'm here without the kids.

"The children are down for a nap, but, uh, Luis is missing his Superman cape. Again." I clear my throat, try to knock out the nerves. "He'll be upset if I don't have it when he wakes up."

Mrs. Hall hums to herself. "The children aren't supposed to play by the offices." She's right. It's one of the few rules Luis actually follows. Most of the time.

I compel myself to laugh, too hard. "I know, right? Can't relax for a minute." Mrs. Hall chuckles as well. It's just as fake as mine. "I'll keep hunting it down."

"I'll leave you to it." I squeeze past her and pace toward the stairs, ready to get back to the children who should be up soon. My heart slows a little with each step away from the office.

I did it. I didn't find anything for the reporter, but I didn't get caught.

I push papers, move books around, open file cabinets.

Halfway up the stairs, I stop.

Did I close the file cabinet?

I shut the desk drawers, cleared off the desk, put the books back. But did I close the file cabinet?

My mouth floods with spit. I don't think I did.

I know I didn't.

If either of the Halls goes in that office, I'm in trouble. Mrs. Hall knows I was right outside the room. She'll know I was snooping.

It's why we surround ourselves with people we hope we can trust.

She might think I've been the one leaking everything to the press. Then it won't matter if she calls the agency or the police. I'm screwed either way.

I can't catch my breath. The writing's on the wall.

Run.

I can't stay at Blackbead. I crossed a line. Got sloppy. Two mistakes I've made before, made again.

I head back downstairs and find Wesley writing up one last grocery list before the storm rolls in. I don't give him a chance to greet me.

"Could you keep Jada and Luis for the rest of the day?"

Wesley frowns. "What's wrong?"

"Not feeling well."

He doesn't answer right away. He knows the protocols for what happens if I'm ill. And calling on him isn't protocol. But he nods. And he says, "All right. I watch 'em."

"Thank you so much. For everything."

"But you come back when you get right, understand?"

Too late.

TWENTY-TWO

I wasn't ready.

My messenger bag slams onto the mattress. I flip it open, start frantically tossing anything important into it. My uncharged Bluetooth speaker. My favorite white shorts that I hadn't yet handed to housekeeping to wash. The sea-glass anklet that Josh bought—stole—for me.

I dump the fresh thermos of bush tea Aaron brewed, leave the red hair ribbon Jada lent to me. I'm not afraid of the duppy anymore. I hate it too much to fear it.

I bend down next to the bed.

The lockbox.

Slowly, I tease it out. There's a pounding in my ears.

I have to tell the others.

Before the reporter does. Before the Halls do.

Can't give Luis and Jada a kiss goodbye. Can't thank Wesley for every delicious dessert he made especially for me. Can't apologize to Gregory for never seeing the difference between the allamandas and the yellow bells.

Run.

I'm out of time.

"I wasn't ready."

If the ghost's here, it doesn't respond. Because now that it's swooped in and ruined my new life every which way, it doesn't have shit to say. No more broken lights or blood bulls or honeysuckle in my nose.

"It should have been my choice," I push. "I wanted to tell everyone when I was ready. You took that from me." I rise to my feet, throw a shirt into the bag. Then a dress. A skirt. "You wouldn't leave me alone. You took everything from me."

Silence.

"Answer me." I slam a hand against the mattress. "The least you could do is answer me."

The duppy's unfazed. This is all its fault, and it doesn't even have the courtesy to respond. To care.

My brain breaks.

There's simply me and the adrenaline and the grinding of my teeth until my jaw aches. I pull a framed art print off the wall above my bed. Swing it to the ground. Glass shatters. Fragments into shards that skip across the wood floor.

"Do you hear me?" I yell. "Do you have any idea what you've fucking done?"

The ceiling fan whirs.

The floorboards creak.

Alone again.

ORA

CARINA: Hey, could I stay with you tonight?

ORA: bigger bed at blackbead no??

CARINA: Need to get out for a while. And need to talk to all the YBs.

Ora takes her time answering. But can I blame her for hesitating? Just because we hung out to say goodbye to Josh doesn't mean we're okay. I should let her be. But the one thing I can offer her—and the rest of the group—is an explanation.

And I'm not sure there's anywhere else for me to go.

> ORA: ok. hurry before the storm get you. we can wait it out.
> ill ask the others.

I leave the key to Ian's office on my vanity.

The house is eerily quiet as I haul my few belongings. The air's sharp with the scent of Dettol. Like it's the first day all over again. I take in shiny floors and pristine portraits, one-of-a-kind rugs, and that massive chandelier in the foyer. Black and white, white and black. There's this chasm in my chest as I hurry past everything. This was supposed to be my home away from home.

When I first arrived, I thought Blackbead was beautiful but silent, like a museum.

I was wrong. Blackbead is a tomb. It's where service and honor go to die.

I slip out through the staff exit. Trek to the backyard, knock on the guesthouse door.

Aaron stands at the entrance like he isn't sure whether he's happy to see me.

"Where's Gregory?" I ask.

"Think he went into town to pick up supplies. Just trimmed some bushes and trees, now need to tie down a few things for safety. Why?"

"Did Ora text you?"

"She did. Ask us all to come by." He studies the darkening sky. "Not sure about that."

"I need a ride to her house. I really hate to bother you, but—"

He waves me off. "Don't worry. I got you." He dips inside, returns with helmets and a jacket for himself. We walk to his motorcycle, and he secures my bag. His hands work with intent, with care.

"Thank you," I blurt.

"For what?"

"For the other day. When you said I wasn't a coward." I push up the sleeves of my sweatshirt. "You were way too kind, but—"

"No, none of that," he says. "I mean, you welcome. But don't need the thanks. Was just speaking truth." He reaches out, waits, then holds my hand in his. For once, the monster inside me doesn't stir. I commit to memory the warmth of his skin against mine. "I know who you are."

I nod. Get on the motorcycle.

I wish he'd never have to know me.

But he will.

We reach our destination: Ora's house for the first and likely last time.

It's a little single-story bungalow painted as aquamarine as the sea. Dents mark up the metal roof. Someone's boarded up the windows. We pull up next to a rough-looking sedan in the driveway. Ora's mom must be home. There are two other cars parked in the front yard—Josh and Simone.

Everyone's here.

Thunder rolls in the distance.

"We goin' in?" Aaron asks, surveying how the palms sway and bend from the powerful gales. Part of me wants to stay here, let the storm sweep me away. But I've done so much running already.

Aaron has a spare key to Ora's place. Knowing this hurts. He lets us in.

The vibe is off the moment we enter. As if the lightning outside has somehow found its way into the house.

As if everyone already knows what's going to happen.

Aaron leads me to Ora's living room. She's posted up in front of the TV, fretting over the weather report—and I've never seen her worry about anything but Aaron. Josh plates a snack platter of breadfruit chips and peppered shrimp, leftover food I'm sure he stole from Blackbead right after they fired him. And what could they do about it now? Simone sits on the wicker sofa and taps anxiously at her phone screen.

They all look up.

Ora breathes a sigh of relief. "You made it. I was losing my head." She stands and hugs Aaron. Then she motions to do the same with me. Hesitates.

God, I hurt us so much.

I tell the room, "We need to talk."

"What every person love to hear," Josh mutters.

Aaron takes a few steps back and faces me. Confused. I want to hold this moment, the moments when he doesn't know the truth.

But he's about to. They all are. And I'm going to lose them.

"I know everything's been weird lately. Everything about me, I mean." I clear my throat, fight for the words. I don't have them. "I think I have to explain."

"You don't have to do anything you don't want," Aaron says. Sweetly. A savior. And he's right. I don't want to.

But it's what's right. They need to hear everything from me, not from Lloyd, not from the Halls.

"And what you explaining?" Simone asks.

I swallow.

"Why I'm here."

TWENTY-THREE

This was me.

Grinning and lost and warm all over. Molly coursing through my veins, throwing vibrant colors and bright lights in front of my eyes. I held Joy's hand as she pulled me through the warehouse full of party-goers, her braided space buns leading the way. People bumped into me, jostled me around, tried to grind their hips into mine, and I didn't mind. It felt good to be close to others. It felt good to have fun.

That's what Joy did. She made life fun.

I hadn't tried molly before. Joy had, because Joy was willing to try anything at least a couple times. And anything's available when you have your mom's money and a generous plug.

Earlier that night, she let me borrow some rave-appropriate clothes, and we jumped in her Audi. Joy popped open the center console, grabbed a baggy, pulled out a little colored pill. She dropped it in my palm.

"I don't want to be high by myself, though," I said.

She quickly rummaged through the console for her little makeup bag. Her caseless new phone vibrated where she'd dropped it in one of the cupholders. "I already took mine. Like a few minutes ago."

"And you're gonna drive?"

"Guess I gotta drive fast," Joy said while fixing her smudged lipstick in her visor mirror. Then she gave me that face, that "you're embarrassing me" face. And maybe I was. But I did my best to keep up with Joy. I could hold my liquor, I loved to flirt with strangers, and if the right music played, I'd dance for hours. But sometimes, it took effort to stay in that headspace. Being chill and carefree came easily to Joy. Everything did.

Joy sighed. Put up the visor. "Rina, just take it. Last hurrah before senior year. It'll be fun."

Fun? I wasn't sure. But she would know.

So I downed the pill.

And thirty minutes later, there I was, strolling through a neon-lit warehouse as if I were floating. Because that's what being in Joy's world was like. Floating. Coasting. A free pass to whatever we wanted, whenever. She made us unstoppable.

And everything Joy had, I got to enjoy. Sips of her drinks, designer clothes she didn't want, jewelry she claimed went better with my warm undertone. After her eighteenth birthday, she pretended to lose her license so I could have it and keep visiting eighteen-and-up events with her. When Joy got a new phone, she passed her old one to me, and it was nicer than anything I'd ever had. She even let me keep the number, stay on the family plan. Because we were close. Like family.

Being around her made me exciting, alive. And I was thankful for that. And envious.

It's hard to be around someone who will always be better than you.

"Oh my god," Joy shrieked. She pointed across the warehouse, past two girls making out in the middle of the room. "That's Mason, right?"

I squinted. "And Noah."

"Shit. Let's go." She tugged my hand and dragged me left. Nothing wrong with Mason and Noah. But we hadn't spoken in months. Noah and I sort of fell out, and it made sense, because he didn't genuinely know me, and I didn't know him. We flirted, made out some. And then

I stopped replying to texts. Or maybe he stopped answering mine. Detaching was easy.

For Joy? Less easy. She cycled through guys weekly because she could. And she always fell hard—mostly for lanky boys who played video games all night. But she fell out of love just as hard. Mason was just one name on a long list.

As we scurried, someone cut between Joy and me. Her hand split from mine. The crowd practically ripped us apart.

"Joy!" She couldn't hear me. Not over the din of the DJ, the screaming and shout-singing of the party.

My high broke. My bra top cut into my ribs, scratched my skin with its beads. The sensation of my hair brushing the back of my neck made me want to scream. My hand was empty and clammy and shaking.

I needed to find Joy.

I wandered the warehouse, aimless. Nothing but spilled drinks, colossal speakers, girls crying. Nothing made sense. I didn't recognize anyone. Violet lights and trance music surrounded me, caged me, broke me to pieces until I started to forget who I was and why I was there. What if I never found Joy?

Someone shoved me. I fell forward.

Landed in some random guy's arms.

I scrambled upright, tried to apologize. When I looked up, though, he seemed just as thrown off as me.

"You're okay. That dude was a prick." He had kind eyes, or it seemed that way in the dark. "*Are* you okay?"

No. "Yeah, I'm good. Just . . . sorry about the . . ."

"It's fine," he said. "All fine." He placed a hand to his chest. Some yellow-and-green abstract design swooped and whirled across his black tee. His shirt pulled across his chest muscles a little, like he worked out a ton. "I'm Sean, by the way."

"Carina."

"Unique." He glanced at the DJ booth. "You into this sound?"

"House is more my thing. Or trap."

"Same, same. You got good taste." He smiled, and I smiled back, because how could I not? It felt like he saw me. Even without Joy nearby to shine her light on me and make me worth seeing, he saw me. And he liked me. Or at least he genuinely liked what I liked. That'd be a first. I felt close. Connected.

Time slowed. Time stopped.

Was that because of the molly? Or him?

"Rina, oh my god, you're okay!"

Joy's voice pealed through the air. She pushed her way through the wall of bodies, pulled me into a hug. Sweat covered me, and I didn't know if it was hers or mine. "Couldn't find you anywhere."

Then she noticed Sean, hands shoved into his jogger pockets. She pulled up her bandeau, straightened her back. "Who are you?"

"Sean." He checked out her outfit, lingered at her chest. I saw it. He liked her. "Just . . . bumped into your friend." His gaze darted between us. "I'll leave you to it."

Joy grabbed the sleeve of his shirt. "No, stay. We don't bite."

Lust at first sight. She saw him, she wanted him, she'd have him. Even though, just a moment ago, he was his own person. And for a second, maybe he was even mine.

"Joy," I whispered, "I think he wants to go."

"Sean, let me buy you a drink," Joy offered. "For keeping my bestie safe from these fucking psychos."

Sean looked at me. I looked back.

And then I turned away.

"Sure, I'll take one."

Joy batted her impossibly long lashes. She got dibs, because she always did. She won, because she always did. And I backed off because I always should. Because I saw what he wanted. What all the guys wanted: Joy. She was inevitable.

But as she walked him to the bar, and I trailed behind, I knew it was also inevitable that they wouldn't be anything serious. Sean just had the honor of being Joy's latest conquest.

And he was. Until he wasn't.

Maybe it was because Sean wasn't Joy's usual type since he liked fresh air and sports. Maybe he wowed her with his brains, because she figured a jock like him would be pulling the same mediocre test scores that the two of us were. Or maybe she thought his dick game was crazy, I didn't know.

But it was different with them. Joy was even willing to call Sean her boyfriend. That title hadn't been used in a year and a half. Yet she dusted it off for him.

So Sean joined our little twosome, came to the parties, hit up the concerts. Joy hung off him all the time, spammed cutesy pics of them on her socials. His contact in her phone read *My Maaan <3*. I thought someone had taken over her body because she'd never behaved this way before.

But I shouldn't have worried. Because Joy was still Joy. Loud as fuck. Wild. Impulsive.

Sean and Joy were like a song constantly changing tempo. They'd break things off, and she'd cry about it on video for hours. Then they'd get back together and our weekly hangout would be canceled so she could spend the night with him instead.

The back-and-forth exhausted me. And so did Joy, honestly. I loved her, but she couldn't love back. She had too much privilege to know how to see real value in anyone or anything. She wouldn't keep something for the long haul when she could always afford to get something—or someone—else.

Those two didn't have anything beyond physical chemistry. He couldn't always keep up with her. Sometimes, if she didn't like Sean's tone, or she wanted to make him jealous, she'd bail or quit responding to his messages. That usually meant Sean was left alone with me. While texting or at house parties. Just us dealing with Joy and connecting over music. Just me and those kind eyes. Seeing me.

Eventually, something started to grow. Inside of me. Something that had been building since the night we met at the warehouse.

I didn't know what it was. Or what to call it.

But it was hungry.

Hungry for something of its own.

Something to claim.

JOY: i have literally been puking for hours

CARINA: Like . . . morning sickness?

JOY: stfu I think my sushi was bad. never eating there again

JOY: can't go to the concert like this

CARINA: Definitely not. Bummer. I wish we could.

JOY: oh you are going

CARINA: ???

JOY: sean isn't answering his phone so he's probably on his way to the stupid venue

JOY: i don't trust him. so you have to go and watch him for me

CARINA: He wouldn't cheat.

JOY: anyone can do anything. don't be fucking stupid

JOY: please just go. will buy you those sony headphones for your service

The idea of spending the night with Sean—without Joy—sent shivers down my spine. Made the creature within perk up her ears.

CARINA: Only for the headphones.

I drove to the venue and cursed my clammy palms the entire ride. Sean waited in the parking lot, surprised when I showed up alone.

"Where's Joy?" he asked.

"Vomiting. Like, a lot. But she'll be fine. And she told us to have fun. So . . ." I gestured to the building. "Wanna head in?"

He could have said no. Could have decided against seeing the show without his girlfriend.

He didn't.

The venue was "intimate," aka small as hell. Exposed brick, neon signs, and the mix of sweat and full-bodied cologne. The stage was the focal point, and everyone crowded before it, shoulder to shoulder, swaying, rolling.

Standing room only.

Half an hour later, the band took the stage. The throng of attendees cheered and surged closer. I'm short; even with my head tilted back, I could hardly see a thing. I got bumped around, debris in a sea of people.

Sean grabbed my arm and tugged me forward. Whipped me in front of him, coiled his arms around my waist to keep me from the squeeze of the audience. And I couldn't help it: I gasped. He'd never touched me like that before. I leaned into him, pretended I was just vibing with the band's energy. The lead singer's voice shot through my chest, took me to some other world made of guitar strums and Sean's tight hold on me.

The being inside me licked her teeth.

Even without the drugs, without the colored lights, I wanted Sean. I liked him. And that was wrong, because he was Joy's. But a feeling never hurt anyone, right? A thought isn't a crime.

The music ramped up. We fell into the swell of it. The fire of it. Sean bent his head down, whispered in my ear. "You loving this?"

The music or his touch?

"You got tense. Relax," he said. "Joy isn't here."

I licked my lips. I wasn't stupid. I knew what he was saying. He was happy Joy wasn't there, groaning and bitching and either starting an argument or getting smashed.

And I knew what he wanted.

Me.

When Joy wasn't around, when it was just us and the music, he wanted me.

Yes.

I don't trust him.

No.

He wouldn't cheat.

Shit.

I couldn't cross that line. Joy asked me to keep an eye on Sean because she trusted me. She needed me.

Sean ran a hand up the side of my torso. Goose bumps popped up all over my body.

Okay. What about what I needed?

What about the fact that Joy and Sean were oil and water, totally incompatible, breaking up every five business days? She'd realize that eventually, wouldn't she?

What about how Joy and I shared everything? Homework answers, phones, pills . . . is a boy all that different?

And what about that hungry, desperate beast within me? Prowling with her claws out. Waiting to feed.

I twisted, faced him. He didn't get a chance to speak. I just kissed him. And all the clichés—fireworks, the earth moving, heart skipping a beat—came crashing in. The second our lips met, I knew I had lied to myself. If Joy discovered this, she would be livid.

In the crowd, people whistled and howled. Some cursed. They came to enjoy the show, the band. I did not care. And by the way Sean was feeling me up, neither did he.

The creature was satisfied. Finally.

And so it began.

JOY: so? how was it?

CARINA: Fine. Boring. You didn't miss much. And you owe me those Sonys.

JOY: did sean act right?

CARINA: He didn't hook up with any randoms, honest.

It was technically the truth.

And I got far living in technicalities. Because how else did I convince myself that I wasn't hurting anyone? Didn't matter what I thought inside that venue. When Sean pressed his body against mine, when I kissed him, I knew. Joy would kill me if she found out.

So I shut up. We went to class, we partied, she cried about her relationship issues, I comforted her. Same as always.

But now, I had Sean. And that made everything okay.

For months.

I'd sneak to see Sean. I'd soothe Joy when she worried he was being sus. I kept the peace, and I was proud of that. Proud to be her closest friend and proud to be with him, even secretly.

One day, in the spring, Joy and I lay in her backyard by the pool. My phone pinged.

SEAN: Thinking bout you.

CARINA: Same. Miss your face.

"Did you figure out your plans yet?" Joy asked.

"For?"

"Summer, bitch."

SEAN: Almost done with the season. We'll see each other soon.

"No. As in, no plans. Just going to rot until classes start in August." Mom and I agreed on two years at community college. She and Dad would figure out how to pay. I would figure out what to do with my life. Wasn't looking forward to it, but school mattered to Mom. It was the least I could do to make her a little happier.

"God, you're boring. For now." Joy turned to me, conspiratorial. "I will give you plans."

> CARINA: Not soon enough. Haven't been alone in like three weeks. Can we video chat tonight?

"Sounds questionable."

"Only a little. Okay, picture this: we kick off the summer with my grad party. My parents caved. They're getting me that BMW." She beamed like she personally financed the car. "And you have to take pictures for me. Nobody else will do it right."

> SEAN: No babe. With J tonight remember? Tomorrow?
> CARINA: OK. I'll be pissed if you skip though.
> CARINA: Not really. I'm just losing my fucking mind.

"And then my gap year is booked ... and guess where I'm going first?"

"Florida?"

"More south."

"Mexico?"

"More ocean."

> SEAN: I'll help you find it. Be patient with me. 🖤

"What does 'more ocean' even mean?"

"Oh my god, *Jamaica*. I'm going to be in Jamaica this summer."

I put the phone down. "Seriously? How?"

"Got this au pair job. It's like nannying? And it's also, like, barely a job because I'm just going to play with kids and stuff my face." I didn't think she'd like the caretaking part, but hey, Joy was always going to do as she pleased. "I figured since you've always wanted to visit, see where your mom is from . . . could spend a week together after the gig, before you're wasting away in gen ed."

That was the kindest thing Joy ever did for me. Genuinely.

"Thanks, girl. You paying for the flights?"

She laughed. "Duh. Like I'd let you fly economy. Don't be fucking gross."

Sean's texts sat on my screen. I read them over and over.

Perfect.

✳

And then that night came.

It was Joy's graduation party, and all I could think about was Sean.

Joy was in her element. Her parents parked her new car in front of the house, even slapped a big red bow on top. The house lights reflected in the BMW's glossy paint. So did Joy's bleached white smile as she posed for pictures. All her friends and acquaintances—and even some enemies—were there. And I did exactly what she wanted. I snapped at least fifty photos, all from her good side, all a bit less polished and cutesy than everyone else's. We even took a few together.

I showed Joy the pics, plus the video I recorded in case she found a cool still in there. She grinned, and her eyes told me that she was a little here, a little not, under the influence of something to make this party more interesting. A girl from our anatomy class pulled on her hand to chat with other guests. "Knew I could count on you, Rina," Joy whispered as she got dragged away. She blew me a kiss.

Joy could count on me.

But the rest of the night was mine.

I found Sean. He stood beside Joy as she chattered with her friends, basically a prop with a heartbeat. He threw the house a glimpse.

We going?

I nodded.

He whispered something in Joy's ear, headed toward the front. I made my way too, through the side door on the deck, so nobody would see us following each other.

I moved through the deserted hallways, passed the *Onward and Upward!* cake on the kitchen island, tried to look casual in case I ran into anybody who should have been outside. But my heart raced. I hadn't seen Sean privately in weeks. All the end-of-year crap, the exams, his sports travel. The beast needed to feed.

I waited at the top of the stairs. On the deck, and by the driveway, and on the front porch, there was so much noise. All for Joy.

"Hey."

Sean slid his hands under my shirt right away. Heat everywhere.

All for me.

"Guest room," I murmured as he kissed me. We hurried down the hall.

Finally alone.

We fell onto the queen-size bed, undressed, and let the night cover us instead. Sean slid his knee between my legs; I wound my fingers in his hair. He trailed kisses down my neck, stole my breath and my mind, reminded me that there were no words to describe that moment, to describe what we were. We weren't fuck buddies or friends with benefits. He wasn't my boyfriend, and I never met his parents. But we were special. We were inevitable.

The bedroom door swung open.

Slammed against a wall.

"What the fuck are you doing?"

Joy's screech echoed across the room.

I covered my bare chest with the top sheet. Joy stalked in, stood motionless at the foot of the bed. Bystanders hung out in the hallway. The girl from anatomy watched, studied even.

"You two?"

"Babe—" Sean started.

Joy jabbed her car keys in his direction. "Do not speak. Don't say a single goddamn thing." She glared at me. "For how long?"

I didn't answer.

"How long?" she asked through clenched teeth. "Tell me."

I couldn't.

Joy's face fell. Like she knew that it didn't matter how long I'd been with Sean. I shouldn't have been with him at all, and that was the problem. Her keys jingled as her body shook.

It was like I'd finally woken up. Which wasn't true. I knew what I was doing, day after day, month after month. I knew she'd be mad. I knew, and I wanted Sean, so I did what I wanted. Just like Joy always did.

But the beast had left. Escaped into the midnight hour, into the woods.

"I can't believe you'd do this to me . . ."

I figured she'd be angry, but I didn't expect she'd be hurt. She'd cried about her grandma dying, the falling-outs with Sean, and that was it. I couldn't imagine a world where I could wound her. Yet I had.

My face flooded with warmth. "Joy, listen to me."

"You don't make demands, bitch." The crowd behind her *ooh*ed in unison like this was some soapy TV show. But this was my life, my real life. "This is what I get for being friends with you, right? You think you can have whatever you want. My clothes, my weed, and—what?—you wanna share dick too?"

"It's not like that."

"Then tell me what it's like. Because it looks like you're just a greedy, shady slut who spent the last four years wanting what I have." She snickered. There was no humor in it. "But why wouldn't you? Can't buy your own shit. Can't pull your own guys. Who would you be if you couldn't bum off me?"

"Joy," Sean said, standing from the bed and scrambling to pull on his jeans. "You need to calm down."

If looks could kill. Joy's was equal parts pained and confused. "Why? Why would you do this? And with her?"

Sean's face softened. Gentle. Remorseful. "I'm sorry. Carina and I had some drinks she made; she talked me into coming up here." He covered his face like he couldn't bear to be seen in his regret. "I wasn't thinking straight, and maybe that's what she wanted. I don't know. It was all a blur, honestly."

I hadn't touched anything but water tonight. I didn't give him shit.

But he lied. He lied so easily. So quickly.

"Don't act like I tricked you, Sean." Defending myself was pointless, though. Joy was hysterical. Curses and callouts filled the air. The crowd became a jury, and the verdict was that I was a manipulative ho.

Everyone pounced on me so fast.

Tears rolled down Joy's face. Her emotions were too close to the surface, intensified by whatever pill she'd swallowed. "You want the BMW too?" She flung the keys at me, and they landed by my thigh. "If I give you the stupid car, will that finally be enough?"

Where were the words to tell her I wasn't using her? That I didn't care about the money, or the designer clothes? I liked being around her. I liked how I felt with her. Even when she was being toxic as hell, I liked her so much that I tried to become her, have what she had.

But I didn't have those words.

I had shame. Humiliation. Anger at what she accused me of, because I was guilty of so much, but not that. Not befriending her for cash. So I hopped out of the bed, still holding the sheet to my chest, trying to cover my half naked body. Someone in the hallway whistled.

"I don't want your ugly-ass car." I hurled the key ring back at her. "Take it. Spin that shit around the block and get the fuck out of my face."

She snatched the keys off the floor, glowered at me. Then she stormed out. Sean followed, still buttoning his jeans.

Hoped she'd crash. Hoped they both would.

After that, my memory gets foggy.

Me getting dressed, dodging all those nosy bitches on the way out, walking ten minutes from Joy's place and then grabbing a rideshare to silently take me home.

I was calm by the time I got to my room. If I could take back the petty stuff I said, I would. So I called Joy. Once, twice, three times. All my attempts went to voicemail.

I texted her before I tried to sleep.

> CARINA: I am so so sorry. You probably don't want to talk to me, and I get that. I know I fucked up. But Sean is playing you. I want you to know the full truth when you're ready. Call me. Please.

She never did.

Early in the morning, Mom crept into my room, the sun pouring grayish light through the window. She sat on the edge of my bed, sat for a long time as if she didn't want to wake me. But I hadn't slept. I couldn't.

She rubbed my shoulder. "Baby girl . . . something happened."

For once, Joy listened to me.

I told her to take the car. She took the car.

She wrapped it around a pole. She died instantly.

Joy was dead.

The room spun and I couldn't move.

Mom held me and I couldn't move.

I called Mom a liar and beat her with my fists and sobbed in her arms until I couldn't move.

That morning brought clarity.

The creature within was a monster. And it being inside me was a sickness. I was sick. I had to be, to do what I did to Joy, to hurt her how I did. To kill her in so many ways, in such little time. I'd never see my best friend again. That was the tragedy I created for myself.

And then came the flood.

The texts, DMs, tweets. Anonymous phone calls. All of it vile.

@UWUPRINCESS07: RIP Joy Milan Carter, our joyful girl. You never deserved this. We will get justice for you. Any way we can, we will.

UNKNOWN USER: 🔪 for the backstabber

VOICEMAIL: You are a waste of oxygen. You're alive and Joy isn't, and ain't that the craziest shit. Your mom really should have swallowed you.

@USER121593: Rot, bitch.

All this anger and one place to put it: toward me.

Even though he fucked around, Sean got to be the heartbroken boyfriend who was taken advantage of by some evil girl. Meanwhile, I lost days of my life. My birthday came and went without so much as a cupcake. A dead girl became my most frequent contact.

CARINA: I didn't get a chance to explain.

CARINA: I'm sorry I made you so angry.

CARINA: Sean lied to me, too.

CARINA: This was a mistake. A huge mistake. You have to believe me.

CARINA: I don't think you do.

CARINA: I miss you so much.

My grief and guilt winnowed my world down to my house.

Then my room.

And then my bed, under the covers, in the dark. My phone—Joy's old phone—turning over and over in my hands.

Trapped.

One day, that phone rang.

Which wasn't new. Since everyone figured out that I had Joy's old phone number, it didn't take long for it to leak. But this wasn't some random caller or an old friend of Joy's ready to curse me out.

The caller ID read *Cultural CareScapes*. Joy's au pair agency.

Why would they be calling me?

I answered. I didn't know why.

"Good morning. This is Hannah from Cultural CareScapes. We're calling to confirm your upcoming assignment."

Right. They couldn't reach Joy on her new line. But they must have still had this number as a secondary contact.

And they must not have known she was dead.

"Could you remind me of the assignment? Please?" My voice didn't sound like mine. It was raspy. Kind of like Joy's.

"Yes, miss. We have you placed with the Hall family in Jamaica starting the third week of June. Is that correct?"

"I . . . think so."

There was a pause. "You received several emails about this," Hannah stated. "With contact information, the Halls' requested length of stay, a request for your payment details . . ."

"My apologies. I've been locked out of that email for a while. It's been quite the headache." Lies. Why was I lying? Why was I pretending to be Joy?

Because it was easier than being myself. At least as Joy, there was something to be excited about.

"Would you consent to a brief security check?" I'd made Hannah suspicious. "We just need the four-digit code you set up when you signed with us."

Four-digit code? That could have been anything. But best guess? "Of course. Should be 8-1-6-1." Our birthdays. August 1 for her and June 1 for me.

Another pause.

"Thank you, Miss Carter."

Miss Carter.

Joy had already done a phone interview with the house manager, paid her agency fees, approved the length of her stay with the Halls—almost everything. All that was left was a final confirmation.

So I confirmed.

"Hannah, could you resend everything to a new email address, please?" I asked. "And update my records?"

Within ten minutes of hanging up, I had a password-protected document full of contact info and a slim bio for the family due to, apparently, Mr. Hall's prestigious position.

There I was again, borrowing Joy's things. This time, borrowing her life. But I needed it more than she did now that she was gone. I needed a way out. Before my world caved in and crushed me the way I nearly wanted it to. Sean lied, and he was living it up. Why couldn't I do the same?

My own name didn't mean anything good anymore. It belonged to the girl who hurt her best friend and got somebody killed. But everybody adored Joy. Even in death, it was as if all her faults faded away, and she became this saint. So maybe she could bless me. With her help, I could start over. Jamaica was the answer.

I held that belief over the next couple weeks. I used my savings to buy a cheap plane ticket. I switched to an inexpensive phone and a fresh number to stop the harassment, packed Joy's hand-me-down cell and old ID. After a couple YouTube videos, I managed to forge some paperwork on letterhead for the Halls' records.

I wasn't proud of any of it. But it was necessary.

The day I left, I sat in the darkness of my room, wearing a ratty white tee and some old off-white sweatpants. I studied the Polaroids pasted to the walls. Half-lit memories in blown-out colors. Clean spaces where Joy's pictures used to be. But the blank areas haunted me anyway. My guilt haunted me anyway.

One final set of messages to her.

CARINA: You've always been the better one.
CARINA: So I'm going.
CARINA: Thank you.

I jumped into a rideshare, one my parents believed would take me to a friend's house. From there, we'd road-trip in her camper van. The car pulled away from the house, and I waited for a swell of relief. Of peace. Nothing came. All I had was what I always had: Her. Looming.

For better or worse, Joy would never leave me.

I'd borrow life from her, and she'd do the same to me.

Forever.

TWENTY-FOUR

The silence is excruciating.

Nobody looks at me. The way their eyes avoid mine horrifies me, leaves a sour taste on my tongue. Their expressions are indecipherable.

I knew this would happen. I knew this would always be how things ended if I couldn't hide my past, become a new me. But knowing doesn't make the reality hurt any less.

No more dancing with Ora. No more sitting on the patio with Josh as he tries to teach me patois. Might even miss Simone side-eyeing me whenever we'd tidy together.

And Aaron.

His face seems all wrong.

No one speaks. Has it been seconds? Minutes? Too long. I struggle to breathe.

"Knew it," Josh mutters. "Knew there was somethin'—"

Run.

"I gotta go," I mumble, my throat thick with regret. Then I rush outside.

The sky's full of dark storm clouds. Droplets pelt the ground, turning dust into mud, wetting the grass in Ora's front yard.

I run.

Away from Ora's house. Away from the rubble of what I blew to pieces. Down the road. No clue where I'm going.

Run.

Legs and arms pumping, lungs burning, a scream sitting in my chest and waiting to be set free. Running is all I know how to do. And I'll still never get far enough away.

I slow to a stop and bend over, hands on my knees, panting. My sweatshirt is soaked through with rain and sweat. I can barely see in front of me. The last slivers of sunlight are gone, buried in dusk and cloud cover. I don't know where I am, but even if I could see, I wouldn't recognize anything.

Because this isn't my home.

This isn't mine. Not an inch of this country was ever mine to claim.

All I've proven by coming here is that self-delusion is powerful.

I thought Jamaica would save me. I thought it'd be different, better, make me feel connected when I was so alone. And at first, I thought I had cracked the code. Because I saw the beauty of this place and the people here. I met friends. I met Aaron.

Yet here I am. For a second time. By myself because of myself.

It hurts more this time around.

I straighten up, stand on the side of the road, pummeled with rain. My head's heavy from my wet braids. A clap of thunder vibrates the muggy air.

Then a streak of lightning bolts through the sky. Bright and jagged, like nothing I've seen before. It illuminates everything around me, and it touches down a few miles away, toward Blackbead.

The lightning and thunder jolt me back to myself. Back to the fact that I'm standing in a massive storm that could get me killed. I feel just enough fear to know I don't want to die out here. Just enough to know I don't want to die at all. No matter how tempting.

I look back down the road, back where I came from.

A pair of headlights barrels toward me.

She took the car. She wrapped it around a pole.

I jump out of the way. But the headlights slow. Someone sticks their head through the driver's side window.

"If you don't get out the rain right now!" Ora shouts over the downpour.

"Gon' catch cold!" Simone says through a rear window. "Come!"

I approach the car and realize it's the sedan Ora's mom parked in front of the house. I try to peek inside. Ora at the wheel. Josh in the front. Simone leaning forward from the back seat, posted up between them.

They were searching for me. They came for me.

"Stupid, get in the car!" Josh yells.

I toss myself into the back.

I'm drenched. I'm cold. I'll probably ruin the seats.

"Not a lick of sense," Simone murmurs. "Less than Rush."

"Seen," Ora agrees as she slowly swings the car around to head back home. "What were you thinking? Just sprinting into the storm? Is this track and field? Use your head."

"I thought . . . you guys hardly said anything." It's all I can utter, and it sounds dumb as hell.

"From day one, what did I tell you?" Ora shoots back. "That you don't seem like a Joy. And from day one, you lied to me—lied to everyone. Did it for weeks. What do you *want* us to say?"

"Your best friend die after she see you fuck her man," Josh adds. "There's nothing *to* say."

Simone kisses her teeth. "Scoob! You so crude with it."

"Well, is true!" He huffs. "All I mean was, we were surprised. That's some dark, dark shit."

My shoulders round. It's like my body can't help but fold, curl up and hide. "I fucked up."

"We know," says Simone. "And you know."

"I'm mad as hell, to be honest," Ora says. "But some wrong choices don't mean you deserve to die in a hurricane." She drives through the rain, hands gripping the wheel tight. "The devil in all of us. You not the first or the last." Ora glances into the rearview mirror. "Is there a towel for the girl anywhere?" Simone immediately starts searching.

By the time we pull into Ora's driveway, it's quiet inside my mind. I made a lot of terrible decisions, hurt so many people, ran and hid and did nearly everything wrong.

But I did one thing right.

I found the Young Birds. Told them the truth. And after everything, they're still here.

Most of them.

Aaron's standing outside, under the shelter of the porch awning. Everyone's reluctant to leave the car. We all pretend it's because of the weather.

But Simone exits first and goes straight for the door. Then Josh.

Ora pauses, tilts her head as if she's going to say something. But nothing comes. Nothing but "Let's go."

We both get out. My heart's in my throat. Aaron stares me down. I still can't figure out where he's at, what he's thinking. "We need to talk," he says.

Josh was right. "We need to talk" sucks to hear.

Ora gives us a long look before she goes inside.

The wind whistles. I can't cope with the silence.

"Being this dramatic . . . some proof I'm definitely Jamaican, right?" All I've got are stupid jokes.

"Don't even know what to call you," Aaron says.

"I'm still Carina. I've always been Carina to you."

"And what does that even mean?" He's always spoken to me in a baby-soft way. This isn't that. "You lie to me, then made me lie with you to figure out the duppy. We spend all this time together, for what? It's like I've been with a stranger."

"I didn't lie about everything. I was only Joy when I really had to be."

"The night at the pool," Aaron snaps. "What happened?"

I don't know what to tell him. So I don't say anything. I retreat. That's what I do.

"Because I told you not to go. And it was like you shut off, just like that. So what went on? Was it me? Or all this with Sean and Joy and them?"

"I wanted to be there. I wanted to be there with you." My teeth dig into the inside of my cheek. "But I thought about everything that happened, and how Monique cheated, and I knew if you found out what I'd done . . . you'd realize you deserved better."

"So you lie."

"I was protecting you."

"You made a choice for me," he presses. "Thought I'd break things off if I knew, so you made sure I don't know. That sound right to you?"

My thoughts are so jumbled, I can't think straight. Did I lie to keep him from getting hurt? Or to keep him by my side? Or to fight off the inevitable? I don't know why I did it. I just knew I needed to, or he'd leave me, and I'd be alone again—without him, without Ora. And I couldn't be alone again.

"I'm sorry." I try to breathe. "But I knew who I was. And who you were. And I thought—"

"What 'bout me? What 'bout what I know? What I think?" He gestures wildly, his face half illuminated by Ora's flickering porch light. "You never ask me, not once. If I thought you and Monique were the same, you'd never know."

He's right.

"So what make you think you know how I felt about you?"

"I don't. I should have asked you."

"Wish you had. Doesn't matter now." He scans my face. "Good night, Carina."

He steps away, gives his attention to the curtain of pouring rain.

Wish you had. Doesn't matter now.

He's done. We're done.

Which is what I always thought would happen. One way or another. Either the beast or the truth would end us.

And I'm still hurting. Imagining the hours we spent together, crossing the island on his motorcycle, joking on WhatsApp, drinking gross bush teas and wearing red ribbons because he asked me to, so I'd be safe from the duppy.

All of it over.

I head into the house.

Ora's standing near the door. Mouth open.

My heart plummets.

She heard us.

Ora could forgive my past mistakes. But she won't forgive me breaking Aaron's heart.

Or hers.

TWENTY-FIVE

I wait for the other shoe to drop.

Ora pulls me inside the house, throws a random robe around me, tosses a towel on the floor to soak up the rainwater.

I expect her to berate me, to curse at me. She doesn't.

"How much did you hear?" I ask.

"Enough." Monotone.

"I am so, so sorry. I didn't mean for anything to happen with Aaron. It just—"

Ora silences me. "It was what I thought," she says. "All the time you alone together. The way he look at you." She hums. Her eyes shine, but she keeps a straight face. "Chicken and me grew up like family. And so it is. It's . . . okay."

"It's not. I know it's not."

"You right. But . . ." Ora squeezes the robe I'm wearing. "Just wish you told me. All this make me feel like . . . Juney was right. Like I didn't know you. Thought you trust me."

"I do."

"If you did, you would have tell me the truth. Joy, Aaron, all of it. Straight up." She sighs. "But it's what you do. You lock up everything like a safe. It make sense."

"I'm sorry. For real."

Ora gives a light smile, shows off that gap between her front teeth. "What are sisters without a little drama, yeah?"

After Joy, I know I don't deserve a friend like Ora. But she's here, and forgiving, and kind. And for as long as she'll have me, I will keep her in my life. I'll try to treat her as well as she's treated me. Even when I didn't earn it. Like right now.

She finds some clothes for me to change into, and when I'm not a drenched rat anymore, she leads me back to the living room. Simone and Josh sit, drinking hot tea and chicken soup to warm up. If they heard me and Ora talking earlier, they don't let on. It feels almost normal, all of this.

Almost.

Maybe the unsettled feeling is me. All my secrets are out there. I've lost Aaron. I'm exhausted in every possible way.

Then Simone clears her throat.

"Since we all being honest . . ." She homes in on me. "I want to apologize, Bambi. Was mad that you thought I could be lying with Mr. Hall. Still am, to be honest. But I see you didn't want me getting hurt."

"I was just . . . worried. And I didn't know how to help." I lean forward. "The Young Birds wouldn't be the same without you."

"Appreciate that." Simone twists a ring on her finger. I don't usually see her in jewelry. "But I'll tell the truth. I was up to something. You just didn't know what."

Josh puts his bowl of soup on the floor. "What you mean?"

"Well . . ." She taps her nails against her cup. "I've been leaking Mr. Hall's dirty laundry to the press."

I'm sorry, what?

It makes a little bit of sense, if that's why Simone didn't like me forcing my nose into her business, searching for info, all of that. I could have blown her cover. "But . . . why?"

She slowly places the mug on the coffee table. "Mr. Hall think charity is smiling at me while I scrub his toilet. The pay small, but I *have* work, so he feel he's helping people like me." Simone massages her palms, her knuckles. "I break my back so he can relax. I struggle so he never will. Burned me up so." Her hands still. "One day, I was cleaning, and heard Dante and his father arguing about money, where it come from, what Mr. Hall do with it. Dante realize the man steal from more than just the staff. He take from his own charities."

That tracks with what I heard. Dante seems so pissed about his dad, so frustrated by how he's perceived compared to who he actually is.

"So why didn't Dante just expose Hall himself?" Ora asks. "Why drag you into it, risk your safety?"

"Since when you care about safety, Rush?"

"Since now! I not going to let you take the fall for no spoiled boy."

"Well, Dante had no proof. So his father laugh in his face and shove him off." Simone stops twisting her ring. "That's when I came to him. Said I'd help find evidence. His father would never look at me twice." She smiles, the most mischievous I've ever seen her. "Hall think I'm stupid, can't understand anything he leave 'round me. Good for me. Bad for him."

"Sneaky girl," Josh says, half-amazed, like he's seeing Simone for the first time. "Then you sweet up big boss, dust some file cabinets . . ."

"Right, right. Take everything, give it to Dante, the news. Do it daily. Man has a lot of issues to expose."

When I ran into Dante after coming home from the rum bar, he was fully dressed at, like, three in the morning. He must have met with someone to hand over information he and Simone had found. He's probably been at this since before I showed up.

I grab Simone's arm. "So, the night I saw you by Ian's office . . . ?"

"Always on the clock, girl."

The deep voice I heard must have been Dante's, not Ian's.

"Dante have some balls after all," Josh admits.

Ora cuts him off. "So, what, everything we done chat 'bout true? Hall lie, steal, cheat? *Kill?*"

Rumors can start in truth, right?

"Him lie, yes. Steal, absolutely. Cheat—on the wife and everywhere else." Simone leans back on the sofa. "A killer, though? That, I don't know for sure. But can't put it past him."

I rub my eyes. Ora is right about one thing: this is all fucking bonkers. And it makes sense, almost all of it. But . . .

"Dante, though? He was working with you?"

"Yes. Why? What wrong with him?"

"Everything you guys giggled about weeks ago," I say. "You all said he was cold and snobby and rude." Even when he and I talked in the garden, it was like the moment I glimpsed a real person, he shut me out.

"Him all those things, won't lie. But also good-hearted when it count, and good to me. For my help, he give extra pay. Needed it since Mama got sick. Helped me work events for the family to keep everyone fed and clothed. More real charity in him than his father." So she really was hustling her ass off 24/7.

"All that time together just for work?" Ora asks.

"Mind your business, Rush. Now can I have a second with Bambi, please?"

Ora holds up her hands and pivots away to safety. She and Josh pretend they're not listening.

"Again, I *am* sorry," Simone says.

"Don't. You were doing what you had to do."

"No, not that," she says. "From the moment you arrive, I treat you different."

"I wouldn't trust me either," I tell her.

"Was more than that. I didn't like you."

Well, shit, she didn't have to say it like that.

"You had it easy," Simone explains. "You come, eat and drink whatever you want, pick up toys, and make three or four times what I make just by playing with the pickney all day." I don't argue that I did more than that. I let her talk. "Meanwhile, I scrimp and save and scrub until my back ache."

She's right. She could take care of Luis and Jada just as well as I did. Hell, I was getting paid for a position I literally stole while Simone's suffering to keep her family from going hungry.

"Didn't think that you might have your own problems," Simone confesses. "Your life seem like sugar. But you know the saying."

"I don't. I'm sorry." Even now, the Jamaican American card is at risk of being revoked.

"Not everything that have sugar sweet." That's true for me. True of the Halls. Even true of Joy, I think.

"You don't have to apologize. But . . . thanks."

"And for what it's worth?" she adds. "I say forget those people in New York. They don't know you."

"They know what I did."

"They *think* they do. They know the exciting parts. But to judge you for what you did at your worst? And ignore what you are like at your best? Selective memory."

Simone has the same graciousness that Aaron used to show me before he knew everything. The same mercy Ora's shown me tonight. And Simone's kind enough to cut me the slack I can't. "But I don't know if I can forgive myself," I murmur. "Joy was my best friend. I betrayed her."

"A little shame is good. Makes you learn, do better. But you can't live your whole life in shame." She holds my hand. This tenderness from her makes me want to cry. "You try save me when I only ever sneer at you. You're a good person, Bambi. When you see that? You'll be free. Truly free."

A clap of thunder vibrates the walls. The storm's moving in.

Josh stands from the tile floor. He's piled his dishes into a neat stack. "I gotta go."

"Go where?" Simone asks. "In this weather?"

"Got a whole heap a food from Blackbead hidden somewhere. Don't want anything to get damaged. Need to protect it from the storm."

"If you die out there, you can't help anyone," Ora snaps. "Don't be reckless."

"The warning don't mean much, coming from you, Rush."

"Why now, Robin Hood?" I ask.

He shrugs. "We all being brave. Can't have you all being more man than me." He grins, that annoying shit-eating grin.

"No bigger man than Scoob," I say.

"Big Man Scoob," Ora repeats. She pulls him into a hug before he rushes out the door in hopes of beating the worst of the wind and rain.

Another rolling boom. "Mama asleep in her room. The boys gone. The house is officially locked down," Ora declares.

So together, we three wait out the storm. Lights flashing, the floor of Ora's house shaking. She checks the windows and doors to make sure the water stays out. But her place isn't built to withstand weather like this. Darkness hangs on the house, on the world outside.

"What if we play a game?" Ora suggests. "Two Truths and a Lie?"

"No," Simone and I answer at the same time.

I'm not sure what to do, what's next, where to go. I ask the powers that be, if they exist, for a sign. Because soon, I'll need to make some decisions and clean up the mess I made. But I don't even know which direction to stumble in.

A sharp crack of thunder sounds. Bright lightning flares through the curtained windows. It's almost as intense as the bolt from earlier, the one that streaked across the sky toward Blackbead House and absolutely could have killed me.

Toward Blackbead.

The light. Freakishly bright and brilliant.

The truth in the light.

The last thing the duppy told me before I bailed.

It's crazy, like everything with that damn ghost. But was the lightning from the road a sign? A message?

An arrow showing me where to go?

I thought I'd need to figure out my next escape route. But maybe it's time to stop running from the truth.

Maybe I need to head right toward it.

I whip out my phone.

"What?" Aaron's ticked when he picks up.

"I know you're mad at me," I whisper, "and you should be, but I need a favor. It's important."

Silence.

"Please."

He sighs. Heavily.

"Where we goin'?"

TWENTY-SIX

The night drenches us in heavy rain.

Aaron drives through the wet streets as carefully as he can. Visibility is low. I'm shivering from the cold air lashing my face. The smell of brine lies everywhere. This might be another mistake, another delusion. One that will give me pneumonia, if I survive at all.

Thunder rolls. I lower my head, try to get a break from the rain smacking against my cheeks. Yeah, this could be a mistake. But what if I'm right? What if there's something left to find? I don't know what that will mean. Maybe I'm just desperate to redeem myself.

The dark sky and the screen of rainfall block my vision. Even with the lights on Aaron's motorcycle, we can't see more than a foot or two in front of us. We're cut off from the rest of the world. I squint, try to focus.

There's something out there.

Between the raindrops, each falling at a slant.

A pair of eyes.

Glowing. Floating.

Glaring.

Impossibly long lashes. Just like Joy's.

Because these are Joy's eyes.

Could the duppy be showing this to me? Maybe. But there's no honeysuckle scent, no rush of heat. So this might just be me.

This might just be my mind unspooling. The angry gaze of my closest friend. The girl I envied. The girl who trusted me and paid her life for it.

You're just a greedy, shady slut.

Even now, the guilt could kill me. For I don't know how long, I wished it would. Because how could I have done all that to her? And so boldly. That hate I see makes sense. I hated me too.

I can't believe you'd do this to me.

I'd do anything to make up for what I did.

But how long can I keep tearing myself apart?

Will that finally be enough?

For the first time, I wonder: How much of that night rests solely on my shoulders?

Simone was right. Some shame is good. I know the mistakes I made, the crappy choices I committed to. No matter how I justified it, I shouldn't have fooled around with Sean. I shouldn't have lied to Joy. I definitely shouldn't have deceived the Halls in order to work in Blackbead House.

But shame should be a moment I pass through. Not a home I live in.

The glow around the eyes dims.

Months ago, I made a decision. I chose to betray my best friend. And I'll have to live with that forever.

But Sean chose to cheat on his girlfriend. Repeatedly.

And Joy chose to get in her car when she wasn't sober. It wasn't the first time. But it was the last.

Joy holds her stare. Then, finally, she goes.

Her eyes vanish.

Something deep in my core settles. None of this matters to anyone but me. To a lot of people, I'm an evil, dishonest bitch, totally unforgivable. I'll be scum forever.

But I know what I did. I know who I am now.

How I've tried so hard to change and do better.

And I will keep trying. As me, Carina Marshall.

I tighten my grip around Aaron's waist. Blackbead House looms on the horizon, lights on.

I will try.

"You distract Ian," I shout over the roar of the motorcycle, "and I'll follow the light." I don't know where the lightning touched down, but I know the duppy is trying to show me something around here. It wouldn't lead me back to this hellhole if it weren't.

"Hope I don't find him," Aaron yells back.

"If you do, punch him."

Aaron parks the bike and we both hop off. The rain's slowed to a trickle, a break in the downpour. Aaron walks toward the staff entrance.

"Wait, Aaron."

He turns. I didn't think of something to say. I don't know what I should say. But anything's better than nothing. "I really—"

He raises a finger to his lips. *Quiet.* "Later," he says. "Let's get it done."

Bet.

I run to the backyard. And there's a trail of smoke, potent even in the light rain. Under the scent of grass and earth, honeysuckle is there. By now, I'd know it anywhere. But there's something else too. It's familiar but I can't place it. I pace a little farther, try to follow where the fumes are wafting from.

And then I see it.

The Halls' enormous mango tree. Struck by lightning and split down the trunk, straight to the roots. The bark smolders. Mangoes burn on the ground.

I race to it, fall to my knees.

That magazine photo, with the *X* burned into the base of the tree. The duppy was always leading me here. Whatever I'm supposed to find, this must be it. I shove my fingers into the soil and claw and dig.

Go. Go. Go.

My hands are raw. But I have to find it. My nails begin to bleed. All I hear is my own heartbeat.

I hit something. I try to clear out more dirt so I can see.

Saliva pools in my mouth.

Bones.

Ivory bones.

A skull. Cracked. A necklace with a pendant in the shape of a flute.

I pitch to one side and vomit.

This is Kelly.

These are Kelly's bones.

She's been here, buried, a secret—for years. Under the goddamn mango tree.

"You."

I jump at the sound and spin around.

Mrs. Hall, unmoving beneath the outdoor sconces, her hair smashed to her bleached forehead from the rain. Her white blouse is soaked and see-through. She's a whole ghoul.

I don't know this woman.

"I knew there was something about you, Carina," she hisses, a slight tremble as she speaks. "I saw your face, those eyes, and I knew something was wrong."

"Stay away from me," I shriek.

"But Ian fought me. He said I was being paranoid. So every night, I watched him be so kind to you. He was so welcoming. And it killed me."

Mrs. Hall slowly steps toward me. I clamber backward on all fours. Where can I go?

"It killed me because I was right," she says. "It's a burden to always be right." Her voice travels through the cold night. I search the ground for a stick, one of Aaron's gardening tools, anything I can use as a weapon. "You came to ruin what my family has fought so hard for. You want revenge."

Behind me, I feel something. Some pruning shears, I think. I grasp them tight in my fist. "I don't know what you're talking about."

"Do not lie to me," she screams. Her whole body shakes. "You come into my home, and you cannot even look at me. You wear her face and lie. But I know you. Kelly's whore child."

I drop the shears.

"That's not me." My mother and I have the same eyes. Large and angry and brown as cinnamon. My legs twitch.

Go.

Run.

I need to go. I need to run. "Just let me leave."

"So you can bring my family to its knees? Like she wants?" she asks. "No. I will not allow it."

Mrs. Hall lifts her arm. In her hand?

A brick from the jerk pit.

I scramble, sliding through mud. The shears cut the side of my palm. I scream.

Pain jolts through my head.

The night's darkness seeps into me.

TWENTY-SEVEN

It's cold here.

Wherever here is.

A soft-focus white void, light coming from nowhere in particular.

Shreds of conversations I can't parse. Music from a time and place long forgotten.

Anxiety ripples through me, and I know that, for once, it isn't mine. It's something in the air. Like whoever was here before me had so much they wanted to say, so much they wished to do. And none of it happened. Now, simply the tension remains.

I'm tired.

"Then rest a little while."

I whirl around. A young woman stands with pretty brown skin and huge eyes and a crimson ribbon woven through her braids. So much of me reflected in her.

"Kelly?"

She reaches out to touch my face. I step back. "Beautiful girl. And I not just saying that 'cause you look like me."

"Ruth is lying," I say.

"Ruth is smart." She shrugs. "Always was."

"I know my mother."

"Yeah, you do, sweetness. And I sure she been a good mother too. Better than I could have been. I'm not strict enough."

"Shut up." I can't hear this right now. Even here, a headache creeps into my skull. "Where are we?"

Kelly glances around the nothingness, like she's curious. Like she just noticed it. "Somewhere," she replies. "Don't know what you call it. Been here a long, long time, though, tell you that."

I take in the sight of her. There's nothing motherly here. She could be my older sister or big cousin, someone I tell secrets to, someone who would sneak out of the house with me to do fucked-up shit.

She's really here.

She's really dead.

And I have no clue how much time I have before she moves on or before I do.

"What happened to you?" After everything, it's all I want to know.

Her face flattens.

"The Honorable Ian Hall happened. Him hire me as a young thing, just eighteen."

To her left, the void transforms. And suddenly, I'm a fly on the wall, seeing the past through Kelly's point of view.

Kelly's family believed she'd be a known name one day. So did her teachers. And her ex-boyfriends. There was something about her. But Kelly didn't know how she'd do it.

And until she figured that out, she was okay being a nobody in the Hall household.

With her hands, Kelly banged out a simple rhythm on Dante's pint-size drum. She could barely hear the beat over his sobs. He pulled at the red shirt she'd tugged over his head that morning; he cried without ever seeming to know what had upset him. At three years old, Dante was a challenge. And that was only one of Kelly's problems.

Someone had noticed her.

"I did watch Ian's boy. And all the while, he did watch me."

She turned to the door—and there stood Mr. Hall. He walked in, hovered by Kelly's side, and pressed a finger to his lips. "Hush now," *he said to Dante.* "I'm not asking you. I'm telling you." *Dante tried to listen, gulping back big breaths, swiping at his tears. Kelly looked up from the floor and smiled at Mr. Hall. With gratitude. He laid a hand on her shoulder. Squeezed, held for a few seconds too long. Then he ambled out of the room and down the hallway.*

Kelly's heart fluttered.

"I loved him. He wanted me. Big difference."

I get it. I wish I didn't, but I do.

"Wanted you until he didn't?"

"I wish it were that simple." She walks around. The image morphs.

Through the bathroom door, Dante's cries pierced the air. Five years old and terrified of everything. Always inconsolable. Even at this age, he needed her comfort. But Kelly needed a minute.

She inspected the test on the white counter.

Positive.

Shocked, but she shouldn't be. She missed getting her shot; he hated condoms. Now here she was, twenty years old and pregnant by a man almost twice her age. If she told the Halls, they'd ask questions.

Or Ian could fire her.

Because this wasn't part of the arrangement. She'd hoped that would change someday, when he woke up and realized how much she loved him, how much he needed her warmth, warmth his wife could never provide.

Dante's screams switched to desperate gasps. Kelly hid the test in her pocket and rushed out of the bathroom to calm him.

Maybe things would be different someday. But not today.

"Carry small, so I hid the pregnancy for as long as I could. When I couldn't, took leave. Said Mama was sick, needed to care for her." She surveys the emptiness, lost in her thoughts. "Hid some more. Until the baby came. Until . . . you. Then I sent you on your way."

Kelly and Ian... and me. Their child. The thought sickens me. Because it doesn't make sense.

"Then who is the person I call Mom? Do you even know her?"

"Of course." Kelly beams. "Big sister always come and save me."

"Sister?"

"Yes. Your auntie. Now your mama."

Mom and I have similar features. But so do me and Kelly. A triangle of women joined by strange blood. "I beg her to take you until I got settled," Kelly says. "Because I couldn't give you a good life yet. I needed time. She agree."

"So you had... me... and then, what? Just disappeared?"

The image dissolves. Kelly winces at the venom in my question. But how else should I feel? Everyone's been lying. Mom's not my mom. Kelly is the family member I thought was missing. How do I feel anything other than rage?

"I went back to work," Kelly says. "Needed money to get you back, take care of you." She presses her hands together, as if she were praying, places them against her lips. "But was young then. And I still loved Ian, body and soul. Spent years at Blackbead, playing with Dante during the day, fooling around at night."

Years? She was a side chick for *years*? "Why?" She had to know he was stringing her along.

"Him paint a pretty picture for me. Of our future. Together, we would be rich and safe." He'd say anything to keep her around. "And one day, I would tell him about you. He'd leave Ruth. Then we'd raise you together. I truly believed that was the plan."

I think of Sean, the wild delusions I had about him and Joy, the way I believed he and I had something special compared to what he had with her.

In the end, he and I had nothing. I wasn't his girlfriend or his lover. I was a buddy to listen to music with. A boost to his ego. Someone to sleep with when Joy was on her period or being a bitch.

There's not much difference between Kelly and me. Just history repeating itself in the most embarrassing way.

Like mother, like daughter.

"You wanted a lot from Ian," I say.

"Too much. I know that now. Probably why it never happen."

"So how did it . . . end?"

A mirage re-forms. "Dante."

"You teased me all day," Ian whispered. "You know that, right?" The warm lights of the reading room surrounded them. Ian toyed with the bone flute necklace she wore, the one he bought for her on a recent trip. Kelly played with her braids and glanced at the all-white bouquet he'd placed on a nearby table. For her. Her favorites.

Ian traced a hand down her arm. Over the curve of her hip.

For the first time, Kelly tensed at his touch.

Once, these brief moments were all she'd lived for. She had been sustained for years on stolen time, whispers, secrets, sneaking. They excited her. Every hour together fed the fantasy she'd created for her and Ian, one where he fell just as hard for her as she had for him. One where he dropped all his playthings, left Ruth, and committed to Kelly with his entire heart. The dream kept her patient.

But after five or six years, patience was hard to find.

Still, his touch usually calmed her. Quieted her fears and frustrations. Lulled her into believing what she needed to be true. All this time devoted to him had to be worth it. How badly he wanted her had to mean something. After all, they were bonded forever, even if Ian didn't know it.

They had a child to raise. Carina had just turned three. Kelly got to watch Dante grow into the smart nine-year-old he'd become. But she and

Ian had missed so much of their own daughter's life in the meantime. How much more time could they let pass while Ian figured himself out?

As if Ian could hear her worries, he kissed her. And one by one, her thoughts flitted away. Like they always did.

And then, something crashed to the floor.

Dante stood in the doorway, Lego pieces dropped everywhere. His eyes zipped back and forth between his father and his nanny.

"What are you doing here?" Ian asked, irritated.

"Why were you kissing Miss Kelly?" Dante shot back.

"Son, I don't know what you think you saw—"

"Does Mom know what you guys are doing?"

"Enough," Ian bellowed. "Stay out of grown folks' business, you hear me?"

Dante's hands tightened to fists. He bolted from the room.

Kelly stepped around the fallen Legos. Ian held her back.

"You're too soft," he said. "He's nine, and he's like this because of how you always baby him."

Kelly pulled her wrist from Ian's grip. "He's still a child. Children get upset."

As Kelly ran, she wondered if he'd treat their daughter this way too. Had she ever seen Ian show Dante love? Real love? Did he know how to be a real man, a real father?

Kelly needed to reconsider some things later.

She raced outside because Dante always wanted fresh air when he was angry. He liked to sit in the garden, breathe in the scent of hibiscus and orchid until he settled down, poke at the little shame bush Gregory planted for Dante's amusement.

But he wasn't by the flowers. Nor the trees. The shame bush showed off its open leaves; Dante hadn't been there.

Kelly peered farther out. Toward the sea.

Dante stood by the cliff's edge.

I've seen this cliff before.

In the vision by the jerk pit. While the Halls took photos. In my nightmares as I envisioned myself crumpled at the bottom of it.

"Dante," Kelly called, "please come here. Come to me." *She slowly approached him. Waves crashed against the rocky shore, drowning her out.*

"*Get away from me,*" *he yelled. He stepped back. Tear streaks stained his cheeks.*

She crept closer. "I know you upset, but we're not safe here."

"*Leave me alone. Leave my family alone." Dante shifted away again. The side of the cliff stretched far down. Dante's eyes widened.*

Kelly feared heights too.

"*Okay," Kelly said, heart pounding. If Dante retreated much farther, he'd fall. "I'll leave. As soon as you want. But you have to come to me first."*

Dante scowled.

He inched himself backward.

No.

Kelly lurched for him. She yanked on Dante's arm. She fell forward.

Dante screamed.

Kelly plunged.

I look away. I can't stomach watching her plummet, seeing her smash against the ground while Dante takes in everything from above.

"I lay there for what felt like forever," Kelly murmurs. It's as if remembering still rattles her. "It hurt everywhere. Till it didn't."

"I'm sorry."

The vision I saw in the smoke was wrong. It wasn't me. It wasn't Simone.

It was Kelly. It had always been Kelly.

But I didn't find her bones under the cliff.

"You didn't die there," I say plainly.

"I did. But I didn't stay there."

Kelly kept her eyes closed. When she dared open them, she followed the moon. Full and crawling across the darkened sky.

Minutes passed. Perhaps hours did. It was hard to know. Time didn't feel the same. Her body didn't feel the same. But her body did feel. Did twitch and ache and writhe atop rocks and crags.

A shadow blocked the moonlight.

Help. Dante must have gotten help.

The shadow hovered. It did not ask if Kelly was okay, where she hurt, or if she could move. It simply took notice.

Kelly tried to speak. She could only cough and cry. Pain reverberated through her body. The next time she opened her eyes, the shadow came into focus.

The bleached skin, the swoop of hair, the nails as sharp as a cutlass.

Ruth.

Her arms raised, a heavy rock in her grasp.

Kelly tried to speak.

Ruth did not allow it.

"And then they moved you. And hid you."

"And I linger. Follow 'em. Had no choice."

They buried her body, probably had Gregory plant that mango tree on top of her, then pretended that love and commitment made it grow. Told us to respect the tree so we wouldn't discover the truth.

"They said you left the country."

"Ruth say that. Next day, she write a goodbye note like it was from me, put it in my room. Said I quit, said I left."

My mind's spinning. "But Dante saw you fall. So, what, he's always known?"

"Be easy on him. He was just a boy. He didn't know. Never did."

"But he *saw*."

"And he cry and scream and get his mother. Bet she say she'd handle it." Kelly sighs. "Guess she did."

"He never asked? Never wondered where the hell you went?"

"You assume so much. Angry like your father." She shakes her head. "Dante ask, plenty. Ruth story never change. Heard it so much, he had to believe it."

With how much he hates his dad, I don't know that he did. Not entirely.

"I didn't like Ruth," Kelly admits, waving the vision away. "But she always take care of everything. Especially her family. She grow it, protect it." She crosses her arms. "Can almost forgive her for that."

Murderers don't deserve forgiveness. Ruth definitely doesn't. And when I thought my selfishness killed Joy, I knew it was true for me too.

"So when I first showed up at Blackbead, what did you want from me?"

"To leave." She's so simple with it that it annoys the shit out of me. "Since I pass, I try to shield anyone the Halls bring to care for the pickney. Scare them out of the home, keep them runnin' for the mountains. Always work." She smiles, sadly. "Until you. You fight me so."

Wish I hadn't. "I can't fight anymore." I've been running for so long. Deep down, I knew I'd hit a dead end eventually. But I didn't imagine it'd play out like this.

"You not done yet," Kelly says.

"I want to be done."

"No," she insists. "You want to fight. You love it. You're just like me." Kelly grasps my shoulder. Her first touch and her last. "Fight a little longer. Live."

A sharp current flies through my body. It sets every nerve on fire, lights up my cells. It's too much.

"Wake up," Kelly whispers.

I'm so tired.

"Wake up."

No more, please.

"*Wake up.*"

TWENTY-EIGHT

Rain.

Rain on my skin.

A pounding in my head.

The sound of frogs croaking. Of someone panting.

I peel my eyes open.

Aaron's leaning over me. He swears when he sees I'm awake.

"Jesus, I thought I lost you," he says. "You hurt? I see blood."

"I'm okay," I wheeze. My voice is scratchy, as if I haven't spoken in years. Glancing around, I realize I'm near the bushes that line the back of the mansion. The torched mango tree looms a few feet away. I think Ruth bashed my head in before dragging me here to hide my body. Because what's another murder when you've already gotten away with the first one? I'm lucky Aaron saw me. "I'm okay. Just . . ."

Something moves in the background, into my line of sight.

Someone.

Ruth.

Creeping closer, soundlessly, makeup smeared.

A brick in her hand. A brick red with my blood. Aiming for Aaron.

She's going to kill Aaron. This crazy bitch is going to kill him.

"No!" I lunge forward. Pain shoots from my head to my toes.

I grip Ruth's arm. Her eyes bulge at me. But she isn't thrown off for long. She pushes back, tries to overpower me.

Ruth's not just smart. She's strong.

My vision blurs from the rain. How do I move? How do I put her down? One foot slips in the mud. Ruth shoves, hard, and I lose my balance.

Aaron leaps in, bumps Ruth sideways with his shoulder. She tumbles into a deep puddle near the mango tree. Grass and muck stick to her blouse, her skirt. Frustration dashes across her face as she sits up. But Aaron's plan worked: he bought me a few seconds to get my bearings.

Aaron rushes Ruth again. She feels around the ground, grabs something.

Whips out the pruning shears I dropped.

Stabs Aaron in the shoulder.

A cry of pain rips from his throat.

It's like tunnel vision. All I see is Aaron, face twisted into a grimace, blood seeping through his shirt.

Aaron folds, tries to hold up a hand to defend against more attacks.

But there won't be any more.

The Halls can't hurt anyone else. I can't let them.

Ruth stalks toward me with precise steps, a quick stride. She raises the shears. Points the blades at me. I shuffle back. But I can't run backward forever.

The cliffs wait.

Electricity surges through me. It pushes and pulls at my insides, makes my stomach flip like I'm caught in free fall.

Let me in.

I don't know what this is. It's overwhelming, this sensation that sparks like fireworks in my fingers and toes.

Let me in.

I'm afraid to let go. To give in.

It's my turn.

Kelly.

I let go. An otherworldly heat races across my skin, sears my ribs from the inside out. And with that heat comes adrenaline. Energy.

Wrath.

I jerk forward and knock Ruth flat onto her back. Mud smears everywhere. I straddle her, press my forearm against her neck, use my knees to pin her down. She grunts and growls, a crazed monster. Tries to thrust her weaponed hand at me.

"No more," I tell her.

"This isn't over."

I push on her windpipe a little harder. Hold steady. "I said"—Ruth gasps a little, chokes—"that's enough."

The words come through forceful and clear. Like it isn't only me speaking.

The shears slip from her hand and hit the ground with a thud. She stares as if she's seeing me for the first time. "Kelly?"

A smile pulls across my face. Kelly is smiling.

Ruth's chin trembles. She's afraid. Afraid she will die tonight.

But I am not like her. Kelly is not like her.

Ruth should be afraid because she will live. And by living, she will suffer.

"Get off her!" Ian roars. He sprints across the yard. Dante's right behind him. Ian charges at me to pull me off. But Dante stops him.

His fist cracks against his father's face.

Ian slumps to the ground, screaming, cursing. "Boy, I will break you."

Dante says nothing.

He punches Ian again. And again. And again.

Until the sirens blare.

Police.

Dante slows, stops. Hisses as he shakes out his sore hand, knuckles raw and bruised. Ian lies in the dirt and weeps.

The street fills with emergency vehicles, cops jumping out to swarm Blackbead. Something between a delirious laugh and an overdue sob racks Dante's body.

He screams. Into the night and the clouds. "Finally!"

It's over.

Finally.

TWENTY-NINE

Blackbead is a tomb, a museum, a bad memory to its core.

I stand in the foyer as people bustle. Blackbead's doors sit open like some gaping maw, and I pay attention to the outline of the door carvings. A great tree with fruit on its branches.

A mango tree.

Servitium et Honorem? Not here.

The chandelier twinkles—in fragments.

Sometime during the night's chaos, the light fell, showering crystal everywhere. The chandelier's silver body sits in a broken heap. Muddy footprints mar the floors. One of the wall sconces flickers, and I flinch.

This was supposed to be my home. The Halls were untouchable.

And all they had to do was lie, steal, kill, and degrade themselves for the honor of having that power for years.

Was it worth it?

My head throbs.

Medics hurried Aaron to the hospital for his shoulder. Dante sits in the courtyard with Jada and Luis, arms wrapped tight around them. Police cars cram into Blackbead's driveway, line the street outside the front gate. I don't know who called the cops or the media, but they're all here. The crowds, the cameras—it's too busy. It's too loud.

Run.

But I refuse to leave until I see everyone go.

It's like observing an hours-long funeral procession. Everybody standing around, shocked and bawling. Everybody marching through the foyer, down the driveway, and into police cars.

Ruth leaves Blackbead first. The crazed appearance is gone; she's escaped deep inside herself now. The mascara's still smeared, hair's still mussed, nails still broken. I don't see the woman I remember, the one who seemed glamorous and regal and in charge. No. Ruth seems pathetic.

This is what a real murderer looks like.

Gregory trots out next. He's as gruff and irritated as ever, yanking on his handcuffs. The escorting officer shoves him toward the street.

Ruth wasn't lying when she said it was a burden to be right. And I was right about Gregory. He buried Kelly, planted the mango tree on top. Tended to it for years. Proudly.

Cops walk Thomas to the foyer. Thomas isn't rattled by the turmoil around him. His clothes fit perfectly; his face remains stoic. He doesn't seem like a criminal. But neither did anyone else at Blackbead—besides Gregory.

"What'd he do?" I ask the officer. My throat's rough and raspy. Thomas glances at me from the side of his eye.

The cop seems to recognize me from earlier. And I remember him too. He had to pry me off Aaron as I wailed and tried to stop his bleeding wound. Maybe that's why he's comfortable answering. "We believe he helped cover up everything, miss. But don't worry. We will take care of this, we promise you." The officer nods before pushing Thomas out the front door.

I don't know if the police will take care of anything, what sort of justice there will be, if any. Nobody here trusts the cops, and Thomas is smart—probably smarter than most. He could wiggle out of this.

But if he really was the key to keeping everything hidden for so long? I hope he fucking rots.

"Please," a desperate voice calls. "I didn't know."

Ian weeps as the police drag him out of Blackbead. His face is covered in black and blue. He stumbles, trips over a chair on the veranda. The metal screeches. Cameras flash. No poise. No grace. Ian's face warps from apparent agony as the cops snap cuffs on his wrists.

"Ian Hall, you are under arrest for embezzlement," declares an officer. But it's as if Ian can't hear him, doesn't care at all.

"I did not know about Kelly," he says, each word clear and pained. "I thought she left because of me, and I regretted it. Believe me. She said she was abroad. She wrote to me for years. The letters are in my office, I have them, believe me."

There's a brokenness in him. Something I recognize in myself. I don't want to share anything with him beyond the DNA he gave me. But the rawness, the hurt? Sounds real.

Those love letters, each written in the neatest handwriting, each missing a return address. Dated for years after Kelly died. Ruth wrote Kelly's goodbye note. She must have faked all those messages too. Kept Ian clueless and pining after the girl who got away.

But the girl was always right here.

Maybe Mother Maud wasn't talking about me when she told Aaron to watch out for a lying woman. Maybe she was warning us about Ruth. A decade and a half of her lies.

My mom isn't my biological mom. Ian Hall, one of the most miserable people I've ever met, is my sperm donor. I spent weeks this summer caring for my half siblings without knowing it, letting my half brother boss me around so I wouldn't get fired.

The world is tilted. I don't know how to set it right. Or if I can. It feels too big for me.

Blackbead falls into stillness. Jada cries outside. She's never been so loud.

In the shadow of everything, I am small and naive. Childlike. My eighteen years aren't enough to process this. I want my parents.

But what would I even say to them? How do I explain this? How do *they* explain this?

Someone rests a hand on my shoulder, and I startle.

"Hey, breathe deep, yeah?" Ora's tone quickly soothes me. I throw my arms around her neck, hold on like she's a life raft. Ora makes sense. Nothing else does. "Cops done with you?"

"Think so," I mutter into her shirt. She rubs my back.

"Okay. Let's take you home, Bambi."

The next morning, the sun's out.

I'm not feeling it.

I lie in Ora's bed, the girl snoring beside me. She offered to set me up on the living room couch. Then her mom called her a bad host and suggested I take Ora's room for myself.

I asked if we could just share. Didn't want to be alone.

My phone vibrates on the nightstand. I peek at the screen.

SIMONE: Don't know what happen last night but call me when you can because I worry

JOSH: yooooo heard sum1 did smash up hall bmw overnite w/ a brick. But if ne1 ask, wasnt me. stay safe bambi

Ah, the flood of messages begins. I start to reply.

But a call comes through.

MOM

Oh, she and Dad have some explaining to do.

I grab the phone and scurry into the hallway so I don't wake Ora. And for the first time in weeks, I pick up.

"What are you doing in Jamaica?" Mom fumes. I haven't heard her speak in weeks. I don't admit I've missed it. Can't admit how it nearly brings me to my knees.

"How do you know where I am?"

Mom kisses her teeth. "How are you going to ask me questions when you weren't answering any of ours? Just photos."

Shit. I had fake road trip updates scheduled to go out through the end of my trip. But then my life exploded, as it likes to do. I got sloppy.

"Wondered if someone took your phone, pretending to be you so we wouldn't check to see if you're okay." Mom hits a sharp pitch. "Imagine our surprise when we search up your phone. And see! You're not even in the country. My heart, Carina Brielle! Thought you got snatched."

Mom has always been big on the Life360 thing. So at the airport, I'd set up a VPN so she could track my fake trip if she wanted. But when did it switch off? When the duppy screwed up my phone at Ian's fundraising banquet, maybe? Has my location really been exposed for so long?

"I didn't mean to freak you guys out."

"You don't know freak out. Not even close." Car horns honk in the background. "Roads a mess... give me your address. We're driving there."

"You're *here*?"

"Our daughter is lost on the island. Of course we're here. So stop back talk and tell us where you are."

I wait outside Ora's house, sit on the stoop and count the palm fronds littering the road. Ora's mom brings me a cup of hot tea while

I scan every car driving down the road. With each passing moment, I grit my teeth, replay the weeks, try to find sense where none exists. Everything circles back to a single question. And only my parents can answer it.

After forty-five minutes, a car rolls into Ora's driveway.

I stand and imagine I'm a stalwart palm tree that hurricane winds could not take down. I can face this. I can face them.

The car doors swing open.

Mom and Dad sprint to me, wrap me in their arms. I want to lean in. I want to let go.

But I can't.

I push them back.

"Why didn't you tell me the truth?"

Dad at least has the courtesy to wince. "Carina—"

"Why didn't *you* tell us where you were going?" Mom cuts in. "Expressly told you not to come. Imagine you got hurt out here, all alone, nobody know where you are."

"I did get hurt. Because of you two. Because you lied for years."

"You don't understand the situation," Dad insists. He looks forlornly at Ora's house, probably worried everyone inside is witnessing us being messy and loud in the yard. And they definitely are.

"Then explain it to me."

Mom pinches the bridge of her nose, forces air out like an angered bull. How can she be mad at *me*? "The plan was to tell you on your birthday back in June. Right?" Mom looks to Dad to back her up; he's too distressed. "But you had just lost Joy. Weren't going out, eating, talking. Your whole world was upside down. Were we supposed to tell you still?"

"But why was it ever a secret? Mom, you *never* mentioned Kelly's name, not once. Do you get how crazy this has been?"

"I told you a family member went missing in Jamaica, didn't I? I told you why I didn't want you here. Because it isn't safe for—"

Dad cuts Mom off. "No, Rina, you're right. We should have been honest. But Kelly wanted us to wait until you were eighteen, or until she could come meet you herself. So we honored her wishes."

"She was my baby sister, Carina," Mom adds, some anguish leaking into her tone. "All those years ago, she reached out for help. Pregnant and scared. I'd do anything for her. Including become your mother."

And she is my mother. Aunt by blood, yes. Pain in my ass, absolutely. But these *are* my parents, shared blood or not. They always will be.

Mom's words irk me, though. She'd do anything for her sister. Yet that same sister died out here, alone. She was hidden for over a decade, and hardly anyone searched for her.

"You came all this way for me," I start. "Why didn't you do the same for Kelly when she disappeared?"

Now it's Mom's turn to flinch. "When I lost contact with Kelly . . . I called her you don't know how many times. Contacted the Halls until they blocked my numbers. Reported her missing to the police because she never would have just vanished like they were saying." She studies her shoes. "Your father thought we should come here, locate her ourselves."

"But you didn't."

"I couldn't. I don't know if you can understand." She sighs. "If we found her, or if we didn't, it'd be . . . hard. And I needed to take care of you. You were all I had left of her."

I remember the red ribbon in Kelly's hair. Like the one I've worn here at Aaron's troubled request. Like the ones Mom loved to wrap around my hair ties until I told her I was too old for that.

Red ribbons that reminded Mom of her sister.

Mom left Jamaica with a sibling and couldn't come back knowing she might not have one anymore. And she thought if she could keep me from coming here, she'd shield me too. Her last link to Kelly.

I do understand. We all fool ourselves, hide from the truth when it's too much to handle. We fear getting lost, drifting.

Like mother, like daughter. Again.

"After a while," Dad says, "we knew we weren't going to get answers about what happened. We had to move on. But we still wanted you to know."

"Then plans changed," Mom murmurs.

Meaning, if I hadn't blown up my life, I'd presumably have known everything by now. Maybe I would have found some other way to come here. Maybe I would have never been haunted by Kelly to begin with.

But that's more speculation than I can handle.

"When we realized where you were," Mom explains, "we believed that ... you knew. Figured it out yourself somehow. Come here to make sense of it."

"We're sorry," Dad adds. "We can't imagine what you've been through."

Tears prick my eyes. Because he's right. He can't. I wouldn't even know how to describe the events of the last few weeks, the ups and downs of my own feelings, the terror I've lived through.

I sob.

This time, they embrace me, and I let them. I fall into their arms. Mom whispers gentle words, holds me with a sweetness I didn't know was possible, a softness she must not have known how to show while trying to protect me. It's comforting.

"We'll try to find a flight that leaves tomorrow," Mom says. "Throw it on one of the cards. Get you home, make it up to you somehow."

"Thank you both, for apologizing." Having Black parents, I know how rarely this happens. "But I'm not done here."

"Oh, don't start," Mom warns.

"No, listen. A friend told me duppies need dead yards to move on. Kelly never got one." I look between Mom and Dad, read the confusion on their faces. "Can you help me put one together for Kelly before we go?"

They grin.

"Of course," Mom says. "Punkin always loved a party."

THIRTY

AARON

CARINA: How are you feeling?

AARON: like a mad woman did stab me. but alive. josh set me up nice at his place for now.

AARON: how are YOU?

CARINA: I'm . . . okay? Maybe? Or will be. Head hurts still.

CARINA: Just glad my parents are here.

AARON: same. happy for you.

AARON: got plans with them today?

CARINA: Eating. Talking. More eating. Why?

AARON: thought we could chat. don't wanna interrupt though.

CARINA: I want to see you.

CARINA: If you want to see me. And even if you don't.

AARON: pick you up in an hour.

The hummingbird garden is still beautiful.

We walk through lush greenery, some resilient flowers in full bloom. Birds chirp, finally safe now that the storm's cleared the island.

The sun's full-out, and the ocean-blue dress I borrowed from Ora pops in the light. Skipped sunscreen because I'm attracted to endangering myself, apparently.

I mean, why else would I agree to come out with Aaron? We walk with so much space between us. After everything, I'm asking for my feelings to get hurt.

And maybe that's okay. Getting hurt won't kill me. It's proof that I'm still surviving, still open, still trying. I don't need anything from Aaron. Can't ask anything of him. I just want to show him the realest version of me. One without secrets.

He deserves that much.

"I'm sorry," I start. "For the other night." Am I apologizing for the grand reveal of my past, or the near-death experience, or the newfound unemployment? I guess all of it. "I didn't think everything would end up like that."

"Dramatic. Very Jamaican of you."

"Please don't remind me of embarrassing shit I've said. And I'm being serious." I pick at the skin of my thumb. "I should have just told you what happened from the jump. Let you make your own decisions."

"Agreed." He stops walking. "But I get it. You carry a lot of things on your mind."

"It was hard to share."

"But you did."

I'm not sure that's something I deserve praise for: doing the right thing *eventually*. "I know you were pissed, but ... thanks for listening. Letting me explain myself."

"Only crime you commit was against yourself. All that punishment, forever? Not healthy, you know?" I definitely do. "Now it's my turn. I'm sorry."

"For what?"

"Making the whole thing about me." He rubs his hand over his chin, presses into the stubble. He's nervous. It's cute. "And for making it seem like I wasn't feeling you anymore."

My heart flutters. Hope.

Hope waiting to be crushed.

Because maybe he still liked me before, but it's different now.

Because he probably wouldn't want to keep talking long-distance. Like, what even were we?

Because whether he says it or not, I probably still remind him too much of his ex.

Aaron looks around, then pulls a flower off a nearby bush. Bright red. Scotch-bonnet red. He tucks the stem behind my ear.

"Know I made a big deal about your past," he admits, "but after everything, I don't care about it. Not anymore. You could have—" Aaron's voice cracks, and he finally meets my eyes.

He seems, well, like he saw a ghost.

Died. I could have died.

"Who you were don't matter. I know you now." He smiles a little, and my chest lightens. "What I don't know is what we doing."

"Talking . . . ?"

Aaron sucks his teeth. "Stubborn. Tell me what's next. Where you going." His expression softens, almost bashful. "Let me meet you there."

My heart stops fluttering. It just explodes.

I grab his face and kiss him.

No guilt. No shame.

Just him and me.

Warm lips on mine. Our bodies pressed together. He wraps his arms around my waist, lets his hands graze the small of my back. The crescendo of a song that's been building for weeks. Maybe it's a poppy love song or some experimental indie tune with no chorus. Doesn't matter. It's ours. And I love it.

When I pull away, his dopey face makes me laugh. I probably look just as ridiculous. Drunk on happiness. On possibility.

On freedom.

"I think you need a new nickname now," I say.

"Brave girl. Okay. What you think? Froggy? Tall Man?"

Not sure. But Aaron's no Chicken. I knew that from the rum bar.

"I'm thinking . . . King."

He smirks. "King? Could get used to that, you know." He grasps my hand, and we stroll through the garden together. Hummingbirds zip and hover on invisible wings. Time drips away like melting ice.

I've made so many mistakes. Aaron will never be one.

Coming to Jamaica will never be one.

For the first time in a long time, the future seems bright. Like something I deserve to explore.

With a grin.

With King's hand in mine.

As hard as I used to party, I couldn't handle nine nights straight, or even seven. So I'm glad we're at the tail end of Kelly's dead yard.

The group's spread out across the section of the beach we've claimed. Tables, coolers, and more booze than I'm comfortable drinking around my parents.

A bonfire blazes and crackles, paints the party in amber light. The acoustic guitar of "Redemption Song" serenades the shore through Bluetooth speakers because we couldn't get a band on short notice—though Josh might play his guitar later. The Young Birds sip on cans of Red Stripe and bottles of water, dance like we're back in that cramped rum bar.

This isn't what I'm used to. But it might be better.

I look around, count the figures. Someone's missing.

"Hey, where's Juney?"

Ora shrugs.

"Guess she got tired before the setup," Josh says in between bites of his meal. "Boring."

Aaron jogs to me, points down the coast with his good arm. "Think she greeting some guests."

Simone walks down the shore, holding Luis's hand on one side and Jada's on the other. I didn't think I'd see them again.

When they spot me, they let go of Simone and sprint. Luis practically body-slams me.

"We missed you," he says. Jada beams and folds her tiny arms around my neck in as big a hug as she can give.

I squeeze these kids so tight. My troublemaker brother. My shy sister.

"You forget someone?" Simone asks. She jabs a thumb behind her, to the party crasher.

Dante stands so awkwardly. Which is how Dante does everything off camera, really. He watches his—our—siblings babble to me at hyperspeed.

"If you'll 'scuse us," Simone murmurs before scuttling away, pulling Aaron and the kids with her. Just me and Dante now.

"I didn't mean to disturb you all," he says. "But it seemed wrong to not speak to you."

"You don't owe me anything."

"We're blood," he replies. "I'm sorry for that. I wouldn't wish my father on anyone." A hit of nausea nearly bowls me over. *His* father. *My* father. That Ian helped create me is still hard to accept. And it's a sick joke from the universe that I wound up in his home, of all places.

On my first day, did Ian see Kelly's face when he looked at me? If he did, was he happy? Did he ever imagine that he might have a daughter out there somewhere?

I'll never know. But does any of that matter to me? No. Ian might be my father, but he's not my dad. My dad's warm and kind and, yes, so goofy. And thank god. I'm lucky. Dad chose to raise me. I get to be his daughter.

"Well, Dante, we're better than Ian." I take in Dante's rounded shoulders, the tentative way he holds himself. Like he's scared to be here, scared to *be* at all. "Work with Badrick, and you'll go farther than your father ever did. You deserve to."

"You're very kind. Or a better liar than I thought. I don't know." Dante shoves his hands in his pants pockets. I wait for him to pull back, pretend he never opened up. "I thought . . . I wondered if what happened to Miss Kelly was my fault."

Never mind.

He licks his lips. "I didn't know if she was alive or dead. But I saw her fall. Because of me. I saw her body. And when my mother refused to speak on it . . ." He opens his mouth; no words come out.

"You worried," I offer.

"I *feared*. For years. I kept a candle lit every day for years to remember her, to apologize if she truly did pass because of me. I was the one upset. The guilty one."

"Because you were better than your family." I dare to rest a hand on his upper arm. He tenses, but he stays with me. "But you can let that guilt go," I say. "Ian and Ruth and everyone else? They're done for. *You* did that. *You* helped."

He nods slowly, like he's considering whether or not I'm full of it. Then, he says, "Only because you came. Thank you for that."

Been a while since so many people have been glad I showed up anywhere. Feels good.

"Gather 'round, everyone," Mom calls, her voice floating down the beach.

"Let me leave you," Dante starts. "Sorry to bother everyone. Hey, let's go!" He beckons the kids. They crouch behind the Young Birds instead.

"You're not supposed to tell people you're leaving a dead yard," I remind him.

"Or else the duppy will follow you home. So they say. You believe in ghosts?"

It's probably better I don't answer that.

"Why don't you stay?" I ask.

"Couldn't intrude."

"You wouldn't. You're blood. You all are."

Dante stills. Then he motions to where everyone's gathering. "After you."

Mom waits to speak until we arrive. Aaron stands beside me, arm around my shoulders. He's solid, warm. Dad's holding the neck of a white rum bottle.

"Well," Mom begins. "Just want to say thank you all for joining us tonight. Normally, would save the speech for the funeral, do all these festivities at home, but . . . my Punkin never liked to do anything the traditional way. She was always special, really."

Mom's eyebrows lower, and she rubs at her collarbone, and I realize too late that she's sobbing. Dad pulls her into an embrace. The rest of her speech gets buried in Dad's tropical-print shirt.

I gently take the bottle of white rum from Dad's hand, pour a splash onto the sand. A gift from here to wherever Kelly is. "For Kelly," I say. And, in my heart, for Joy too.

Joy should have lain on this gorgeous beach herself, felt the warm sand on her skin. Should have cracked jokes with the big-hearted people here, my friends who would have been hers too. Joy should be traveling the world and living that big life she was meant to live. My mind used to torment me with all the realities I wouldn't get to have. Now, it tumbles thinking about all of Joy's.

But I know Joy. What could really keep her from doing whatever she wanted? Even in death?

So I pour one out and hope she's happy. Hope she's seeing the world somehow, in her own way.

Hope she knows that I will always miss her.

Folks raise their drinks, bow their heads, applaud. "For Kelly."

I join Mom and Dad, make it a group hug. I worried I'd feel differently knowing who my parents truly are to me. And I do. Just not how I thought I would. I feel closer to my parents. Grateful that I landed two people who love me so much. Everything changed, yet nothing did.

Finally, we celebrate.

Everyone peels off to dance and drink themselves silly. The sun continues its descent as Josh, Aaron, and Dante light up some lanterns to illuminate the beach. I follow my parents away from the festivities, to the shoreline, and we watch the sea. Waves lap at my bare feet, the silt and sand covering my toes. I still want to live by the water someday. But that can wait. Standing beside it is good enough for me.

An Irie Blaze deep cut and too much static blast through the speakers. Fate somehow led me to Blackbead, to the mother I didn't know was here. And this is how our time together ends. With this little dead yard. It isn't enough. It's too simple. The beach is too bare. After everything she went through, Kelly deserves more. But this is the best I could do. I wish Kelly could tell me what she thinks. If she likes this dead yard despite how basic it is.

I stand between Mom and Dad, and Mom turns to look at me. Really stares. "What?" I ask.

"I wish Punkin could see you now," she says quietly. She tears up again, and I almost spin away because I don't want to cry too. But I face her. I stay. Because that confusing wall between us is finally gone.

It's like I finally see her. "I wish my sister knew how brave you became. How determined."

A rush of heat covers me from head to toe.

Honeysuckle grazes my nose.

I never mentioned the duppy to Mom. Never knew if she'd believe me, or if she could handle it if she did. But I still want to tell her the truth, the truth I know deep in my soul.

"She knows."

We behold the ocean, wide and endless. The future creeps ever closer and asks me what I'll do with it. I don't answer because I can't. I don't know, have no plan, and that's okay. But I know one thing for sure.

No more running.

No more escaping.

It's time to fight a little longer.

It's time to live.

ACKNOWLEDGMENTS

Putting one's work into the world can be frightening. It requires confidence that, I admit, I haven't often had. Fortunately, I'm lucky to have had people who believed in me long before I could fathom doing the same.

First, so much gratitude for my editors Lexy Cassola and TJ Ohler. Thank you for your time, your insight, and your enthusiasm. I think we've made something truly special. And I'm excited to do it again soon!

And to Tiff Liao: You've always been a fierce advocate for me. Whenever I lost hope, you talked me through my troubles and helped me get back on track. Having the opportunity to work with you in this capacity was a dream. I wish I had the words to show my appreciation for years of encouragement and real-deal advice. But I hope what I've written above will suffice. Thank you.

My deepest thanks to the wonderful team at Zando: Molly Stern, Andrew Rein, Ashley Alberico, Sarah Schneider, Kayla White, Nathalie Ramirez, Anna Hall, Amelia Olsen, Natalie Ullman, Chloe Texier-Rose, Julia McGarry, Emily Morris, and Christopher King. And thanks to Tal Goretsky for your efforts in designing my cover.

Endless love to the entire Working Partners/Dovetail Fiction crew. To Lynn Weingarten, Marianna Baer, Blair Thornburgh, and Anna Carey: I appreciate each of you for the hours, energy, and hard work put into this book. Your contributions made *Honeysuckle and Bone* what it is today, and I hope I've made you proud. Special thanks to Chelsea Eberly: You're a legendary agent *and* you are magical. You were key to making this dream come true.

I've had a couple fabulous writing mentors and advisors, some for years, and others for days. All important to me.

To Paula Chase-Hyman: Thank you for mentoring me and meeting every anxious, perfectionist thought I had with honesty. You held space for me when I was knee-deep in those early days of grief, and for that, I appreciate you and send you love.

To Jennifer Jacobson: You were the first person to ever read a full manuscript of mine. You said we needed to find a way to keep me writing despite the hardships I was experiencing at the time. I hope you're proud to see that I am, in fact, still writing. Thank you for seeing me.

Over the years, support also came from some stellar organizations. My gratitude to We Need Diverse Books for awarding me a Walter Dean Myers Grant in 2018. This was the first time I ever felt like my writing might have promise, and I'm still honored. Thank you for believing in me.

Biggest thanks to the Highlights Foundation, which has provided me both education and respite since 2019. At a time when courses, workshops, and writing retreats weren't accessible to me, the Highlights Foundation opened the door.

And my love to my Highlights Diversity Fellows, who have cheered me on even when I've tried to hide: Daria Peoples, Krystal Song, Narmeen Lakhani, Nathalie Alonso, Adriana De Persia Colón, Pamela Courtney, Jacqueline Barnes, Gerry Himmelreich, and Jessica Galán. Thank you all. You're amazing.

My small circle of friends has somehow always included the best people in the world.

To Jas Hammonds: I've said this before, but I'll say it again—I'm so glad Pitch Wars helped us find each other. I've been screaming about your writing since 2018, and I will read everything you write forever. Because you deserve the world. You deserve to be seen! I'm your fan, and your friend. Thank you for holding space for me. Thank you for encouraging me and hyping me up. Thank you for being you.

To Samantha Herrick: From fifth grade to right now—I think this is for life! We've come a long way from reading and writing fanfic, right? You've been there for all of life's ups and downs, and I'll never have the words to express how much you mean to me. I'll be your sister for as long as you'll have me. I love you the most, bestie. And please send pictures of the book shrine. I'm daring you to actually build it.

My thanks to my family, in the States and in Jamaica, for your excitement and eagerness.

To Casey and Bonnie: Thank you for the daily support. The pep talks, the rides to this or that, the all-nighters, the delicious "eat your feelings" meals. You've kept me grounded. Thank you for taking care of me. I know I don't say it enough, but I love you both dearly.

To Mom: Thank you for having faith in my abilities. Thank you for answering all my questions. Thank you for reminding me to keep my eyes on the prize. Thank you for being excited when I didn't know how to be. Thank you for making me laugh. I hope I can fly you back to Jamaica someday. Then you can show me everything you wanted me to see. Thank you for being my mom. I love you.

To Dad: I'm still mad that you're not here to hold this book yourself. I want to know what you think of the cover, or the author photo I chose. I wonder if you're proud of what I've done. I could have read a bit of the book to you. But I want to believe you've somehow already seen every word I wrote. I want to believe you've been looking over my shoulder and guiding me. I think you've helped me achieve this dream, in your own way. Thank you for loving me, in every life. Visit me sometime.

My love and appreciation to everyone I didn't name. If you were once special to me, then I'm grateful for you. Thank you for being a part of my story up till now.

And finally, to my readers: Thank you for reading Carina's story. Thank you for giving me a chance. I hope our time together was as beautiful for you as it was for me. And I hope we meet again someday.

ABOUT THE AUTHOR

Trisha Tobias is a writer, editor, and Fordham University graduate. She is a recipient of the 2018 Walter Dean Myers Grant and a 2019–2021 Highlights Foundation Diversity Fellow. Trisha lives in North Carolina. *Honeysuckle and Bone* is her debut.